The deep, resonant tone of Mr. Stratford's voice filled the room, making it seem smaller, more intimate.

The soft glow of the lamp on the nightstand brought them closer together. They probably looked like a family.

Dix jerked upright. She hadn't come to Stratford's mansion to become part of his family. She'd come to protect this family.

She glanced around, wondering where Leigha's mother was and why she wasn't there, taking care of her child.

Fontaine had told her she would be the bodyguard for the Stratford family. From what she could tell, that family consisted of two people. Father and daughter. And the daughter called her father Mr. Stratford.

Why?

As her father read, Leigha's eyes closed. Dix backed away from the bed, her hand clenching around the damp cloth. Her goal was to leave the room and perform the search of the giant house for any weaknesses in entry and exit points.

She'd almost made it to the door when a little voice said, "Please don't go."

* * *

Dear Reader,

With a heavy heart I wrote this book, knowing it was the last in the Devil's Shroud series. I've grown to love Cape Churn and all the members of the Stealth Operations Specialists team who've made this little town their home. I'll miss Sheriff Taggert and his wife, Nora, and sheriff's deputy Gabe McGregor and his talented artist wife, Kayla. We won't be going back to McGregor B and B to sample Mollie's best clam chowder or sit on the porch with Creed and Emma, Nova, Jillian or any of the other characters we love as we stare out over the beautiful Pacific Ocean at sunset.

I hope you enjoy this last installment as we bring back Andrew Stratford, the eccentric billionaire, his daughter, Leigha, and the newest addition to the Stealth Operations Specialists: former army ranger and MMA fighter Dix Evans, as she finally finds a place to call home, a little girl to love and a man who has the patience and ability to help her through her own issues.

Enjoy discovering the secrets of Stratford House and the beautiful Oregon coast, and thank you for coming along for the ride!

Elle James

DEADLY FALL

Elle James

HARLEQUIN®ROMANTIC SUSPENSE

Recycling programs
for this product may
not exist in your area.

ISBN-13: 978-0-373-40194-9

Deadly Fall

Copyright © 2017 by Mary Jernigan

This edition published by arrangement with Harlequin Books S.A.

For questions and comments about the quality of this book, please contact us at CustomerService@Harlequin.com.

HARLEQUIN®
www.Harlequin.com

Printed in U.S.A.

Elle James, a *New York Times* bestselling author, started writing when her sister challenged her to write a romance novel. She has managed a full-time job and raised three wonderful children, and she and her husband even tried ranching exotic birds (ostriches, emus and rheas). Ask her, and she'll tell you what it's like to go toe-to-toe with an angry 350-pound bird! Elle loves to hear from fans at ellejames@earthlink.net or ellejames.com.

Books by Elle James

Harlequin Romantic Suspense

Deadly Reckoning
Deadly Engagement
Deadly Liaisons
Deadly Allure
Deadly Obsession
Deadly Fall

The Adair Legacy

Secret Service Rescue

The Adair Affairs

Heir to Murder

The Coltons of Oklahoma

Protecting the Colton Bride

Visit the Author Profile page at
Harlequin.com for more titles.

This book is dedicated to my readers, who buy my books and let me live the dream of writing full-time. Without you, I'd still be commuting to work wearing business clothes and tight shoes instead of working at my desk in my yoga pants, barefoot.

Also to my family, who puts up with my late-night writing, taking my laptop on vacations and letting the cooking and cleaning go when I'm on deadline. They know I'm working and try to get along without me.

I also dedicate this book to my little dogs who remind me to get out of my chair and take them outside. They keep me company during the day when I'm writing and are just happy to be with me. Okay! Okay! I'm getting up. Sheesh! You could at least have let me finish my dedication...

Chapter 1

"Leigha?" Andrew Stratford called out.

The old mansion had been quiet for too long.

"Leigha?" he said a little louder.

He glanced up from the computer terminal, having spent the last three hours day-trading, buying as the prices on several of the stocks he had his eye on dipped to an all-time low.

He'd made his fortune on Wall Street. Since the accident, he'd left it all behind and moved to Cape Churn, Oregon. Giving up the high-stress job of managing the fortunes of other people to only managing his own portfolio had been a decision he'd never regret.

Not that he'd had much of a choice. With the scars he'd acquired, his high-powered, beautiful clients would be less likely to come to entrust their money to him. So intent on being the wealthiest, most beautiful people money could buy, they wouldn't have the courage to face a man with a wicked scar running from the base of his jaw up to his eye. The burn scars on his right hand would be a deal breaker in a society where a good handshake was a measure of a man's character.

But the main reason he'd come back to Oregon was the reason he rose from his desk.

"Leigha," he called out.

Now that he had a daughter to look after, he couldn't live the fast-paced, late-night lifestyle he'd been living for the past ten years as one of the most eligible bachelors in New York City. And, frankly, he didn't want to. He'd burned the candle at both ends with a high-powered job and a jet-setter lifestyle. Sure, he'd amassed a fortune, but what else did he have to show for it?

Andrew stretched. He needed to get up and move. His housekeeper, Mrs. Dottie Purdy, had ducked in an hour ago saying she needed to stock the pantry and Leigha preferred to stay and play.

Normally, Leigha played in the big mansion with Brewer, her black Labrador retriever. Andrew could count on the reassuring sound of little feet and canine toenails clicking across wooden floors. For the past fifteen minutes there had been nothing. No sounds, no squeals of delight or soft-spoken tea parties in the salon two doors down from Andrew's office.

Silence used to be calming when he was a bachelor without a care in the world. Now that he had Leigha, silence was disconcerting.

The little girl was always into something. Though

she was abnormally solemn, she was a natural-born explorer and adventurer. She reminded Andrew of himself at that age. His nanny had despaired of keeping up with him. Unfortunately, Stratford House perched on the edge of a three-hundred-foot cliff. If she wandered too far from the house, Leigha could fall to a very grisly death on the jagged rocks below.

On that thought, Andrew hurried from his office and out into the mansion's huge entry hall. "Leigha!"

He listened, hoping to hear an answering call in the little girl's high-pitched voice.

More silence greeted him.

The mansion had three living areas: a massive formal dining room, fifteen bedrooms and a full basement complete with a wine cellar. The child could be anywhere inside.

Andrew went room to room on the main floor and then stood at the base of the sweeping staircase. "Leigha!"

Again, no answering call.

Had she gone outside without telling him? Andrew's pulse quickened. A glance through the window made his chest tighten. While he'd been busy working at his desk in the study, a cold, gray fog had crept in from the Pacific cloaking Cape Churn in what the locals called the Devil's Shroud.

"Damn," Andrew muttered and hurried for the door. If Leigha had gone out when it was clear, she might now be lost in the fog.

Andrew burst through the massive front door and ran out onto the marble portico. "Leigha! Brewer!"

A dog barked in the distance, the sound coming from the back of the house, farther along the coastline, sounding too near to the edge of the cliffs for Andrew's comfort.

Andrew broke into a sprint, trying to remember just how many steps past the garden led to the cliff's edge. He'd contracted a local handyman to erect a decorative wrought-iron fence, but he had to wait for the man to finish renovations on another home before he had time to start the work on the fence and other repairs around Stratford House. In the meantime, Andrew worried Leigha or guests might walk off the cliff in a dense fog, such as the one now hiding the treacherous shoreline.

"Leigha? Brewer?"

Again the dog barked.

Andrew slowed, knowing he was close to the edge of the cliff. He would be of no use to Leigha if he fell off. But the thought of the child being out there in the damp fog, her foot slipping on a wet rock, made him hurry as quickly as he could.

Andrew nearly walked into a tree trunk clinging to the ledge.

As he stepped around it, something moved. A shadowy figure detached from the tree and slammed into him.

Andrew's forward momentum shifted sideways, sending him over the edge of the cliff. He dropped ten feet, hit a jutting boulder, his arms wind-milling the air, grasping at the fog for purchase to keep him from falling three hundred feet to the rocky shoreline. His hand tangled in a tree root. Closing his fingers around it, he held on. Damp with the mist, the root slid through his hand. He grabbed with his other hand and held on tightly. When his body fell below his hands, his arms felt as though they were being ripped out of their sockets. But he managed to arrest his downward plunge.

Andrew clung to the root, his breath caught in his throat as he held on, his hands wrapped around the root, his feet dangling in the air.

For a long moment he hung in midair, thankful for the stalwart tree and its tenacious hold on the rocky cliff. Then he raised his legs, kicking out his feet, searching for ground to dig his toes into. Using the tree roots, he inched his way up the side of the cliff until he was back where he'd started before he'd fallen over the edge.

Or rather, before he was *pushed*. No tree in the span of Andrew's lifetime had ever managed to shove him over a cliff.

As he dragged himself up onto the path, he braced himself, prepared to fight for the ground he could stand on. Fog swirled around him but nothing jumped out.

Staggering to his feet, Andrew pressed on, more afraid than ever for Leigha.

Brewer barked again, closer to him and far too close to the cliff's edge for Andrew's liking.

"Mr. Stratford?" a tiny voice called out.

"Leigha?" Andrew's heart pounded against his ribs and he strained to see through the thick fog.

"I'm here. I got lost," she said, her voice wobbling.

"Stop," Andrew ordered. "Stay right where you are.

But keep talking to me so that I can find you." Andrew moved forward, careful not to get too close to the ledge.

"I'm scared," Leigha said, her voice thin and shaky.

The Labrador materialized out of the fog and walked toward him.

Holding on to the dog's tail was the little girl Andrew obviously had no clue how to care for. He swept her up into his arms and hugged her tightly. "Thank God."

Leigha wrapped her arms around his neck. "Brewer and I were playing with my friend. Then the clouds came in and I couldn't see my way back home."

"You have *me* now. I'll make sure you get back," he assured her.

"I held on to Brewer's tail," Leigha said. "He knows the way. He was leading me home when we found you."

The big Lab leaned into his leg. His tongue lolled and his tail thumped against the hard ground.

Andrew glanced down at the dog. He'd never had a pet. As a child growing up in New York City, his parents refused to have an animal in their apartment. When he was old enough to make his own decisions, he got caught up in making a living, and then powered on to make a fortune. A pet didn't have a place in his intensely busy life.

Now he stared down at the dog that seemed to be smiling up at him, daring him to smile back.

"Brewer is happy to see you," Leigha said. She placed both of her small palms against Andrew's cheeks and turned his face toward hers, undaunted by his scars. "Mr. Stratford, why are you bleeding?"

"I tripped and fell." Andrew swept a damp strand

of blond hair out of Leigha's eyes, leaving a streak of blood across her forehead.

Leigha captured his hand. "You have a boo-boo on your hand, too. You need to go to the doctor."

For the first time since his fall over the cliff, Andrew felt the pain of a cut on his hand. The way it was bleeding couldn't be good.

"I'll take care of it when we get back to the house," he assured her.

Leigha leaned her head against his shoulder, her pretty little brow puckering. "Mr. Stratford, are you going to die?"

He snorted. "Not today, Leigha. Not today."

"Tomorrow?" Her fingers curled into his shirt and held on as he walked in what he hoped was the direction of the mansion, his attention focused on sounds and any movement. Holding Leigha in his arms, he was doubly aware of his responsibilities toward the child.

Someone had pushed him over the cliff. But who? And why?

When Stratford House finally appeared in front of him, he sighed and hurried through the back entrance, into the large kitchen.

"There you are." Mrs. Purdy stopped in the middle of unloading a bag of groceries and set the can in her hand on the counter. "What happened to you?" she cried. Grabbing a kitchen towel, she rushed over to him.

Andrew lowered Leigha to the ground in time for Mrs. Purdy to grab his hand.

"Good Lord, you look like you got into a fight," the older woman said.

"It's nothing," he said, trying to calm his house-keeper.

"Nothing?" She frowned and led him by the hand to the kitchen sink. "That cut is deep enough it might require stitches. And I don't know how they go about stitching over burn scars."

"A bandage will do." He let her drag his hand under running water and winced as pain shot up his arm. He jerked his hand back, but the woman stubbornly held on.

"You need to have a doctor look at this. I'll wrap it up, but you'll continue to bleed if you don't have it stitched."

"Please, Mr. Stratford. Please go to the doctor." Leigha touched his arm and stared up at him. "I don't want you to die."

"I'm not going to die," he insisted. "And I'm not going to bleed to death."

Mrs. Purdy crossed her arms over her chest and stared him down. Then she tipped her head toward Leigha. "If not for yourself, do it for Leigha."

Outnumbered, Andrew sighed. "Okay. I'll let a doctor look at it. I'll make an appointment for tomorrow."

"Today," Leigha said.

"We'll go to the ER in Cape Churn." Mrs. Purdy wrapped a clean kitchen towel around his hand. "I'll drive."

"I'm perfectly capable of driving myself to Cape Churn."

"You're bleeding like a stuck pig. You might get dizzy." She held up her hand. "I won't take no for an answer."

"I'm going with you." Leigha clutched his sleeve.

"And I'm driving," Mrs. Purdy insisted.

"Do I have a choice in this matter?" Andrew asked.

"No!" Mrs. Purdy and Leigha answered as one.

Thus outmaneuvered, Andrew found himself loaded into the passenger seat of Mrs. Purdy's minivan and driven all the way to the Cape Churn Hospital emergency room.

Once inside, he was whisked back to an examination room. Mrs. Purdy and Leigha waited in the ER lobby. As the door closed between them, Andrew noted Leigha burying her face into Mrs. Purdy's sleeve, her eyes clouding with tears. The child appeared terrified for him.

He had to admit, he was terrified for her. After nearly falling to his own death, he realized how easily it could have been Leigha. The thought of finding her body smashed against the boulders made him sick to his stomach. He sat on the edge of the hospital examination bed, pain throbbing through his hand with each beat of his heart.

A nurse carrying a clipboard stepped into the room. "Hi, Mr. Stratford. I'm Emma Jenkins. I'll be your nurse. What brings you here today?" She set the clipboard on the bed beside him and took his injured hand in hers, unwrapping the dish towel. "How'd you get this cut?"

Andrew's first instinct was to retract his scarred hand. Instead he stared at the gash. "I was pushed over a cliff."

Emma blinked. "Say again? Someone pushed you over a cliff?"

He nodded, more certain than ever it hadn't been a ghost or a blast of wind in the fog. "Someone pushed me over the cliff behind my house."

"Do you want me to notify the sheriff? He can send a deputy out to take your statement while we stitch the wound."

Though he didn't like anyone invading his privacy, Andrew nodded. If someone had pushed him, he couldn't ignore it. What if that someone tried to push Leigha? "I think that would be best."

Emma waited until the doctor appeared before she slipped out to make that call. Within minutes, a sheriff's deputy appeared.

"Hi, I'm Gabe McGregor. I believe we've met once before."

Andrew nodded, his lips thinning. "You came to my house when you were looking for a murderer, several months ago." They'd questioned him as a suspect. "I'm glad you caught him."

"You and me both," Gabe said. "I'm sorry I had to question you on that case."

"Don't be. I understand. I was the new guy in town." Andrew gritted his teeth as the doctor stuck a needle in his hand to deaden the area around the cut.

"So tell me what happened." Gabe pulled a notepad and pen out of his front pocket.

While the doctor and Emma cleaned and stitched the wound, Andrew recounted what had happened.

"And you didn't see a face?" Deputy McGregor asked.

Andrew shook his head. "It happened so fast. I stepped around the tree, and the next thing I knew, I was clinging to a tree root, thankful for that tree and the root, or I wouldn't be here to tell you the story."

The deputy's brows drew together. "I'm sorry it happened to you. I'll follow you home and have a look around the area. Maybe there will be some footprints."

"It's not safe in the fog. Besides, the cliff edge is primarily rock and moss. That tree on the edge is the only one there. How it found enough soil to grow as big as it is still astounds me."

"Any idea who might want to hurt you?" McGregor asked.

"No. And it's got me concerned. I found a loose board on the outside step yesterday. At first I didn't think anything of it. I just got out a hammer and fixed it. But when I did, I noticed the board wasn't old or weatherworn. It looked like someone loosened it. I brushed it off as an overactive imagination. But after being shoved off a cliff, I'm rethinking it."

"I knew your grandfather." Emma used a wad of sterile gauze to sop up the excess blood from around the wound as the doctor sewed another stitch. "Though the ME ruled his death as accidental, I thought it pretty strange the old man who'd walked two or three miles a day, and had a healthy heart the last time I could get him in for a checkup, should fall over dead on one of his walks. The ME said his heart was fine. He'd died from the fall. Hit his head on a rock."

Andrew leaned forward. "Are you saying someone murdered him?"

Emma raised both of her hands, wad of bloody cotton and all. "I'm not saying anything. Just the facts."

"Look, all I know is I came to Cape Churn because I thought it would be a safer, quieter place to raise Leigha. I didn't want her to grow up in the concrete jungle where I grew up. She deserves a place where she can run and play." Not a park with a nanny and polluted air.

Andrew knew he was far from the father Leigha deserved, but he wanted her to have a normal childhood, where she could play outdoors, have a pet and be happy.

"Cape Churn can be all of that," Emma said. "I've lived here all my life and love all the cape has to offer. The community is supportive and the summer activities are what most kids dream of. I'd love to teach Leigha how to scuba dive, when she's a little older."

Andrew's heart warmed at the offer. "I want all of that for her, too."

"I feel a 'but' coming," Deputy McGregor said.

"But, after what happened today, I'm rethinking my decision to bring her here. After I nearly fell to my death, Leigha told me she and the dog were playing with her friend. A man. When I asked her about him, she said he's been visiting her every day."

Emma, the deputy and the doctor all frowned.

"Have you had a talk with Leigha about stranger danger?" the doctor asked.

"I have." Andrew snorted. "She said he's not a stranger. He's her friend."

The doctor completed the last stitch and held the strand out straight.

Emma used a pair of scissors to snip it close to the knot.

The doctor set his tools on the tray. "I'll leave you in Emma's capable hands. I have other patients I need to attend." He peeled off his gloves and gave Andrew a stern glance. "Try not to fall off any more cliffs."

After the doctor left, Emma cleaned the area around the wound. "Have you considered hiring protection?"

Andrew frowned. "I've never hired a bodyguard. Where would I start?"

Emma shrugged. "I don't know."

"What about the people Creed, Nicole and Nova work with?" Deputy McGregor asked. "Could they help?"

"Normally they work bigger issues," Emma said. "You know, save-the-world kind of problems." She glanced across Andrew's head at the deputy. "But maybe they have someone who could help while Mr. Stratford goes through the interviewing and hiring process." She turned her attention back to Andrew. "Do you want me to ask?"

"Do you trust them?" Andrew asked.

Emma nodded. "With my life."

"How about with the life of your child?" He captured Emma's gaze and held it.

She nodded. "Absolutely."

"Then yes. If I could get someone on a temporary basis that is trustworthy, it will give me time to look for a full-time bodyguard."

Deputy McGregor closed his notepad and slid it into his pocket. "Tell you what… We're having dinner at McGregor Manor tomorrow night. Why don't you and Leigha come? You can discuss it with some of the members of the SOS team then."

Andrew frowned. "SOS?"

"Stealth Operations Specialists," Emma clarified. "They're like the FBI and CIA, only better. Somehow they've opened a branch here in Cape Churn. You should come. You can meet all of them, and maybe by tomorrow night they'll have an answer for you. Or they might have a suggestion of who to hire for the job of bodyguard to you and Leigha." Emma wrapped a bandage around his hand. "Keep that out of water for a couple of days. In a week you can come in and I'll remove the stitches. Otherwise, I'll see you tomorrow night."

Emma gave him the routine discharge instructions and a prescription for antibiotics and sent him out to the lobby, where Leigha and Mrs. Purdy waited.

Leigha ran to him and hugged him around the legs. "I was so scared."

"I'm fine." He patted the child's head and lifted her up on his uninjured arm. "Since we're in town, why don't we get some ice cream at the Seaside Café?"

Leigha clapped her hands together. "Yes, please."

The smile on Leigha's face made warmth spread across Andrew's chest. He never ceased to be amazed at how much one little human being could make him feel more important than an entire office building of employees.

He vowed to keep this little girl safe, no matter the

cost. If it meant hiring a bodyguard, he'd do it. But it had to be someone special. Someone he could trust completely. There weren't many people he knew who fit that bill. How was he going to trust a stranger to fill that role?

Chapter 2

Dixie Reeves pulled into the parking lot of McGregor Manor. The lovely old home perched on the edge of a cliff outside the small community of Cape Churn, Oregon. In just under twenty-four hours she'd gone from being unemployed to having a job, to getting her first assignment.

What she was supposed to do as a bodyguard to a rich man was beyond her. As a squad leader in the Army, she'd been responsible for her soldiers, the first all-female squad of Airborne Rangers.

She'd done her best as a leader among her peers until one of their special operations had gone bad. They'd been caught in the middle of a firefight. Dix, manning a .60-caliber submachine gun, had remained behind, laying down cover fire for her squad, allowing them to escape. When she'd run out of bullets, she hadn't had time to put her handgun to her head before she was captured.

Dix shook off the memory of the week she'd spent in hell in an enemy camp where she'd been humiliated, tortured and beaten repeatedly until the Navy SEALs were sent in to extract her.

That was over three years ago. Her life had changed dramatically. Processed out of the Army, she'd spent two of those years as a member of the Mixed Martial Arts fighting community. But the nightmares still lingered.

Dix stared at the lush landscape damp from the previous night's mist, so foreign to the deserts of Afghanistan and Las Vegas she might as well have been on another planet.

From what she'd been told, the building in front of her had once been a rich man's home, but had been turned into a bed-and-breakfast by the remaining members of the family. As a home, it was larger than anything Dix had ever lived in. As a bed-and-breakfast, it was quaint and had a heck of a view of Cape Churn.

Her new boss, Royce Fontaine, had tracked her down to her small apartment in Las Vegas, where she'd been sorting through what was left of her belongings after donating most of them to a local women's shelter. He'd said he'd been following her career. At first, she'd assumed he'd meant her career as an MMA fighter. She'd done pretty well, winning one championship after another, focusing all of her anger and frustration into her fists.

Her opponents didn't have a chance. The women she'd fought had never been through the intense training she'd survived as one of the first women to pass the Army Ranger training program. Nor had they been tortured in an enemy camp. The anger had fueled her fists until one day she'd gone too far and left an opponent comatose with a very slim chance of recovery.

Royce thought she'd be a good fit for his team. Dix wasn't so sure. But with no other skills to add to her résumé, what else was she fit for? She might have gotten a job as a security guard at one of the casinos, but the noise bothered her, making her head ache and the tensions to multiply.

So, now she was going to be a member of the SOS team. What exactly did an agent with the Stealth Operations Specialists do? Royce had told her, *Anything that needed to be done.*

Then he'd gotten word from one of his other agents that a wealthy man needed bodyguard services on a temporary basis while he interviewed and hired one he could trust.

"But what does a bodyguard do?" she'd asked Fontaine.

And he'd answered, "Whatever needs to be done."

"Not helping," she muttered as she walked toward the bed-and-breakfast. Hopefully the other members of the SOS team could shed light on her responsibilities. She couldn't afford to lose this job. It might be the only offer she got, and the pay was good. As far as she could tell, all she had to do was keep a rich dude alive.

How hard could that be in the States? They didn't have Taliban or Islamic State fighters…at least, not that she knew of.

"Hello. May I help you?" a female voice called out from the front door of the manor.

Dix shaded her eyes and squinted. "Is this the Mc-Gregor Bed-and-Breakfast?"

"It is." An auburn-haired woman stepped out onto the porch and smiled. "I'm Molly McGregor, one of the owners. Do you need a place to stay tonight?"

"I don't think so," Dix said. "I'm supposed to meet someone here."

The woman frowned. "Meet someone? Anyone in particular?" she asked, her smile warm and welcoming.

"Royce Fontaine sent me. Does that name ring a bell?"

Ms. McGregor's eyes widened. "You're D. Reeves?"

Dix nodded. "Dixie Reeves."

The bed-and-breakfast owner clapped a hand over her mouth, smothering what sounded suspiciously like a giggle. She dropped her hand, a sparkle dancing in her eyes. "We've been expecting you."

"We?" Dix didn't like the sound of that. A single contact was all she'd been led to believe would be waiting for her in Cape Churn.

"Yes," Molly continued, cheerful and happy, something Dix couldn't begin to relate to. "The gang's all here. We thought you'd be here an hour ago."

"My plane was delayed by weather over Vegas or I would have been here sooner."

"No worries. I kept your dinner warm." She waved a hand. "Come inside. Everyone is waiting for you."

"Everyone?" Dix halted with one foot on the bottom step. "I was told to meet my contact here." After quit-

ting the MMA circuit, Dix had no desire to step in front
of a crowd of people ever again. Whether it was a throng
of three thousand or a party of five, she wouldn't perform like a trained monkey to the delight of others. In
her mind, being a bodyguard was being invisible until
she needed to step forward to protect her client. She'd
actually looked forward to being invisible. No celebrity
status. No paparazzi. After dropping out of the MMA,
she never wanted to be in the public eye again.

"The entire West Coast office of SOS agents is in
attendance tonight. You'll get a chance to meet all of
them." Molly grinned. "Don't worry—they won't bite.
Unless you try to take their clam chowder. I managed
to save a bowl for you."

"If it's all the same to you, I'd prefer to meet my
contact out here, get my marching orders and go on to
my client."

Molly's smile slipped. "Oh, okay. But your client is
inside, as well. He's having clam chowder, too." The
woman's smile returned. "You might as well have dinner with us. I think your client gave his housekeeper
the night off from cooking."

Dix squared her shoulders and continued up the
steps. She wasn't getting out of the dog and pony show.
"I don't mean to be rude, but I'm here to work, not so-
cialize."

"Is that our newest SOS agent?" A dark-skinned
man, with brown-black eyes, a full, sensual mouth and
a slight Hispanic accent, stepped through the front door
behind Molly and slipped his arm around the redhead's
waist. He frowned, his head tilting to one side. "Dix

Reeves? *The* Dix Reeves?" His face split into a wide smile. "Are you a guest of the bed-and-breakfast?"

So much for being invisible. Dix sighed. "No, I'm not here to stay. I'm here on work-related business."

"Dix, this is Casanova Valdez. Or Nova for short." Molly turned to the man. "Nova, this is the agent Royce sent."

Nova's frown deepened. "I don't understand." He flicked a hand toward Dix. "That's Dix Reeves, one of the most talented MMA fighters ever."

"MMA?" Molly asked, her brows rising. "I'm sorry— is that another one of your military acronyms?"

Nova laughed out loud. "No. It stands for Mixed Martial Arts. Dix, here, is at the top of her game." He reached out a hand. "It's an honor to meet you."

Dix held out her hand and, with a firm grip, shook Nova's.

"Wait—what did you say?" Nova didn't release her hand. "You're the agent Fontaine sent?"

With a nod, Dix extracted her hand. "That's me."

"But you're with the MMA."

"Not anymore. I quit a week ago."

"That's a shame. I watched your last fight against Peggy Pounder. You threw some wicked punches and kicks. I don't think I've seen anything quite that intense."

Her lips thinned. *Intense* was one way to describe the fight. *Insane* was closer to the truth. She'd had a particularly bad night's sleep, plagued by nightmares from her time as a guest of the Taliban. She'd gone into the ring, not to claim a championship, but to beat the demons out of her head.

She'd nearly killed her opponent.

Molly touched Nova's arm. "Was that the fight you were watching last weekend?"

Nova nodded. "Incredible."

Molly's brows knit, her smile fading. "Didn't that woman end up in the hospital?"

Dix's belly clenched. "Yes. She's still in a coma. It's not one of my prouder moments." Dix stared at Nova. "Are you one of Fontaine's agents?"

With a grave nod, Nova answered, "I am. But I'm not your contact. That would be Tazer. She's inside."

"Good. I'd like to get on to my assignment."

"Well, that's the place to start." Nova held open the door. "Just follow Molly. And don't forget to try her amazing clam chowder. It's *muy bueno*."

Molly entered the manor first. "Everyone is in the dining room."

Dix followed, bracing herself for more questions than she was ready to answer. If Nova recognized her, she hadn't done a good job of blending in. She'd have to buy some hair dye and go from blonde to brunette to hide her identity. In the meantime, she squared her shoulders and turned toward the sea of faces in front of her.

The men pushed back from the table and stood.

Molly turned to her. "Everyone, this is D. Reeves. Otherwise known as Dixie Reeves or—"

"I'll be damned." A woman sitting at the other end of the table stood. "Dix Reeves. Mixed Martial Arts World Champion." The woman had long blond hair, combed straight and hanging in a soft curtain down her back. In tan slacks and a cool, white-cotton blouse, she could have been a model for one of the fashion magazines. She stepped away from her seat and rounded the table, a smile quirking the corners of her lips. "Fontaine sure knows how to pick them." She stopped in front of Dix and held out her hand. "Nicole Steele. But my friends call me Tazer."

Dix shook the woman's hand, surprised at the firmness of her grip. "Sounds like an MMA call sign."

Tazer shrugged. "Suits me. I guess you could say I earned it." She raked her gaze over Dix. "So, you're going to be Andrew Stratford's bodyguard." She let the smile spread a little wider. "Makes sense."

Dix pulled her hand free of Tazer's grip. "I'd like to get on to my assigned duties, if that's possible."

Tazer grinned. "More than possible."

Dix glanced around at the faces all staring at her. Which one was the rich man she was supposed to protect?

Tazer chuckled. "It's none of the men at the table. Mr. Stratford stepped out to take a call. He'll be back in a minute. As far as I know, you start your assignment immediately."

"In the meantime—" Molly pulled out a chair "—have a seat and a bowl of chowder. I won't take no for an answer."

The pretty redhead might be smiling and sunny, but Dix suspected she was as tough as the muscular men seated around the table. "Yes, ma'am." Before she could sink into the chair, a deep, resonant voice spoke from behind her.

"I'm sorry. I need to leave. Leigha isn't feeling well. If you could send the bodyguard over when he gets here, I'd appreciate it."

"As a matter of fact, your bodyguard is here." Tazer hooked Dix's elbow and turned her around.

Dix stared at the most beautiful man she'd ever laid eyes on. He stood half turned toward the exit, only one side of his face visible. While all the other men in the room were dressed in jeans or khaki slacks, this man wore a dark suit that appeared to be tailor-made to fit his body to perfection. His dark hair was shortly cropped, showing a bit of a wave. And those ice-blue eyes…

Then he squared off, spinning to fully face the room of people. A jagged scar ran from the edge of his jaw all the way up to the corner of his eye.

Dix drew in a sharp breath. She hadn't expected such a magnificent man to have such a wicked scar.

His dark brows drew together into a V over his nose. "Where is he?"

"Not *he*," Tazer said in a slow, deliberate voice. "*She* is here and ready to go to work." She shoved Dix forward a step.

The gentleman shook his head, his eyes tapering into little more than a slit. "I don't understand. I asked for someone who could protect me and my family." His gaze raked over her. "I don't need another female in my household. I need someone strong and capable of protecting Leigha."

Her shock at the rugged scar on his face morphed

into anger roiling deep in her belly. Dix let it bubble up to the surface. Yeah, she was probably overreacting, but she'd put up with more gender discrimination than most women, and had to fight and claw her way through every leg of the journey that had brought her this far. "Just because I'm female doesn't mean I can't defend myself, or take care of you and your family." She planted her fists on her hips and lifted her chin. "Go ahead. Try to take me down."

"Uh, Dix, I'm not so sure that's a good idea," Nova said. "He's the client."

Andrew Stratford raised a hand. "It's okay. I don't think she's the right person for the job. If she can prove she is, I might reconsider." He gave her a narrow-eyed, assessing glance. "I don't want to hurt you."

She snorted. "Oh, sweetheart, you're not going to hurt me." *I might hurt you*, she thought, but kept the comment from coming out. "Aren't you afraid I'll wrinkle your suit?"

Tazer's lips tilted upward. "Mr. Stratford, you might be biting off a little more than you can chew. My boss wouldn't send someone who couldn't do the job, and Dix is more than qualified. I've seen her dossier."

"I can't trust her with my family until I know she can handle the job."

Tazer shook back her beautifully groomed hair. "Okay, but take it out in the yard. You don't want to damage Molly's dining room."

Molly bit her lip. "I don't want you to damage yourselves."

Another man stood and clapped his hands together. "I've gotta see this."

"Creed, don't encourage them." A sandy-blond-haired woman stood.

He shook his head, a smile spreading across his face. "You're a nurse. If someone gets hurt, you can stop the bleeding until the ambulance gets here."

"That's right," Nova said. "We have Emma. She can stabilize the loser until the ambulance gets here."

Mr. Stratford waved a hand toward the door. "Ladies first."

Dix fumed at his condescension, but swallowed her anger and focused on teaching this man not to judge a book by its cover, or a woman by the color of her hair or the size of her body. With her head held high, she marched through the living area and out the front door, letting it close in the man's face.

She didn't stop until she was standing on the ground in front of the manor.

Footsteps behind her indicated Stratford had followed her.

Before she could turn to face him, strong arms circled her, clamping her own arms to the side.

Used to facing her opponents in the MMA, the sudden attack brought back memories of being held in captivity, bound tightly, unable to fight her way out. Panic almost set in. Two years of therapy came to her rescue. She breathed in and out, forced the bad thoughts to the back of her mind and shut the door on them. Then her thoughts flashed to the best way to extricate herself from the man's strong hold.

"If you can't defend yourself," he whispered against her ear, "you can't defend me or my family."

Dix drew in another calming breath and let her body go limp, a complete deadweight in his arms.

Stratford staggered backward.

She slipped downward, bunched her legs beneath her and planted her feet in the dirt. Then she twisted her body, taking his with hers, flinging them both to the ground.

As they fell, his grip loosened to break his fall.

Dix rolled over, grabbed his arm and jerked it up and behind his back, forcing Stratford onto his belly. She straddled his hips, sat on his back and leaned over to whisper in his ear. "Sorry I wrinkled your suit, Mr. Stratford. I'm also sorry I wasted your time. And, for the record, I'm not interested in protecting someone who doesn't trust my ability to do the job. Thank you for the opportunity but no thanks. I'll find another job."

Dix released his arm and stood, stepping over his prone body. She turned back to the people gathered on the porch, clapping and cheering for her. She shook her head and repeated, "Thanks, but I don't want the job."

The cheering died down. Tazer descended the stairs, her brow furrowing. "What do you mean you don't want the job?"

"I don't. Mr. Stratford obviously doesn't think a woman will suffice. I've fought my share of gender discrimination. I'm done." She started toward the rental car, wondering how long her savings would last after she paid Fontaine back for the flight and the car rental.

Before she'd gone four steps, a leg shot out and swept

her off her feet. She landed hard on her back, the air knocked from her lungs.

Stratford straddled her hips, grabbed her wrists and yanked them above her head, pinning them to the dirt. "Sorry I messed up your hair and smudged your makeup, but you can't quit until I fire you."

Dix gasped, her lungs remembering how to inhale. "I'm not wearing makeup. And it's too late. I already quit."

He shook his head. "I don't accept your resignation."

"You don't have to." She shoved at him and lifted her leg sharply, attempting to knee him in the back. "It's not negotiable." She grunted.

"I need someone to protect my family." He scooted back on her thighs, trapping her legs on the ground. "Despite your bad temper, I want you to do it."

She opened her mouth to protest.

He released one of her wrists and pressed a finger to her lips. "I don't have anyone else. I need someone temporarily until I can hire a full-time replacement. At least give me that."

"I'm not your *man*," she bit out.

"Call me crazy." For the first time since she'd met the man, his lips twitched in something akin to a smile. "I don't want a *man*. I want *you*."

Chapter 3

Andrew wasn't sure what made him tackle the female. Not only had he pinned her to the ground, he'd insisted she take the job. He told himself it was her stubborn determination to prove herself that had pushed him past his concerns. The heat of her thighs straddling his hips and the way she'd pressed her breasts against his back had nothing whatsoever to do with his decision. Though his skin still tingled and the warmth of her breath on the side of his neck lingered in the cool night air.

The plain facts were that he needed someone to keep track of Leigha and keep her safe from whoever was trying to hurt him. What worried him more was the secret friend Leigha went on and on about. Should the person actually exist, he had no business hanging around a six-year-old without her father's permission. Until Andrew had a permanent fix for the situation, Dix Reeves would have to do.

And even if she were as attractive as she was tough, he wouldn't hold that against her. He rose to his feet and extended his hand to the woman on the ground.

She shoved it aside, easily rolled to her feet and brushed the dust from her jeans. She moved like an athlete, with a spring in her step. Fast and strong, the woman could be an asset. At the very least, she'd be a good temporary solution to his needs. Tomorrow he'd log on to the internet and search for reputable bodyguard services. "If you're ready to leave, I need to get home. As I mentioned, Leigha isn't feeling well and I don't like leaving her for very long with only Mrs. Purdy to protect her."

Dix crossed her arms over her chest. "What part of 'no thanks' did you not understand?"

Ignoring her refusal, he walked to his SUV and climbed in. "Follow me. The road can be hard to find in the dark. And by the looks of it, the Devil's Shroud is moving in."

Dix shot a glance from Andrew to Tazer. "What's he talking about?"

Tazer nodded. "He's right. By the time you get back to his place, the Devil's Shroud will make it very difficult to find your way." Her lips twisted. "The folks around here have a flair for the dramatic. The Devil's Shroud is what they call a thicker-than-pea-soup fog that blinds anyone trying to find their way through it. If you live here long enough, you will undoubtedly experience it firsthand. Probably tonight."

Molly stepped forward. "They say that when the

Devil's Shroud rolls in, you can count on evil coming along with it."

Dix snorted. "Well, I should be able to find my way to town and a hotel before it gets that thick."

With a shrug, Molly glanced toward Andrew. "You might try saying 'please.'"

Andrew pressed his lips together. As one of the most powerful traders on Wall Street, he'd been used to giving orders and having people follow them without question. Since *the accident*, he'd left that world behind. But that world hadn't completely left him. He swallowed the desire to tell everyone to go to hell and forced out, "Please."

Dix's brows puckered and a smile curled the corners of her mouth. "Wow. That's the best you can do?"

He growled before he could stop himself. "Take it or leave it."

She hesitated, her gaze sweeping him from head to toe. As he expected, her perusal slowed on the scars he'd acquired in *the accident*.

Andrew fought the urge to turn his face away as well as to hide his hand from her all-seeing eyes. But he stood fast, refusing to back down. She'd see the scars on a daily basis; she might as well get used to them now.

When her gaze reached his toes, she looked up and nodded curtly. "I'll take it. But only on a temporary basis." She pointed a finger at him. "And not for you, but for your daughter. Hopefully she doesn't have her father's bad temper."

Andrew slipped into the SUV without saying another word. He didn't wait to see if she would follow, but pulled out of the gravel driveway and onto the paved highway.

Lights shone into his rearview mirror.

He let go of the breath he hadn't realized he'd been holding and focused on driving through the increasingly thick fog along the curvy coastal highway leading toward his estate.

When she got too far behind, he slowed and waited. By the time he reached the turnoff to his driveway, the fog had completely taken over. Andrew waited for Dix to turn in behind him before he hit the button to activate the automatic gate opener. The gate remained open long enough for both cars to pass through. Then he was leading the way along the twisting drive to Stratford House, the mansion his grandfather had left to him.

Not until he was right in front of the structure could he see the lights glowing a hazy yellow from the main living room and one of the upstairs bedrooms. The rest of the house lay in shrouded darkness.

In the fog, the house resembled one of those Gothic buildings in a horror movie. Andrew wondered what Dix was thinking. Would she turn around and leave? Or would she accept the challenge, creepy house and all?

He got out and waited for her rental car to pull to a stop next to his SUV.

Dix climbed out of the vehicle and stared up at the three-story mansion. "This is where you live?" she asked. Her gaze shot to him.

"It's my home," he said.

"It's big enough to be a hotel. No wonder you need

help keeping track of your daughter. Someone could easily get lost in that house."

"It was my grandfather's," he said, surprised at the defensiveness in his tone.

"Did he have a large, extended family, aunts, uncles and cousins who moved in with him?"

A smile pulled at the corners of Andrew's lips. "No. He built it for his wife, whom he loved dearly."

Dix shook her head. "Why?"

"Some say they had hoped to fill each room with children. Others think my grandfather and my grandmother liked making love in a different room every night. It gave them a multitude of options."

Dix's cheeks blossomed into a pretty shade of pink and she turned toward her rental car. "I'll have a look around the house. As big as it is, it has to have multiple entry and exit points."

"It does."

She lifted a gym bag from the backseat of the car and straightened. "Do you check each one of them every night?"

"I do. It takes approximately fifteen minutes to check and secure all of them." He held out his hand. "I can take that for you."

She shook her head. "I can manage."

"Where are the rest of your things?"

She lifted the bag. "This is it. I travel light."

Andrew stared at her. She didn't wear makeup and her blond hair was straight and neatly brushed. Jeans, a powder blue T-shirt and a slightly worn pair of running shoes made up Dix's outfit. She looked like the girl next door. No. More like the tomboy next door. So completely different from his ex-lovers. Some of them had to have a new pair of shoes for every outfit. Several families could be supported for a year on the amount they'd spent on footwear alone.

He strode to the front door, inserted a key and threw open one side of the massive double-door entrance. Andrew waved his hand. "Ladies first."

Dix's eyes narrowed but she stepped past him into the three-story foyer.

"Wow, it's as massive on the inside as it is on the outside." Even though Dix spoke softly, her words echoed against the walls and marble floors.

Andrew closed the door behind him and twisted the dead bolt. "My grandfather and grandmother had a flair for the dramatic."

"No kidding." Dix spun in a circle. "Yeah, I can see where you could lose a kid in this."

Andrew had been coming to his grandfather's house since he was a small child. He was used to the grandeur. Seeing it through Dix's eyes, he could understand how overwhelming it could be. Especially if you were tasked with protecting the occupants of such a large building.

"Oh, good. You're home." Mrs. Purdy, his housekeeper, hurried down the sweeping staircase. "Leigha was asking for you."

"Any improvement?"

Mrs. Purdy's lips pressed together. "None. She's still running a temperature despite the anti-inflammatories and cool compresses. I think she's a bit delirious, as well. When you didn't come after she called, she asked for her imaginary friend."

In the months Andrew had taken over the care of his daughter, he'd only had to contend with a case of the sniffles and an odd nightmare or two. Never a fever and delirium. "Should I call the doctor or take her to the emergency room?"

Mrs. Purdy shook her head. "Her fever has only been up to 102 degrees. If it goes higher, you should take her to the hospital. For now, she needs to sweat it out." The older woman glanced back up the stairs. "I'd stay, but Mr. Purdy wasn't feeling on top of the weather himself." For the first time, the woman noticed Dix. "I'm sorry. I didn't see you back there." She held out her hand. "I'm Dottie Purdy. And you are?"

Dix held out her hand and opened her mouth to reply.

Before she could, Andrew cut in. "Mrs. Purdy, this is Dix Reeves. She's an old friend who will be staying with us for the next couple of weeks."

Mrs. Purdy smiled and shook Dix's hand. "Oh, that's just lovely. This big old place needs more people to fill it up. I'll be sure to add a plate to the dinner table tomorrow. Anything in particular you prefer to eat, or allergies to anything?"

"I'm pretty open to anything," Dix said. "No allergies."

"Great." Mrs. Purdy beamed. "Then I'll see you two tomorrow. Call if you have any questions about Leigha. My children all went through fevers and upset stomachs a number of times. They all came through just fine." She waved her hand. "Cool compress. Her next dose of Tylenol should be in four hours. Rub a little mentho-lated cream on her chest if she gets stuffy. Other than that, stay with her. She seemed a little sad and frightened tonight."

Andrew almost stepped in front of Mrs. Purdy to block her from leaving. "Are you sure I'm qualified for this? Should I call a nurse, anyone with more experience?"

Mrs. Purdy patted his scarred cheek. "You have as much experience as most new parents. You'll do fine. And I'm sure Miss Reeves will help."

"Me?" Dix touched a hand to her chest. "I don't know anything about sick children."

"All you have to do is stay with her. Check her temp and keep her calm." Mrs. Purdy glanced at her watch. "I really must go. It will take me quite a while to get home in the fog."

Panic threatened to overwhelm Andrew. He'd had a nanny for Leigha in New York City. And Mrs. Purdy did most everything for him since he'd arrived in Cape Churn and secured her services. He was completely unqualified to deal with a sick little girl.

Mrs. Purdy didn't stay to argue. She was through the door and gone before Andrew could order her to stay. Not that she would. Mrs. Purdy wasn't one of the Wall Street interns he could order around. She did things when she was good and ready, on her own schedule, in her own way. And she kept his house in order.

Dix crossed to the door and twisted the lock behind Mrs. Purdy. "If you'll tell me where I can drop my things, I'll start my inspection of the house."

"I'd like you to start your inspection in Leigha's room," Andrew said.

"Oh, no, you don't. You just want me to take care of your kid." Dix held up her hands. "Just because I'm female doesn't mean I know what to do with a sick child. She's your little girl. *You* fix her."

A weak cry came from above. "Mrs. Purdy? Mr. Stratford? I don't feel good." Sobs followed.

Andrew's gut knotted. So, he didn't know how to take care of a sick little girl. He'd wing it. Leaving Dix standing in the entryway, he took the steps upward, two at a time, and entered the third doorway on the right. The room closest to the master suite.

Leigha lay in the queen-size bed, a small figure swallowed by puffy, cotton-candy-pink blankets. Her long blond hair fanned across the pillow and her face was even paler than normal. Brewer lay at her feet, his chin between his paws, his tail thumping against the comforter.

"Hey, Leigha. Mrs. Purdy had to go home."

She stared up at him, her eyes wide. "Who's going to take care of me?"

Andrew sat on the edge of the bed and brushed a strand of hair out of her face. His hands felt so big and clumsy next to her delicate features. God, he wished Mrs. Purdy hadn't left. "I guess you're stuck with me."

Footsteps sounded outside the bedroom door.

Andrew shot a glance over his shoulder.

Dix peeked in and added, "And me."

Leigha's eyes widened. She reached for Andrew's hand and whispered, "Who's she?"

Andrew waved his hand behind him, urging Dix forward. "Leigha, this is Dix. Dix, this is Leigha."

Leigha's brows lowered. "What is she doing here?"

Andrew hated lying to the child, but he needed her to trust Dix. "Dix is my friend, and she's come to stay with us for a little while. I'm counting on you to show her around. This place is so big, she might get lost."

"I don't feel like showing her around. My tummy hurts."

"You don't have to show me around today, sweetie." Dix entered the room and came to stand beside Andrew. "Maybe when you get better?" She reached out her hand to the dog. "Is this your dog?"

Leigha nodded.

"What's his name?" Dix asked.

"Brewer."

Dix scratched behind Brewer's ears. "Does Brewer like to listen to stories?"

Leigha frowned up at Dix. "Brewer's a dog. He doesn't always understand people."

Andrew hid a grin. His daughter wasn't going to give Dix an inch. She'd have to work for a connection.

His new bodyguard walked over to a shelf and thumbed through the colorful books. "I bet he likes it when you talk to him, doesn't he?" Dix lifted a book off of a shelf. "Do you think he would like it if I read to him?"

The little girl closed her eyes. "He might." She reached for Andrew's hand and squeezed it, uncaring that it had burn scars and didn't feel like a normal hand. She didn't mind that he wasn't perfect. She always seemed glad that he was just himself. His heart swelled. This little girl he hadn't known he had until a year ago was his.

"What would he like to listen to?" Dix asked.

"He likes the book about the island and the blue dolphins."

Andrew almost laughed out loud. From claiming Brewer was just a dog to admitting the animal would like to listen to the book *Island of the Blue Dolphins*, Leigha had come full circle.

Score one for Dix. Despite her claim that she didn't know anything about children, she'd gotten Leigha to come around to her way of thinking without having to order her to do so.

Andrew nodded. "I'll let you three get to it." He started to rise but was stopped by the little hand holding his.

"Please stay, Mr. Stratford." Leigha stared up at him with glassy blue eyes, her face flushed and her body hot.

"Tell you what…" Dix handed the book to Andrew. "Let your father start the story, while I get a fresh cloth to cool your face."

"But Brewer wants to hear *you* read," Leigha said.

"And I will. After I get something to cool you down." Dix drew an X across her chest. "Cross my heart."

"Okay." Leigha turned to her father.

Outmaneuvered by the woman, Andrew opened the book. "Where should I start?"

"At the beginning." Leigha closed her eyes and lay back against the pillow.

Andrew started reading.

Dix disappeared into the room's adjoining bathroom

and returned with a damp cloth. She folded it several times and laid it across Leigha's forehead.

Andrew couldn't help noting how gentle Dix was with his little girl. The woman was a natural with kids. While he read, Andrew studied Dix out of the corner of his eye.

Without makeup and her hair hanging loose around her shoulders, she wasn't a classic beauty. Her shoulders and arm muscles were well-defined and taut. She didn't have an ounce of fat on her body. Whatever she'd done before going to work for Fontaine, she'd kept physically fit. No, she wasn't like Tazer, a woman who could pose for a fashion magazine. Nor was she bone-thin, like so many runway models who looked like they could use a big hamburger or treatment for an eating disorder.

No, Dix was what Andrew would call a healthy, granola girl, adept at hiking up hills without breaking into a sweat. She might even be capable of scaling cliffs with her bare hands.

But at that moment she was showing a side of herself she probably didn't know she had. A side that made Andrew look at her in a whole new way.

The tenderness with which she applied the cool cloth to Leigha's brow and cheeks was nothing short of maternal. She moved slowly, carefully patting Leigha's face as she smiled down at the child.

So engrossed in watching Dix's movements, at one point, Andrew forgot to read.

"I'm not asleep yet." Leigha opened her eyes. "Please keep reading."

"Sorry," Andrew said, shaking aside his obsessive desire to watch Dix's every move.

Dix chuckled low in her chest.

The sound made Andrew warm all over and he wanted her to do it again. He jerked his attention back to the book and read each word, without really seeing them or absorbing the story.

As he ended the first chapter, Andrew realized two things.

Leigha had fallen asleep and Dix had chinked away a piece of the wall he'd erected around himself.

That would not do. The woman was a hired hand. A temporary one at that.

The sooner he found a replacement bodyguard, the better.

Chapter 4

Dix smiled down at the little girl with the spun-gold hair splayed out on the pillow. She remembered a picture of herself at about Leigha's age. Her hair had been long and wavy, and she'd been full of curiosity and mischief. Her mother had never been able to keep up with her. Looking back, she was surprised she'd lived through some of her more dangerous escapades.

If her mother had known where she'd been exploring, she would have had more gray hair. To the young Dix, life had been one big adventure.

Joining the military had been a logical choice for Dix. She related better with men than with women, and she'd always liked getting dirty and shooting guns with her father. In fact, she liked fishing, hunting, yard work and anything her father had liked. Housekeeping, cooking

and laundry had been her least favorite things to do growing up. She'd been happiest outdoors in the sunshine.

So why did her heart skip several beats and then
tighten in her chest when she stared down at the little
girl lying against the cool sheets, her body warm from
fever?

Something she'd never felt before welled up inside.
A fierce desire to protect this small creature so depen-
dent on adults to keep her well and alive. Was this how
parents felt about their children? While her mother had
wanted to hold her back, she'd done it out of a desire to
keep her safe. Her father, on the other hand, had wanted
to share his love of the outdoors with her, to show her
some of what she could do if she broadened her mind
beyond the walls of their little house in the country.

The deep, resonant tone of Mr. Stratford's voice filled
the room, making it seem smaller, more intimate. The
soft glow of the lamp on the nightstand brought them
closer together. They probably looked like a family.

Dix jerked upright. She hadn't come to Stratford's
mansion to become part of his family. She'd come to
protect this family.

She glanced around, wondering where Leigha's mother
was and why she wasn't there, taking care of her child.

Fontaine had told her she would be the bodyguard
for the Stratford family. From what she could tell, that
family consisted of two. Father and daughter. And the
daughter called her father "Mr. Stratford."

Why?

As her father read, Leigha's eyes closed. Dix backed
away from the bed, her hand clenching around the damp

cloth. Her goal was to leave the room and perform the search of the giant house for any weaknesses in entry and exit points.

She'd almost made it to the door when a little voice said, "Please, don't go."

Dix turned to find Leigha staring across the room at her, her cheeks flushed, her eyes glassy.

"Your father will stay with you," Dix pointed out, hating to disappoint the girl but feeling the need to escape. This sweet little family scene threatened to choke her. After all she'd been through, she doubted seriously she'd ever have children of her own or be the mother they needed.

"But I want you to stay, too," she said, her voice trailing off, a single tear slipping from the corner of her eye. "I don't feel good." She raised her little hand, reaching for Dix.

Mr. Stratford stopped reading and turned to add his gaze to his daughter's.

Her heart contracting, Dix couldn't step through the door and leave when the little girl had asked her so sweetly to stay.

She sighed. "I'm only going to wet the cloth again and make it cooler. I'll be right back." Dix changed direction and headed into the bathroom. There she turned on the cold water and dipped the cloth beneath. While she soaked and squeezed the excess out, she stared at her reflection in the mirror.

I can't do this.

Fighting in the MMA had given her an outlet for her

anger and sorrow. Without it, she had no way to channel the energy or to push aside the pain.

This father and daughter pair already had her gut tied into a very twisted knot and she hadn't been there for even a day.

Dix's parents had died in a helicopter crash while touring the Grand Canyon. She'd been deep in Army Ranger training on the field training exercise when it had happened. The training officers hadn't told her until she'd completed the most challenging portion of the exercise.

No one had been there when she'd graduated, nor had she had the opportunity to celebrate because she'd gotten right onto a plane and flown to her home state of Texas to attend her mother and father's funeral.

Going home had been the hardest thing she'd ever done in her life. The house hadn't been the same without her mother and father in it. She'd listed it with a Realtor, packed a few photo albums, her great-grandmother's antique candy dish and given the rest of the furnishings and clothing to a local charity.

She hadn't had much time to manage it all before she'd had to report back to her new unit only to ship out within two weeks to the war zone.

All of those memories were still raw, even though it had been years.

Dix glanced down at the cloth she'd squeezed so much it barely retained any water. She dampened it and started over. A minute later she returned to Leigha's bedroom and draped the cloth over the girl's forehead.

"You came back," she whispered and reached for

Dix's hand. She pulled her closer until Dix was forced to sit on the side of the bed.

The little fingers in hers were too warm. She wondered how long it would take for the fever to break. If it didn't, they might be making an emergency trip to the hospital before the night was over.

Mr. Stratford glanced up, his gaze connecting with Dix's.

A sharp stab of awareness coursed through Dix's veins. She averted her gaze and stared down at the little hand resting in hers.

Stratford started another chapter of the book, his voice droning on until Leigha finally slept.

Dix slipped her hand free of Leigha's and stood.

"You can go. I'll take it from here," Mr. Stratford said.

With a nod, Dix left the room. Once in the hallway, she dragged in several deep breaths before she started down the stairs and took her time going through each room on the ground floor, checking windows and doors to ensure they were all secured.

All the while, she thought of the little girl and her father in the room upstairs. Other than a housekeeper and a dog, they seemed incredibly alone in the huge old mansion. How sad. Even if the mansion was a family inheritance, she would have converted it into the hotel it seemed more suited for or she'd have sold it. The McGregors had the right idea converting their big old house into a bed-and-breakfast. At least it was full of people, not dark and lonely.

All of the doors and windows on the first floor were

secured. In the kitchen, she found a door leading into the basement. She flipped the light switch. A yellowed bulb gave an eerie glow that barely lit the stairs halfway down. Hollywood had given basements a bad reputation. Everyone knew a lone female going into the basement by herself was a bad idea. It never ended well.

Dix snorted. Having trained in snake-infested swamps as well as having significant experience in hand-to-hand combat and mixed martial arts, she didn't consider a basement a threat. But she wasn't stupid. Dix grabbed a butcher knife from a drawer and descended the stairs. At the bottom, she found another switch. When she flipped it, bulbs lit at different locations. Some appeared burned out.

The space below the mansion was almost as extensive as the first floor, broken up by thick posts, crates, old furniture, a room set up as a wine cellar and stacks of cardboard boxes. A veritable maze. Scattered around the outer walls were tiny windows and one exit leading to a trapdoor that probably opened out into a garden. She pushed against the door. It held firm, no matter how hard she tried to open it. In the morning she'd check it from the outside. She suspected it had a padlock holding it in place. The small windows were locked and, other than a creepy feeling, the basement appeared secure.

As she started for the stairs, something moved in the shadows with a scuffling sound. As big as the house was, it might have a mouse or rat problem.

A shiver slipped down Dix's spine and her hand tightened around the handle of the butcher knife. She inched forward, her ears straining to pick up the sound again.

If she could pinpoint the direction, she might actually find the culprit.

There it was again. Only this time it sounded more like a footstep. Dix ducked behind a stack of boxes and waited. Whoever it was shouldn't be sneaking around the basement. If it was Mr. Stratford, he would have announced his presence, wouldn't he?

Or was he like her, wondering who would be sneaking around a basement so late at night? Dix opened her mouth to say something, announcing her presence. She didn't want to startle the man. He could be carrying a gun and react by shooting first, asking questions later. Before she said anything, she shut her mouth and remained silent. The footsteps faded away into silence.

Dix waited several minutes before moving again. Why hadn't Stratford said something? If he'd come down to the wine cellar, he would have passed her stack of boxes. But no one had walked past her hiding place.

Shrugging the tension from her shoulders, she stepped out from behind the boxes, calling herself every kind of fool. She knew better than to let a creepy old mansion scare her. It was just a building. She'd performed sweeps of many buildings in her Army career. The difference being she'd carried an M4A1 rifle, worn protective gear and had a trained team backing her.

She had just placed her first foot on the bottom step leading up to the kitchen when the lights blinked out.

The darkness in the basement was so complete, Dix couldn't see anything but the sliver of light beneath the door to the kitchen at the top of the stairs. But, wait—how could the light be on in the kitchen and not in the basement? Someone had to have turned out the lights or a breaker had tripped to cut the electricity to the lights where she stood.

The sound of wood crashing against the concrete floor made Dix jump. She stumbled against the riser, nearly stabbing herself with the butcher knife as she scrambled for a handhold. She found her footing and raced up the steps toward the slim bit of light finding its way beneath the door.

At the top, Dix held her breath, twisted the knob, flung open the door and burst into the kitchen, running into a solid wall of muscles.

A strong hand wrapped around her wrist, holding it and the butcher knife at a distance.

"Didn't your mother ever tell you not to run with a knife in your hand?"

At the sound of Stratford's voice, Dix sagged against him, at once relieved, quickly followed by chagrin that he'd found her running out of a scary basement because of a noise. Some bodyguard she'd prove to be if his house gave her the willies.

She pushed her free hand against his chest, inhaling the faint yet tantalizing scent of aftershave. "Thank you, but I was doing fine until you stepped in my way."

He chuckled. "Where were you going, brandishing that butcher knife?"

She pulled her hand free and tilted her chin. "I was headed to the drawer to put it away." As if to prove out her lie, she walked to the drawer where she'd found the knife and slipped it in. Gathering her wits, she turned to face him, her brows rising. "I have a question."

"Try me. I might have an answer."

"Where's the breaker box?"

His brows dipped. "Why do you ask?"

"The lights went out in the basement while I was down there checking windows and doors."

His frown deepened. "The breaker box is in the basement. I had the wiring upgraded several years ago. Since then, I can't recall having issues with breakers being thrown." He walked to the door Dix had stormed through a moment before and flipped the light switch. The light came on. "Seems to be working now."

Dix's face heated. Could she have hit the switches by accident?

"I'll check the breaker box, just to make sure. But if this light is on, the others will come on, as well. The basement is all wired to the same breaker."

Dix nodded. "I'd feel better if you did check. Perhaps there's a short in one of the wires."

Mr. Stratford descended the steps.

Dix followed, wishing she'd brought the butcher knife.

A wooden chair that had been stacked on top of an old table lay on the ground, its legs broken and splintered. She could have brushed by, dislodging it from its perch. But that still didn't explain the lights extinguishing when they did.

She followed Stratford to a metal box mounted in the wall. He opened it, ran his finger down through the labels until he stopped on the one marked Basement. He flipped the switch and the lights went out.

The breath caught in Dix's lungs and she strained to

hear the sound of footsteps, like she had a few minutes before. Silence stretched until another loud click heralded the lights coming back on.

Stratford turned to her. "Seems to be working fine."

Great. She looked like an idiot. But that didn't bother her as much as the memory of shuffling footsteps when she'd been hiding behind the cardboard boxes.

She didn't believe there was a real problem with the electricity. The problem was that something or someone had to have flipped the breaker to make all of the lights in the basement go out at once.

"Besides you, me and Leigha, are there any other people who live in this house?"

Stratford shook his head. "No. Mrs. Purdy comes in every day to cook and clean for us. But that's it."

Dix nodded. She'd be sure to carry a gun with her whenever she entered the basement. If for nothing else, to shoot at the rats.

"Any more questions?" he asked.

"Yes." She stared up into his eyes. "Where will I sleep?"

Stratford cupped her elbow in his hand and led her toward the stairs. "I have Leigha in the room next to mine with an adjoining door. I'd like for you to sleep in the bedroom beside hers."

Dix nodded, her skin tingling where his hand rested on her arm. In a structure the size of Stratford House, she could have been assigned a room in a completely different wing. She was glad he put her close to Leigha for the child's sake. But being close to the man added an entirely different dimension to this task. "One more question."

His lips quirked on the corners, making the wicked scar less menacing. "Shoot."

"Where's Leigha's mother?"

The hint of a smile vanished, replaced by a fierce frown. "Why do you need to know?"

"I was sent to protect the family. I assumed husband, wife and child. If I'm to protect the entire family, I need to know who that consists of."

"All you need to be worried about is making sure Leigha is safe. I can take care of myself."

Dix persisted. Stratford wasn't happy about something and he was avoiding a direct response. "Your wife?" She held her breath, part of her hoping there wasn't a wife. The other part of her wondering why she cared. She'd just met the man.

"Leigha's mother is dead."

Andrew turned away from Dix and marched up the steps to the kitchen. He didn't wait for her to follow. The sooner he got away from her, the better. All the old rage roiled up in his belly, threatening to take him to that dark place he'd lived in when he'd been in the hospital suffering the pain of skin grafts. All because of Jeannette and her horrible, hateful revenge.

A hand on his arm slowed him to a stop. He breathed in and out like a bull preparing for the charge, but he refused to face Dix.

"As a bodyguard, I feel like the more I know about you, Leigha and this place, the better equipped I'll be to take care of all of you. I'm sorry. I didn't mean to step over the line. I didn't know."

"I told you—I don't need anyone to take care of me. Focus on Leigha. She's the one who needs you. Not me." He shrugged her hand off his arm.

"I'm sorry. Losing your wife is hard enough without someone dragging up the memory. You must have loved her a lot."

Fury surged upward. Andrew was powerless to hold back. He spun, gripped Dix's arms and shook her. "Jeannette wasn't my wife, and I can honestly say that I hated her with every fiber of my being. Any mother who could willfully set fire to the apartment she shares with her daughter, and then stand by watching it burn with her daughter inside, is a monster. I'm glad she's dead." He shook her again. "Do you hear me? I might rot in hell, but I'm glad she's dead."

Chapter 5

Dix lay in the bed one door down from Leigha, her arms sore from where Andrew had squeezed so hard he'd left bruises. Yeah, they hurt, but nothing like whatever it was Andrew had gone through. She assumed the scars on his face and hand were caused by the fire Leigha's mother had set.

Though he'd answered the question about a wife, he'd left so many more unanswered. Was Leigha his daughter? If so, why did she call him "Mr. Stratford"? Question after question spun through Dix's mind to the point she couldn't go to sleep.

She rose from the bed and padded barefoot down the hall to Leigha's room. Pushing open the door, she entered. A night-light shone in a corner, giving just enough light for Dix to see everything in the room, including the little girl in the middle of the big bed.

Leigha stopped beside the bed and laid her hand on Leigha's forehead. Thankfully, the fever seemed to have broken and the child appeared to be resting comfortably.

Grateful Leigha was better, Dix turned toward the door.

"Stay with me." The little girl's voice stopped her before she could take a single step.

Dix smiled down at her and brushed a strand of golden-blond hair away from Leigha's brow. "Why aren't you sleeping?"

"Sometimes I get scared," she said, taking Dix's hand in hers.

"Are you scared now?"

She pressed Dix's hand to her cheek. "Not when you're here with me."

Dix's heart melted a little at the girl's puppy-dog eyes. "Sweetie, you don't even know me."

"My friend said I could trust you."

Dix's hand tightened around the child's. "Your friend?"

The child nodded. "He said you're one of the good guys."

Dix perched on the side of the bed, wishing she'd stopped long enough to pull on a pair of jeans. The extra-large T-shirt didn't seem fully adequate should Leigha's father choose to come in and check on his girl. But then, Leigha had Dix's hand and didn't seem willing to relinquish it anytime soon. "How does he know I won't hurt you?"

She shrugged. "He just does." Leigha scooted to the far side of the bed and threw back the blanket. "You can lie down, too. I won't kick."

With her legs cooling in the night air and Leigha still holding tightly to her hand, Dix caved. She slid between the sheets and laid her head on the pillow beside Leigha.

The child immediately rolled into her side and rested her head in the crook of Dix's arm. "You smell like flowers."

Dix smiled. "It's probably the soap from the bathroom."

"I think it smells good on you." Leigha snuggled into Dix's side and laid her arm over Dix's stomach.

Dix sniffed the girl's hair. It had that soft, clean smell of baby shampoo. "You smell pretty good yourself."

Leigha hugged her. "My friend thinks you're pretty."

Dix stiffened momentarily and then relaxed. She supposed many children had imaginary friends to keep them company when they were lonely. "Does your friend have a name?"

She nodded, her eyelids drooping. "Bennet."

"Do you play with your friend often?" Dix asked.

"Every day," she whispered, her voice fading as her breathing grew deeper.

For a long time, Dix lay with the little girl nestling against her. She listened to the sounds the mansion made, creaking like an old lady's knees as she settled in for the night.

A few days on the Oregon coast keeping track of one little girl who could very easily steal her heart wasn't bad for her first gig as a Stealth Operations Specialist. She would ease into her role and learn more about the man who'd engaged her and his expectations of the bodyguard he'd hired.

The black Lab, lying at the end of the bed, rolled over onto her foot, completely relaxed. Acceptance by two of her clients had been accomplished. Now all she needed was to win the approval of the head of the family, one darkly brooding, deeply scarred man who didn't mince words or waste time. But he did read to his daughter when she wasn't feeling good, and he cared enough to hire someone to keep her safe from an unknown threat.

Tomorrow, Dix would ask him who might have it in for him and the exact nature of the inciting incidents that had set him on the course to finding a bodyguard for his daughter. In the meantime, her charge was to protect Leigha. With the little girl sleeping soundly against her side, Dix let her eyes slide closed.

Just as she was about to drift into sleep, a waft of cool air caressed her skin. Her eyelids fluttered open and she stared up at a man with black hair and dancing blue eyes, a smile curling his lips. His clothes appeared to be from another era. Wearing a dark suit and a fedora, he could have been a gangster from the early nineteen hundreds.

Was she dreaming? She blinked and the image was gone.

Dix gasped and jackknifed into a sitting position, her heartbeat thundering against her ribs.

Leigha lay with one hand tucked beneath her cheek and the other reaching out to Dix. Brewer lifted his head as if to question her for waking in the middle of the night. Then, as if his head were too heavy to hold up, he let it drop back to the blanket and sighed.

Had an intruder been in the room, surely the dog would have let her know or at the least been agitated.

Convinced the man she'd seen was nothing more than the beginning of a dream, Dix lay back on the pillow and willed her pulse to slow. Dreams of bygone eras had to be the norm for guests of Stratford House. The structure and the furnishings conjured ghosts of the past. If not real aberrations, then those dreamed up in the minds of present-day inhabitants. No wonder Leigha had an imaginary friend.

Dix finally relaxed. The day had been full of revelations and tomorrow she'd learn more about her new assignment. For now, sleep claimed her, sweeping her into a dream that spanned a continent and swept her out to sea in a mobster's yacht.

Andrew lay in his bed, tossing and turning, drifting in and out of sleep. He fought the lure of the recurring nightmare that had plagued him for almost a year. But every time he closed his eyes to sleep, the dream returned, filling his night with memories of that awful day. Pulling him back into that flaming inferno of Jeannette's apartment building—an image he could never erase from his mind. He'd go into the blaze to rescue the daughter he hadn't known he had until that day he'd gone into hell to bring her out.

Jeannette had been a willing partner, but she'd failed to tell him she was married when they'd met in a bar in

New York City. He'd been drunk, celebrating a Yankees win, when she'd invited him to her hotel room.

One night of sex he couldn't even remember, and six years later he'd gotten a call from a woman he couldn't recall, claiming he had a daughter.

When he'd called her bluff, Jeannette had told him she couldn't afford to keep the brat since her husband had left her. If he didn't take her, she'd leave her in the apartment where she couldn't afford to pay rent.

At first Andrew chose to ignore the call. After all, he was a wealthy man. The woman could be scamming him.

When she'd called a second and third time, more desperate than the first, she described a tattoo Andrew had on his right butt cheek. She claimed the child had his blue eyes. She couldn't keep her. Her landlord had threatened to evict them. With nowhere to go and no way to support a child, she had no other choice but to end it for both of them.

At that point, Andrew couldn't ignore the woman. A child's life could be at stake. He coaxed an address out of her and, in the middle of the night, he'd raced to the apartment building in a ramshackle section of the Bronx. When he arrived, smoke billowed from a window on the third floor of an eight-story building.

Women in bathrobes and men in boxer shorts herded small children from the building as Andrew ran inside and up the stairs to the third floor. Alarms blared but the sprinkler system never came on.

Choking on the acrid smoke, Andrew pulled his T-shirt up over his mouth and nose and pressed on, arriving at the *door to the apartment where most of the smoke seemed to be coming from. He tried the handle. The door was locked. With the potential of a child being trapped inside, Andrew threw his shoulder into the door. It didn't budge. He kicked and kicked until the door frame splintered around the dead bolt and the door swung open, emitting a cloud of black smoke.*

Andrew crouched low and ran inside. His eyes had stung and his lungs had burned. He found Jeannette throwing a burning blanket over a couch.

When she saw him, she screamed and tried to run past him. "You didn't want her. Nobody wanted her."

Andrew grabbed her by the arms. He didn't recognize the woman like she was, her hair tangled, her face streaked with soot. He didn't care if the child was his or not—she didn't deserve to die in a fire lit by a crazy woman. "Where is she?" he shouted.

"You can't have her. No one can have her!" The woman kicked him hard in the shins.

His grip loosened and she flung herself away from him. Before he could catch her, she ran screaming into one of the two bedrooms and slammed the door.

The other bedroom was completely consumed in flames. Andrew prayed the child hadn't been in there. He focused his attention on the room into which Jeannette had run.

This door didn't take long to breach. Two hard kicks and it crashed open. Andrew searched through the thickening smoke and couldn't find the woman or the child.

Then he heard a whimper from beneath the bed. He crouched below the curtain of smoke and spied Jean-

nette holding on to a little girl. The child coughed and cried, "I'm scared, Mama!"

"Shut up!" Jeannette yelled. "Shut up!" She pulled her deeper beneath the bed.

Andrew reached in to grab the girl, but Jeannette lashed out with clawlike fingernails, scratching his arm. He pulled his hand back, but the heat of the blaze behind him pushed him to try harder. "Don't do this to her, Jeannette. Let's get out of here. I'll make sure you're all taken care of."

She spit at him and clutched the child closer. "No! You can't take her from me."

"You wanted me to get her. I'm here now. Let me take her."

"No one wanted her. No one cared about me. We're leaving this world and taking this stinking apartment building with us."

Andrew couldn't stand by and let that happen. He grabbed what he could. His finger wrapped in the woman's hair and he dragged her out into the open. She let go of the little girl and fought like a wildcat.

The child slipped back beneath the bed. Andrew couldn't take care of her until he subdued the animal Jeannette had become.

He grabbed her around the middle and held on.

She freed one of her hands and raked her nails down the side of his face.

Pain seared through him, but he didn't let go. He carried her to the apartment door and shoved her out into the hallway, peeling her claws off of his arms. She had been like an octopus, clinging to him, refusing to let him return to rescue the girl.

Finally, he freed himself, slammed the door in her face and ran back into the thick smoke. He staggered into the bedroom, his eyes burning so badly he could barely see.

Dropping to his hands and knees, he crawled under the bed, grabbed the girl by her leg and dragged her out.

She cried, coughed and wrapped her arms around his neck, burying her face in his shirt. "Help me!"

When he turned toward the exit, the flames leaped. By then the blaze was so hot, Andrew felt as if he and the child would be cooked alive if he took a step back into the living room. He closed the bedroom door, grabbed a chair and flung it through a window. Smoke poured out into the night. He kicked the jagged shards out of the way and leaned out, hoping for a breath of fresh air.

Several emergency vehicles were parked on the street below, lights flashing, and the first responders were unloading equipment. Some ran toward the burning building.

People huddled in small groups, pointing upward to the window through which Andrew leaned. He wished he and the girl could be counted among them. Instead of hanging out a window, uncertain of their fate.

An explosion behind him nearly knocked him and the child over the ledge.

Two firefighters leaned an extension ladder against the wall of the building and one man started up. When he neared the top, he reached for the child.

The little girl refused to let go. Andrew finally peeled her arms from around his neck and handed her to the firefighter. Step by step, he eased back down the ladder, careful not to drop the girl.

The door exploded behind him and Jeannette ran in, carrying a flaming blanket. She tried to throw it at Andrew, but it tangled in her arms and caught her hair on fire.

Screaming, she ran around in circles, trying to pat the fire out with the blazing blanket.

Andrew tackled her, slapping at the flames with his bare hands. Pain seared through his skin. Jeannette pushed him off, ran for the window, hiked herself up over the sill and flung herself out.

Numb from pain and the smoke filling his lungs, Andrew dragged himself back to the window and over the ledge. One hand had been burned so badly he couldn't use it to hold on to the metal ladder. One rung at a time, he eased himself downward. Ten feet from the ground, his body and lungs gave up the fight. He fell the rest of the way, landing beside the limp body of the woman who'd condemned her daughter to death. Then he passed out.

A sound woke Andrew from the nightmare. He sat up, drenched in sweat, and pushed his hand through his hair. Why couldn't time heal his mind? Surely a year was enough to push the horrible event from his memories.

Another noise penetrated the lingering haze of his

dream and he tilted his head, straining to pinpoint the direction. It was coming from Leigha's bedroom.

He flung back the covers, leaped from the bed and ran through the connecting door, skidding to a halt at the foot of her bed.

Leigha lay sleeping peacefully, her body curled into the side of Dix's.

Dix's eyes were open and she had a finger pressed to her lips. "She's fine, just wanted someone to hold her," she whispered.

Andrew let go of the breath he'd been holding and relaxed. Seeing the two of them lying there so close made him realize just how similar they were. Leigha had golden-blond hair. So did Dix. Leigha had blue eyes like him, that clear ice blue. Though Dix had moss green eyes, on first impression, she could pass as Leigha's mother.

Andrew's chest tightened and he squeezed his fists, the pull on his scars a painful reminder he wasn't the man he used to be. Scarred and besieged by horrific nightmares, he wasn't fit to be anything to anybody. Leigha was his only concern. Making her life better, giving her the happiness she deserved after what she'd been through, was his number one priority. Andrew was surprised the child didn't have more nightmares than she did.

Andrew backed up a step, determined to return to his room and forget how different he'd pictured his life. Then he remembered why he'd come into the room in the first place. "I heard a noise. Did you?"

Dix's cheeks flushed with color and her gaze darted

to a corner. "Sorry. I was having a bad dream. I might have called out."

With a nod, Andrew took another step backward. "I know how it feels," he muttered. A little louder he said, "Sleep well." And he left the room, almost running back to his own.

For a long time, he lay in the bed, unwilling to go back to sleep, knowing the nightmare would return. Instead he filled his mind with the image of Leigha and Dix holding each other. It warmed his heart and eventually allowed him to drift into a deep, dreamless sleep. Deep down, he knew it was a mistake to frame that image in his mind. Dix was a temporary solution, not to be confused with a permanent relationship. That could never happen.

Chapter 6

"Dix?" a tiny voice whispered in her ear.

Dix tried to brush the sound away with her hand.

Little fingers caught her hand and held on. "Dix, are you awake?"

"No," Dix answered, trying to pull her hand free. She opened her eyes and closed them immediately as sunlight assaulted them with cheerful brightness. "Please tell me it's not morning."

A little giggle sounded beside her and a warm, soft body squirmed against her side. "Okay, I won't tell you. But you have to get up soon. My tummy is rumbling and I smell bacon."

Dix inhaled the mouthwatering scent and the rest of her body came alive. "Wow, that does smell like bacon." She rolled over to face Leigha. "What are we waiting for?"

"Last one to the kitchen is a rotten egg." Leigha leaped out of bed and ran for the door.

"Last one *dressed* and down to the kitchen is a rotten egg." Dix rolled out of the bed, onto her feet, and raced for the bedroom door. She ran out into the hall and smacked into a wall of muscles.

She staggered back but a hand on her arm kept her from falling. She glanced up into the twinkling blue eyes of Andrew Stratford. For a moment he looked familiar. Then she remembered the more rakish image of a man with similar hair color and those sparkling blue eyes. She rubbed her hand over her eyes and looked again. No, it was her client, Mr. Stratford. Perhaps her mind had played tricks on her with the ghostly image of a mobster Andrew Stratford.

"Are you all right, Miss Reeves?" His hands on her arms tightened.

"I am. And I can stand on my own."

Immediately he released her and dropped his arms to his sides. Then his brows rose into the tuft of hair that fell over his forehead. "Do you always run around half dressed?"

Heat burned in her cheeks as Dix remembered she'd gone to bed in an oversize T-shirt and not much more. The hem more than covered all of the important parts, but it only came down to just below her bottom, with a long expanse of legs left bare. "I was just headed to my room to dress."

A whirl of pink flashed by her, long curls flying

out behind as Leigha darted between them and ran for the staircase. "I'm not going to be a rotten egg!" Her little feet moved in double time as she descended the staircase.

"Slow down!" Stratford yelled.

"Can't," Leigha responded. "You wouldn't want me to be a rotten egg, would you?"

Dix chuckled.

Her client frowned. "What is she talking about?"

"I told her the last one dressed and down to the kitchen would be a rotten egg." Dix shrugged. "I guess that will be me. If you'll excuse me, I'll put on something more presentable."

His frown deepened. "Do that."

Dix turned and started for the door down the hall, but something made her turn back to her client. "You know, you look a lot more approachable when you smile." She held up her hand to stop him from saying anything. "Just saying." Then she ducked through the door and closed it behind her. She didn't require a response, and she knew it wasn't her place to tell the client he had a grumpy face. But, boy, it transformed when he smiled. That smile practically made her heart flutter and her knees grow weak.

Hmm. Maybe it was better if he continued to frown. She didn't need the distraction of his smile muddying her perspective.

She threw on a clean, if wrinkled, T-shirt and a pair of blue jeans, slipped into her brogan boots and pulled her hair back in a ponytail. Satisfied she was ready to work, she eased open the door to the hallway. Thankfully, Stratford wasn't there for her to crash into again. She found standing so close to him to be very unnerving. The breadth of his shoulders and the incredible blue of his eyes made her feel a little off balance, not quite on her game.

Dix followed the smell of bacon to the kitchen.

Mrs. Purdy stood at the stove, ladling a spoonful of scrambled eggs onto a plate. "Oh, there you are. Miss Leigha has been talking nonstop about you."

Dix drew in a long, deep sniff. "Is that bacon I smell?"

"No, it's rotten eggs," Leigha piped in and giggled. "I beat you down."

"And so you did." Dix rubbed her hand over the little girl's hair. "I'll be smelling like rotten eggs for a week."

"Don't be silly. That's only pretend." She smiled up at her. "Are you staying here forever?" Leigha's gaze shone up at Dix, her brows high and her expression hopeful.

"I don't know about that, but I'm here now and I'm going to be with you all day." Dix patted the child's cheek. "How does that sound?"

"Great!" Leigha said, bouncing in her seat.

Dix turned toward the housekeeper. "Is there anything I can do to help?"

"No, ma'am. You just sit there and keep Leigha company while I serve up your breakfast." Mrs. Purdy leaned toward Dix. "I'm just glad the little sweetheart is feeling better this morning."

Dix snorted. "You'd never know she'd been sick last night."

Mrs. Purdy sighed. "Oh, to be so young and resilient again." She handed Dix a plate piled with fluffy scrambled eggs, bacon and biscuits. "Enjoy."

"This isn't all for me, is it?"

"Honey, you'll need all the energy you can get to keep up with that one." Mrs. Purdy tipped her head toward Leigha.

"Surely one little girl won't be that much trouble."

"Not at all, but she's constant motion. If you try to keep up with her, you'll be going from the time she leaves that table until the time her head hits the pillow." Mrs. Purdy turned back to the skillet. "Trust me. I speak from experience."

Dix sat across the table from Leigha. "Is she right? Are you constantly on the go?"

Leigha looked up, wide-eyed. "Who, me?"

"Are there any other little girls in this room?" Dix asked.

Leigha glanced around and shrugged. "No."

"Then that would mean you."

Her brows dipped and she puffed out her chest. "I don't get into trouble."

"But I imagine sometimes you disappear?" Dix queried.

Leigha's frown deepened. "No, I don't." She held up her arm. "I can see me." She stared up at Dix. "Can't you?"

"Yes, but—"

The little girl didn't wait for Dix to explain. She looked past Dix and asked, "Can you see me, Mr. Stratford?"

"I certainly can."

The deep voice behind Dix made her jump.

Footsteps brought the man around the table to ruffle his daughter's hair.

Dix tensed with a forkful of eggs remaining poised halfway to her mouth. The air around her seemed to sizzle with Stratford's presence.

"I see Mrs. Purdy has been busy this morning. She's the best cook on the entire Oregon coast."

Mrs. Purdy laughed. "I wouldn't say that. I can stir a pan of eggs and make a mean lasagna, but I'm not quite as good as Nora Taggert."

"Mrs. Taggert's got nothing on you," Stratford insisted.

"You know best." Mrs. Purdy shifted her spatula in the pan full of eggs. "Speaking of which… You remember I'm leaving at noon today. I'm taking my husband in to Portland for a doctor's appointment. I won't be back until tomorrow. You'll have to fend for yourself for dinner tonight."

"No worries, Mrs. P.," Stratford said. "I can open a can of beans."

"I can burn toast on a good day," Dix offered. She really was terrible in the kitchen. "I can make a decent salad. Basically, I'm hopeless at anything that requires an oven or stove."

Mrs. Purdy turned to face Dix. "You three should go out to the Seaside Café and sample some of Nora's fine cooking. Then you can judge for yourself who's the better cook."

Dix noted the frown descending on Stratford's face. Already he was shaking his head.

Leigha bounced in her chair. "Mrs. Taggert has ice-cream cones. Please, Mr. Stratford. Please can we go?"

"I don't know," Stratford said.

"It's been months since you got out of this old monstrosity of a house," Mrs. Purdy pointed out. "It would do you good." She turned to Dix. "And you need to show Miss Reeves around town. If she's staying for a while, she needs to know where to find things."

Dix glanced up at Stratford and almost grinned at his discomfort. She found the fact interesting that a man as strong and handsome as he was didn't like leaving the house.

He lifted a hand to his scarred cheek, his lips pressing into a line. "Miss Reeves can take Leigha. I'll stay home. I have work to do."

"Oh, pooh. That's your code for 'I don't want to.' Your friend needs someone to show her around the town. As her host, you have a responsibility to do that. No, you should have the decency to give her a tour of Cape Churn. Show her where to find groceries, the drugstore, library, sheriff's office and anywhere else she might need at a moment's notice."

The more Mrs. Purdy pushed, the deeper Stratford's frown grew.

"If she ends up watching out for Leigha, she needs to know these things." Mrs. Purdy crossed her arms over her chest.

"Okay. I'll do it." He pointed at the stove. "You're burning my eggs."

Mrs. Purdy threw her hands in the air and spun back to the stove to rescue the eggs, muttering, "Wouldn't have burned them if my boss wasn't so darned stubborn."

"I heard that," Stratford said. "I'm in the same room."

The housekeeper scraped the eggs onto a plate loaded with bacon and carried it to the table. "Good. I wanted you to hear it. You're a stubborn man, Andrew Stratford. As stubborn as your grandfather."

"And my father," he added, taking his seat at the head of the table. "I'd rather be stubborn than a pushover."

Mrs. Purdy snorted. "You only need to be smart enough to know when to use that quality and when to let it go."

Dix fought the chuckle threatening to rise up her throat. Watching the big, strong Andrew Stratford battle it out with a five-foot-nothing housekeeper and lose was highly entertaining.

"I'm done eating. Are you?" Leigha glanced across the table at Dix.

"Almost." Dix really didn't want to leave the table while Stratford and Mrs. Purdy were going at it, but she had a job to do, and her name was Leigha.

Shoving the last bite of eggs into her mouth, she carried her plate to the sink, grabbed the two pieces of bacon from it and hurried after Leigha. To stir the pot, she paused on her way past Stratford. "I'll have Leigha dressed and ready by five thirty this afternoon."

Stratford had just lifted his fork when he glanced up. "Ready?"

"Seaside Café? Dinner?" She shook her head. "You wouldn't disappoint your daughter, would you?" Dix didn't wait for his answer. The fact that his brows met in the middle was what she had hoped for.

Mrs. Purdy smothered a chuckle by the sink.

Brewer trotted after Leigha, leaving the temptation of bacon in the kitchen. If Dix wasn't mistaken, the dog stayed with Leigha to protect her as much as Dix would. Which reminded her... She needed to talk to Stratford about the expected threats before they ventured too far out of the house. She needed to know what to be on the lookout for. Otherwise, she'd be more or less walking into the Devil's Shroud blindfolded.

Andrew's gaze followed Dix out of the kitchen. The woman might be tomboyish, but the sway of her hips was purely feminine.

"I like her," Mrs. Purdy said. "I think it will be good for Leigha to have another woman around her."

He pushed back from the table. "Don't say it."

"What? That the girl needs a mother?" Mrs. Purdy smiled. "Okay. I won't. But it's true."

"She has me."

Mrs. Purdy's brows rose. "A girl needs a mother to show her the ropes of being *female*."

"Not the mother she had."

"Agreed. But someone who's strong and independent and can show compassion." Mrs. Purdy nodded. "Sounds like Dix, doesn't it?"

"You just met her," he said, carrying his plate to the sink.

"I have a good sense of who people are. Dix is the

real deal. She seems honest, open and a good influence for Leigha."

"As long as she keeps a close eye on her. I don't want her getting lost in the woods again."

Mrs. Purdy wiped the counter clean and nodded. "If anyone can keep up with Leigha, Dix can."

"I hope so. I have work to do this morning and can't hold her hand while she makes sense of the estate."

Mrs. Purdy raised her hand. "Leigha's the expert there. She'll show Miss Reeves all of her hiding places."

"I hope so. She hasn't shown them to me."

"Because you don't spend enough time with her. She needs a father as much as she needs a mother." She raised her hands. "Not that I'm telling you how to raise your daughter. You're the boss. You know best." She waved her hands at him. "Now, out of the kitchen so I can finish cleaning up. I have a few more chores to tend to before I leave for Portland, and you have a business to run."

If he was the boss, then why did he feel he didn't have any control over his housekeeper? His employees on Wall Street would never have spoken as frankly as Mrs. Purdy telling him how to run his household. But then, he had all the experience on Wall Street and none raising a little girl.

Shaking off the sense he wasn't doing it right, he marched to his office and went to work. So, he wasn't as attentive as usual. He could still put in a good bit of day-trading and increase the value of his portfolio for the hundredth time.

His thoughts strayed to Leigha and Dix, wondering

where they were and what they were up to. By noon, he hoped to have his work squared away. Perhaps then he could ask his daughter to show him where all the hiding places were. If she refused to show him, he could demand that Dix take him there.

He almost laughed at himself. Dix? Taking commands from him? Well, she had to have followed orders somewhere in her military career, or she wouldn't have made it as far as she had. The dossier Tazer had shown him indicated Dix had been an Army Ranger, as well as a Medal of Honor and Purple Heart recipient. He wondered what wounds she'd sustained to receive a Purple Heart. The thought of her being wounded made his fists clench. And when he clenched his scarred and now re-injured hand, the pain reminded him to quit thinking about Dix and get to work.

An hour later he pushed his chair back from the desk and went in search of his daughter and the bodyguard. If he couldn't keep his mind on task, he might as well join them in their exploration of the property.

He wandered through the halls, listening for the sounds of female voices. The vacuum whirred in the upstairs bedrooms, but that was the only sound he could hear. Where had they gone?

He stepped out of the front door and looked around. He didn't see any sign of Leigha, Dix or Brewer. Andrew frowned. What was the good of having someone watch over Leigha if she disappeared with the child?

A sheriff's vehicle rumbled up the sweeping, paved drive and pulled to a stop in front of the house. Gabe McGregor and an older man emerged.

"Good morning, Mr. Stratford. I'm Sheriff Taggert." He climbed the steps and held out his hand. "How are you feeling today?"

"Fine." *If I could find my child and the woman who is supposed to be looking out for her.* Andrew held up his hand, displaying the stitches. "I hope you don't mind if we don't shake."

"Not at all," the sheriff responded.

Andrew glanced to the right and left, hoping to catch a glimpse of his daughter and Miss Reeves.

"I read through McGregor's report about the attack on you two nights ago. We'd like to look at the area in the daylight. Perhaps there is some evidence we could have missed in the density of the fog from last night."

Andrew nodded, unable to ignore the two men. The sooner he helped them, the sooner he could find the ladies. "I'll take you to the exact location." He turned and walked around the house, through the garden and out to the edge of the rugged cliff.

McGregor and Taggert followed.

"Any more incidents since two nights ago?" the sheriff asked.

"No." The lights going out on Dix in the basement could have been anything. Since she hadn't been attacked, she'd probably suffered through a freak short. He'd have an electrician come check the panel and the wiring.

Once he led the lawmen to the spot where he'd been attacked, he got a good look at it with a different perspective—looking down at what he'd gone over and had to climb up. A chill rippled down his spine. He was lucky to be alive.

They checked around the tree, enlarging the circle a little at a time, staring at the ground. The rocky ledge didn't give them much of a chance to find footprints. Thirty feet out from the tree, they entered the forest where the ground was covered in evergreen needles and moss. Again, not good for finding footprints. But then, maybe they weren't looking for footprints.

A bark sounded from the direction of the house.

Andrew glanced around to see Brewer bounding his way. Leigha and Dix hung back, moving toward them at a more sedate pace.

Before he reached Andrew, Brewer slowed, his tail wagging.

Andrew bent to scratch behind the dog's ears.

Brewer then moved on to the sheriff and his deputy, sniffing hands and wagging his tail.

Sheriff Taggert and Deputy McGregor crossed the ground and rejoined Andrew.

"Didn't find anything, did you?" Andrew asked.

Taggert shook his head. "I didn't expect we would. But we have to look in case the perpetrator left a calling card, a scrap of cloth, some DNA…anything."

"Unfortunately, he didn't leave a trace," McGregor confirmed.

"Gentlemen, I'm sorry to waste your time." Andrew herded them toward the house.

"Investigating a crime is not a waste of our time," Taggert argued. "We wish we could be of more help. Gabe said you didn't know of anyone who might be mad at you or want you off the property. No disputes over property lines, no ex-wives looking to take you to the cleaners, former business partners who might have a gripe?"

Andrew shook his head. "I'm the sole heir to the Stratford estate. Never been married. No ex-girlfriends stalking me and no former business partners with a complaint."

Taggert sighed. "For the time being, you might want to stay away from the cliff's edge at night or in the fog and grow eyes in the back of your head. Wish we could help more."

"Thank you for taking the time to come out to investigate," Andrew said.

By then they'd reached Dix and Leigha.

Andrew's daughter held tightly to Dix's hand and stared up at the sheriff and his deputy. Brewer sat at her feet, leaning into her body. She reached out to run her hand over the animal's fur, stroking it slowly.

"Hi, Leigha." Deputy McGregor squatted beside her and scratched Brewer's ears. "Do you remember me?"

Leigha nodded, her eyes wide and wary.

Brewer nudged McGregor's hand and then rolled over, exposing his belly.

The deputy laughed and scratched the dog's belly. "I like a dog that knows what he wants."

"Brewer likes to have his belly and ears scratched," Leigha said.

"I'll remember that the next time I visit." The deputy smiled at the little girl and stood. "Miss Reeves, my sister Molly had good things to say about her meeting with you last night. I wish I had been there." His lips turned upward on the corners and he cast a sideways glance at Andrew. "I hear I missed a show."

"You didn't miss anything," she said.

"Well, I'm glad you're here to help Mr. Stratford and his daughter."

"It's my pleasure." She smiled, and the few floating clouds that had been blocking the sun cleared, leaving the big blue sky wide open and the sun shining brightly.

Something woke inside Andrew he thought long dead. Something he didn't expect or want to wake. But now that it had, he couldn't make it go away. His heart swelled and his chest tightened.

Dix smiling hit him like a ray of sunshine.

Damn the woman to hell.

Chapter 7

After the sheriff and his deputy left the estate, Dix followed Leigha back into the house, fully aware of the man two steps behind her. Every nerve ending shivered in anticipation of him touching her arm, her back, somewhere on her body.

But he didn't. Instead he opened the back door to the house and held it for his daughter and Dix.

She swung as widely as she could to get around him without actually bumping into him. Why she went to such lengths she couldn't guess, but somewhere deep inside she knew that if they touched, all kinds of electric impulses would zing through her body and confuse her more than she already was about this man.

Leigha skipped ahead to the kitchen, giving Dix time to confront Stratford about what had happened to bring

him to hire a bodyguard. Royce had said something
about being pushed off a cliff. After having been out to
the cliff Stratford had been showing the lawmen, Dix
could see why that was such a big deal. How he'd survived was beyond comprehension. The three-hundred-
foot drop to the boulder-strewn shore would have killed
a lesser being.

She stopped in the hallway and faced the man.

His head was down and he didn't notice she'd stopped
until he ran into her. He reached out to grab her arms
and held her steady.

"Sorry. I should have let you know I was stopping."

He slowly lowered his hands, removing them from
her arms. "I should have been watching."

"So, tell me what happened to make you think you
needed a bodyguard." She tipped her head toward the
door. "You don't strike me as someone who would call
the law unless it was the last resort."

"Someone pushed me over the cliff two nights ago
during a really thick fog."

"Are you sure it wasn't an accident?"

"If someone barreled into you like a lineman on a
football field, would you consider it an accident?"

Dix shook her head. "Did you see his face?"

"No." He hooked her elbow and led her toward the
kitchen. "I'm not worried for myself. I worry for Leigha.
She's an innocent. She can't tell who is friend or foe."

"Understandable. She's a great kid."

"Did she show you all of her hiding places?"

"Not yet. I think she's still trying to decide how far
she can trust me. We did the tour of the third floor.

This place is huge. Have you considered transforming it into a hotel?"

"Absolutely not."

"But it would be incredi—"

"No." He stopped at the entrance to the kitchen. "I value my privacy. Opening it to other people will put my daughter at too great a risk."

"This place needs to be full of people. It's too big for just the two of you."

"It's my home now. I brought Leigha here so that she could grow up in a small community, not the big city. Cape Churn is a nice little town."

"I wouldn't know. All I know about it is what I saw when I drove through yesterday and straight out to the McGregor B and B."

"You'll see more this afternoon when we go into town for dinner."

Dix hid a smile as she stepped through the kitchen door.

Leigha carried a plate full of sandwiches to the table. "Mrs. Purdy made lunch. But she's leaving now, so we have to clean up."

Dix hurried to take over for the housekeeper. "We've got this. I might not be a cook, but I can make a pretty decent sandwich."

"They're already made. All you need to do is come up with your drinks. Chips are in the pantry." Mrs. Purdy removed her apron, hung it on a hook near the back door and then looped her purse over her arm. "I'll see you tomorrow. Enjoy dinner at Nora's café." She dropped a kiss on Leigha's head and breezed out the door, leaving the kitchen silent in her wake.

Dix filled glasses with ice and water from the tap, setting them on the table.

Stratford grabbed an assortment of bags of potato chips from the pantry and laid them on the table.

Leigha grinned. "This is almost like a picnic." Her smile faded a little. "I've never been on a picnic. But this is nice."

Dix stared at the little girl, her eyes wide. "No picnic?" She glanced at Leigha's father. "Well, Dad, how can we remedy this serious lack in her upbringing?"

The man stood beside his daughter, his brows twisting. "What do you mean?"

"I mean we're going on a picnic." She took a sandwich out of Leigha's grip and wrapped it in a napkin. "Show your father where he can find a blanket you don't mind getting dirty while I pack this food into something we can carry."

Leigha leaped from her seat, grabbed her father's hand and practically dragged him out of the kitchen. "Hurry! We're going on a picnic!"

Minutes later Dix had found a basket in the pantry, packed the sandwiches inside, a few water bottles, two bags of chips and napkins. By the time Stratford and Leigha returned with a blanket, she was ready.

"Are you coming with us?" Dix asked her client.

Leigha looked up at her father, her eyes big...hopeful.

He nodded. "Of course. You have my sandwich, and I'm starving."

Leigha clapped her hands and grinned from ear to ear.

Dix's heart filled with some of the joy Leigha was experiencing. She'd gone on quite a few picnics with her parents. It was one of the many things she missed about them.

By dying young, her parents would never know their grandchildren. And Dix's children would never know their grandparents. Shoving aside the sad thoughts, Dix fought to recapture Leigha's joy and led the way out of the house, checking right and left for any threats.

Stratford locked the door behind him and quickly caught up. "I know just the place."

The three of them marched into the woods. Brewer ran ahead, chasing birds and small animals.

Stratford seemed to know the woods better than Dix expected.

"I used to spend my summers here with my grandfather. We explored, he took me fishing, and we even camped in these woods. Sometimes we'd pretend to be treasure hunters and search for pirates' gold in the caves among the cliffs." He shook his head. "I loved doing all the activities I couldn't do from our apartment in New York City."

"You grew up in the city?" Dix asked.

"I did. My parents both worked for large corporations that had home offices in Manhattan."

Dix could imagine the adventurous little boy trapped in a concrete jungle. No wonder he'd chosen to bring Leigha to Oregon.

They ventured deeper into the woods until they came to an open glen with a burbling stream running through the middle.

Dix couldn't have found a better spot. The three of them spread the blanket and anchored it with the basket and a couple of rocks. A gentle breeze blew in from the Pacific, keeping the air cool and the sky clear.

Leigha took charge of the basket and passed food to them, while Stratford held Brewer back from stealing all of their sandwiches.

When they'd had their fill, Dix closed the basket and stretched out on the blanket, staring up at the sky between the branches of the trees.

Leigha and Brewer ran off to play on the edge of the creek.

"This place is beautiful. I don't know how anyone would want to leave it for the city," Dix said in a reverent voice, caught up in the beauty of the Pacific Northwest.

Stratford lay on the opposite side of the blanket, his hands linked behind his head. "My father and grandfather had their differences. I contend they were too much alike—both very stubborn."

"What about your mother? Didn't she like living in Cape Churn?"

"My parents left shortly after their wedding and never looked back. I didn't know I had a grandfather until he showed up one day and asked to see me."

"What?" Dix turned to face him.

"Like I said, my father and grandfather didn't always get along. My grandfather knew my father wouldn't come back and settle at his estate in Oregon and he needed to have someone to leave Stratford House to. The need for an heir, and a promise to my grandmother, made him swallow his pride and fly all the way to New York City. The man hated to fly. He did it to ask my father to let me come spend my summers in Oregon."

"So you ended up coming to live here." Dix faced the sky again.

"Not right away."

"Not until Leigha." Dix watched the little girl playing with the dog. Her hair shone brightly in the afternoon sun.

"I remembered how much fun it was to explore and have free rein to do what I wanted at my grandfather's house. I also remembered what a big deal it was to go to a park for what they called fresh air in Manhattan." He leaned up on an elbow, his gaze following Leigha. "I couldn't do that to her. She deserved better."

Dix enjoyed the quiet conversation so different from the cold, stony silences the man had subjected her to in the beginning. "Why does Leigha call you 'Mr. Stratford' instead of Father or Daddy?" And with that one question, the warmth left the air and quiet, like a deep, deep chasm, stretched between them. "You don't have to answer that." She sat up and slipped the water bottles into the basket. "We should head back before it gets too dark. Besides, Leigha will need a bath before we go out to dinner. *If* you still want to go." Dix was rattling on, and she knew it, but she didn't know how to stop until Stratford laid a hand on her arm.

"I don't mind answering," he said. "I didn't know Leigha existed until she was already five years old."

"A year ago."

He nodded. "And she didn't know she had a father."

"Her mother kept her from you?"

"Leigha is the result of too much liquor and a one-night stand. Not one of my prouder moments." He sighed. "But I can't regret it."

Dix nodded toward the little girl laughing at the dog. "You have Leigha because of it. Five years is a long time for her mother to keep her from you. Are you sure she's your daughter?"

His lips thinned and a fierce frown pushed his eyebrows downward. "My name is on the birth certificate."

"Her mother could have lied. They have DNA tests they could conduct to prove lineage."

Stratford pushed to his feet, placed the basket on the ground and waited for Dix to move to the side.

She rose and lifted one end of the blanket while her client took the other, and they met across the hems, their hands touching, an electric shock running up Dix's arms into her chest. Her gaze captured his and she knew. "You don't want to know for certain, do you?"

"My name is on the birth certificate," he repeated firmly. "That's all I need to know."

A glance at Leigha reinforced his conviction. That would be all she'd need to know, too. The little girl was what was important. Making certain she had a loving, happy, healthy environment to grow up in was all that mattered.

But that niggle of doubt crept into Dix's thoughts. Holy hell. What if Leigha wasn't even Stratford's daughter?

Andrew had enjoyed the picnic up to the point where Dix had challenged Leigha's lineage. After what Jeannette had tried to do to the child, Leigha had been in the hospital for a week, recovering from smoke inhalation and the trauma of being caught in a horrific apartment fire.

He'd insisted on the best care and treatment money could buy. Moving her to a private room in one of the most reputable children's hospitals in the city was only a fraction of what he'd done for her. He'd been there every day that he could, putting off his own surgery until Leigha was in the clear. With his hand and face bandaged, he'd probably scared her more than reassured her. But someone had to be there when she'd cried for her mother, unable to understand why she wasn't there.

His heart had broken into a million pieces when tears fell from her eyes, soaking the sheets. He'd wanted to take all of the pain from her and make her life better. When she'd asked who he was, he didn't feel like he'd earned the right to tell her he was her daddy. So he'd said he was Mr. Stratford, her friend.

Leigha had accepted it and calmed down. She looked forward to his visits with her every day. In the meantime, Andrew had had his lawyers do whatever it took to transfer guardianship of the little girl to him. Whether it was through lawful or criminal channels, they were able to produce a birth certificate bearing Jeannette's name as Leigha's mother and Andrew Stratford as her father.

Everything else was a formality. With an overburdened foster care system, the judge had ruled in favor of granting custody to the biological father who had proved he could afford to support the child.

He'd hired a nanny to care for Leigha while he'd

gone through several surgeries on his hand. When he could get away, he'd packed up what he wanted from his apartment, loaded Leigha onto a chartered plane, and the two of them had left New York City behind to start a new life together.

They'd been in Oregon for over eight months. Andrew hadn't known what to expect, but he was no closer to building a good relationship with his daughter. He didn't know how. They'd lived in the same house and shared meals, but Leigha had withdrawn into a very quiet, reserved child. Until Andrew had brought a wiggly black puppy home from town.

Brewer had helped Leigha out of her shell a little, and she'd transferred all of her love and attention to the dog.

By then, enough people had called her his daughter that she had to know he was her father. But still, she hadn't called him Daddy.

And he hadn't been much of a father to her. Sure, he'd given her a better place to live than in that ratty apartment in the Bronx, but he hadn't shown her the love he knew she needed.

He didn't know how to. His parents hadn't been the demonstrative type. Hugging was almost a painful necessity on rare occasions.

Watching Dix gather their things, he felt a little stab of jealousy at how easily she'd fit into Leigha's life. Seeing them lying in the same bed the night before had been bittersweet. They'd looked like they were mother and child. It had warmed his heart and left him cold at the same time.

Leigha needed a strong female influence in her life.

Dix, with her background in the military and her MMA fighting, would make an excellent role model. She could even teach her how to defend herself should someone attack her.

What left him cold was the possibility Leigha wasn't his child. If not his, whose was she? Some deadbeat who wouldn't want her anyway? Wasn't that what Jeannette had screamed at him? Nobody wanted Leigha.

Jeannette had been wrong. Andrew wanted her more than anything he'd ever wanted in his life. More than that, he wanted her to be happy. Rather than risk losing her after what they'd survived together, Andrew preferred to live with the burning question. Was she his biological daughter?

Chapter 8

Andrew carried the basket and the blanket and led the way back through the woods to Stratford House, more somber than when they'd set out on their little adventure. As they neared the path leading past the high cliffs, he glanced down at the water below. Had he died, what would have become of Leigha?

He'd had his attorney set up a trust for Leigha. Everything he owned would go into that trust to be paid out to his daughter over her lifetime. No matter if she was his or not, she'd get everything he owned as it was spelled out in his will. But if he died, he had no one to leave her with. He hadn't made any friends since he'd been back in Oregon, rarely leaving his house to go into town.

For Leigha's sake, he needed to remedy that oversight

and find someone he felt confident could raise Leigha with the love and kindness she needed. After being pushed over the edge of the cliff, he couldn't guarantee he'd be alive to see her all the way to maturity.

Dinner out in Cape Churn might give him the opportunity to work toward finding godparents for his daughter. He needed a backup plan to ensure Leigha's future happiness.

They returned to the house without incident.

Andrew left Leigha and Dix in the kitchen unloading the leftovers from the basket into the refrigerator. He checked his email and phone messages and then headed upstairs to his bedroom, where he showered and slipped into black slacks, a silver button-down dress shirt and the black leather shoes he used to wear when he went out to the nightclubs in Manhattan. Though most folks dressed more casually in Cape Churn, Andrew wanted to look good. He skipped the tie, leaving the top button undone.

He was surprised at how nervous he felt at going out in public. Before "the accident" he'd gone out practically every night of the week. He really had no reason to feel nervous. So he had a scar slashing across his face and his hand was mangled with burn grafts and now stitches. At least he still had his life and that grafted hand had helped save him from falling to his death.

He squared his shoulders and stepped into the hall.

Leigha came out of her room a second later, smiling. She wore a pretty powder blue sundress and white sandals. Her hair was pulled back on both sides with a yellow barrette. She spotted Andrew and her eyes widened. "You look like a handsome prince," she exclaimed and ran to wrap her arms around his waist.

"Then you must be my princess." He lifted her up into his arms, trying not to wince when he disturbed the stitches. "May I have this dance?"

She giggled and laid her hand in his damaged one.

Andrew danced around the corridor with his daughter in his arms. It might be silly to onlookers, but it felt right to him. And the smile on Leigha's face was worth looking like a fool.

When he made another turn, he caught a glimpse of someone standing in the hallway and he came to a halt, his mouth falling open and his pulse slamming through his veins. "Miss Reeves?"

"Dix!" Leigha squirmed out of Andrew's arms and ran to Dix. "You're like a beautiful fairy princess."

Dix's face flushed a pretty pink, complimenting the flowing white-fabric dress that draped off her shoulders, hugged her waist and fell in soft layers that floated down to her knees. Every time she moved the skirt swayed around her like wisps of clouds. "You must be my fairy princess sister, then. You're adorable." She bent to kiss the top of Leigha's head.

"Come see Mr. Stratford. He's our prince." Leigha grabbed Dix's hand and pulled her toward Andrew.

Dix stopped in front of him and smiled. "Well, aren't we dressed up for a night on the town?"

"Indeed we are." He offered his arm to Dix and his hand to Leigha. "Shall we?"

Dix nodded and placed her hand in the crook of his arm.

They descended the grand staircase like royalty.

While the ladies waited in the foyer, Andrew went out to the garage and brought out his black SUV and swung around the front of the house.

He and Dix buckled Leigha into a booster chair in the backseat. Then Andrew followed Dix to the passenger side of the SUV and held the door for her.

She hesitated getting in. "Just so you know, I'm armed, should anyone try to hurt you or Leigha."

"Armed?" His gaze swept over her body, his brow rising. He couldn't see any sign of a handgun on her.

She slid her skirt up her thigh, exposing a strap around her leg with a holster and an H&K .40-caliber pistol. Some men might consider her carrying a weapon somewhat intimidating. Andrew found it sexy as hell. He wanted to slide his hand up the inside of her thigh and touch the cold, hard weapon lying against her warm, soft skin.

He held the door while she climbed in, her dress hiking up as she settled in her seat. Once again, Andrew had a clear view of her legs. Tanned and smooth, with well-defined muscles and narrow ankles, they would wrap nicely around his waist. He resisted the urge to reach out to trace his fingers along the length of those sexy legs. She was his employee. He was her client. He risked losing her as a bodyguard if he crossed the line.

His body tense, his groin tight, Andrew closed the passenger door, rounded to the driver's side and got in.

The trip to town took only fifteen minutes. The sun was setting as they pulled into the parking lot of the Seaside Café. The sun's rays glittered like amethysts across the bay, turning gentle waves into sparkling jewels.

Many cars filled the parking spaces. He had to search for an empty one. Which meant the café would be busy and full of people. For a moment he considered turning around and going back to the house. After spending the past year as a recluse, he didn't look forward to entering a crowded room full of people who would stare at his face and hand.

"I want chocolate ice cream," Leigha said, bouncing in her booster seat. "Please."

One glance at his daughter's shining eyes and Andrew knew he couldn't disappoint her. He unbuckled his seat belt, sucked in a deep breath and got out of the SUV.

Dix was out and already unbuckling Leigha's belt by the time Andrew made it around to the passenger side.

Leigha took Dix's hand and grabbed Andrew's uninjured hand and swung between them all the way into the café.

"Welcome to the Seaside Café," a friendly voice called out. A woman with gray hair, wearing a soft yellow summer dress and a crisp white apron, hurried toward them, carrying menus. "Three?" She glanced behind them.

"Just three," Andrew said.

The woman's smile widened. "Three it is. I'm Nora Taggert. Are you all new in town?"

Andrew swallowed a groan.

Dix chuckled and hid it with a cough.

"Nora, honey, this is Andrew Stratford." Sheriff Taggert disengaged himself from a seat at a counter and joined Andrew and Dix. "He's the owner of Stratford House." The sheriff held out his left hand to Andrew. "So glad you came to town. My wife makes the best meat loaf in the state."

Andrew carefully shook the sheriff's hand with his injured one and released it.

Nora swatted playfully at her husband. "Oh, go on. It might not be the best in the state, but everyone tells me it's the best around *here*."

The sheriff nodded to Dix. "Miss Reeves is here to help look out for little Miss Leigha." He squatted on his haunches and grinned at Andrew's daughter. "Isn't that right?"

Leigha stepped closer to Dix, nodding.

Dix dropped a hand to Leigha's shoulder and squeezed. "We're getting to know each other."

"We went on a picnic today," Leigha offered softly, her eyes lighting up.

"A picnic?" Nora beamed. "I love picnics. Did you take sandwiches or fried chicken?" She held out a hand to Leigha, who took it and let her lead her away to a table in the corner. Dix followed close behind.

"Sandwiches," Leigha responded.

Andrew realized by keeping to his house, he was depriving Leigha of company and social interaction. He resolved to fix that, as well.

"Everything okay out at the house?" Sheriff Taggert asked.

Andrew nodded. "No further incidents."

"Glad to hear it." The sheriff's mouth firmed into a straight line. "But don't let your guard down."

"I won't." Andrew stepped around the sheriff and joined the ladies at the table.

"Six years old!" Nora exclaimed. "Such a grown-up little lady. Are you excited about going to school next fall?"

Leigha glanced up at Andrew. "I don't know."

"We've been home-schooling," Andrew said. "Mrs. Purdy has been very helpful."

"I should think so." Nora smoothed her hand over Leigha's hair. "As a retired teacher, she's an excellent choice." She laid menus on the table and stepped back. "What would you like to drink?"

They gave their orders.

Nora returned with their drinks and took their orders. "While you're waiting, why don't you show Leigha the koi pond we installed on the back patio?"

"Would you like that?" Dix asked.

Leigha's brows dipped. "What's a koi pond?"

"They're like really big goldfish."

Leigha's eyes widened and she clapped her hands. "May I?"

Dix glanced across at Andrew. "Care to join us?"

He shook his head. "I'll stay and hold the table."

Leigha slipped out of her chair and let Dix take her hand as she led her to the back of the café.

Andrew sat back and looked around at the people gathered at the café. Some appeared to be tourists, early for the summer season. Others looked like regulars, there for coffee and pie.

At the table beside him, two young men leaned over

a map, talking excitedly. Andrew couldn't help over-hearing their conversation.

"The dive boat captain is ours for the week. We have to make this venture count."

"No kidding," the other young man agreed. "I'm spending the rest of my college money on this. If we don't find something soon, I'll be working at my father's machine shop for the rest of my life."

"The data is all there. We just have to spend some time in the water to locate the ship."

"What if they got the jewels to shore before they scuttled the yacht?"

"Then it has to be somewhere nearby. I'm not giving up. We've spent too much time and money researching this."

Andrew's curiosity was captured. He wanted to know what boat they were searching for and what jewels they expected to find.

The front door opened and a couple entered with a blast of cool air.

A slip of paper blew over to land at Andrew's foot. He lifted it and studied the drawing. It was a detailed sketch of Cape Churn. Other landmarks were noted ringing the coastline, including Cape Churn Marina, McGregor B and B and Stratford House. An *X* marked a spot in the water just off the coast from Stratford House.

"Sir, do you mind?" The sandy-blond-haired young man from the table beside Andrew stood beside him. "That's my drawing."

Andrew handed the drawing to him. "Treasure hunting?"

The young man shot a glance at his partner, who looked enough like him they could be twins.

The other guy shrugged and answered, "Trying."

"You from around here?" the guy standing asked.

Andrew nodded.

The young man stuck out his hand. "I'm Jared Kessler." He jabbed a thumb over his shoulder at his partner. "He's Joe, my brother."

Andrew raised his bandaged right hand, displaying his stitches. "Are you two related?"

Jared dropped his arm, his lips twisting. "Yeah, we're twins."

Joe scooted his chair closer to Andrew. "Do you know if anyone lives in the big mansion on the cliff?" He pointed to Stratford House.

Andrew choked back his laughter. "Yes. Someone lives there."

"We want to call and ask him if he'd mind if we looked around the caves along the shoreline," Jared said.

"Yeah," Joe added. "We don't want some trigger-happy landowner shooting us for trespassing."

Andrew dipped his head to hide his smile.

Jared dropped into his seat and pulled it closer. "We've been studying the history of Cape Churn and the Oregon coastline for the past two years as a project for our major."

Andrew's grandfather had read a lot about the early inhabitants of Cape Churn. He'd told Andrew stories about pirates of the Pacific Northwest and the rumrunners of the early twentieth century. "The West Coast is said to have been a pirates' haven back in the seventeenth century."

Jared shook his head. "Oh, we aren't going back that far."

"We've concentrated our research on a pair of thieves and rumrunners known as the Bonnie and Clyde of the Pacific Northwest—Peg and Percy Malone."

Andrew stiffened. His grandfather had told him stories of the antics of the pair with whom the Stratfords were rumored to be related. "What exactly are you looking for?"

"News articles dating back to the late 1920s followed the exploits of the Malones. They were crafty rumrunners who transported kegs of whiskey from British Columbia to San Francisco."

"And you're looking for a lost shipment of whiskey kegs?" Andrew shook his head. "That's a lot of research for old barrels."

Joe shared a grin with his brother. "That's not all they did."

Andrew knew the stories. His grandfather had repeated them time and again as they'd sat on the back patio watching the sun set on Cape Churn. But he let the twins tell their version, their eyes bright, their bodies tense with excitement.

Jared leaned closer, his voice dropping lower. "The Malones were also jewel thieves. One shipment of whiskey was supposed to be delivered to a wealthy San Franciscan, Willard Jameson, who owned a number of speakeasies and jewelry stores."

Joe picked up the story. "Rumor had it the man paid off the local law enforcement. They seized the shipment as soon as the Malones pulled into port. The Malones escaped, learned of Jameson's betrayal and vowed to get their revenge."

Jared glanced around the room and spoke in a hushed voice. "They broke into one of Jameson's jewelry stores, took all of the most precious of gems, including the Star of Nairobi, a special diamond Jameson had imported to make a wedding ring for his fiancée."

Joe jumped in with, "They stole one of Jameson's fastest yachts and headed north in the middle of the night. Reports from the coast guard indicated a light flashing by during the night as far north as the southern tip of Oregon, but the authorities never spotted the yacht during the daytime."

"A friend of a friend of the Malones wrote a fictional account of the couple and published it."

"Fictional?" Andrew asked.

Jared nodded. "Only we think it was based on the truth. It was published years after the theft occurred. The Malones disappeared after that last run, never to run rum again."

"The newspaper from that time reported that Jameson offered a reward for anyone with any information leading to their arrest." Joe shuffled through a file and pointed to a photocopy of an old newspaper report. "In the editorial comments, an anonymous writer said Jameson had put a price on their heads for anyone who would assassinate them."

"Others say Peg got pregnant and they went into hiding, changed their names and started over." Jared sat back. "But the Star of Nairobi never surfaced."

"And how did you end up in Cape Churn searching for the Malones?" Andrew asked.

"In the book, the author referred to the Malones as Margaret and Percival. We researched court and church records and went online with ancestry sites looking for people who fit the age and description of the Malones."

"And?" Andrew prompted.

"And we found Margaret and Percival Mason. Here in Cape Churn. They had one daughter, Rowena Mason, who married Thomas Stratford."

"Of the Stratford mansion on the cliff," Jared finished.

"And you think Stratford might know where the Star of Nairobi can be found?" Andrew asked.

Jared shook his head at the same time as his brother. "We think they hid the jewels and forgot about them. The Masons died in a car crash when Rowena was twelve years old. She was raised by members of the church."

Dix and Leigha emerged from the back of the café and started toward them.

Andrew wrote his phone number on a napkin and passed it to the Kessler twins. "You can reach Stratford at that number. He doesn't like trespassers, so be sure to call ahead before you enter his property."

"Thank you," Jared said. "But what is your name?"

"Andrew." A smile tugged at his lips. "Andrew Stratford."

Dix and Leigha arrived at that exact time. The twins scooted their chairs back to their table, grinning and talking quietly.

"Did we interrupt something?" Dix asked.

Andrew shook his head. "No. How was the fish-pond?"

"Great!" Leigha said and then told him all about the different colored koi she'd spotted.

Dix's eyes narrowed and her gaze alternated between Andrew and the two men sitting at the table beside them.

He'd fill her in later on the treasure hunters. He wanted her take on them. Would she think they were dangerous? Could one of them have been the one to push Andrew over the cliff?

He didn't think so, but then, he really had no idea who might have done it. He didn't know many people in the area, as evidenced by Nora Taggert's mistaken assumption that he was new to town. He had to fix that, for Leigha's sake. And as soon as they caught the man responsible for pushing him off the cliff, he might consider letting Leigha go to the public school in Cape Churn. She needed friends to play with. Andrew felt like a fish out of water when it came to parenting.

He would ask Dix if she knew of a manual that could help him figure out what he was supposed to be doing.

Chapter 9

Dix polished off a healthy slice of Nora's famous meat loaf and would have had a beer, but felt she needed to have all of her wits about her, so she'd opted for ice cream instead. Being a bodyguard to a little girl was a huge responsibility she couldn't take lightly. The nudge of the handgun strapped to her thigh reminded her to stay alert.

The two young men who'd been talking with Stratford eventually packed up their maps and left the café, waving to her client as they walked out the door.

Now that they were gone and Leigha was happily licking her cone, Dix posed the question. "What were you talking to those two guys about?"

Stratford sat back in his chair and studied the rounded mound of ice cream on his cone. "Treasure."

Dix frowned. "Your ice cream as treasure, or are those guys searching for treasure?"

"Both." He licked the cone and sighed. "We need to come have dinner here more often."

"Yes, please." Leigha licked her cone, getting a spot of chocolate on the tip of her nose.

Dix's attention latched on to the way Stratford attacked his cone, studying it carefully before licking it in just the right spot. That look of intense concentration from his incredibly blue eyes and the long, deliberate stroking of his tongue on the creamy dessert made a tingle ripple through her body and pool low in her belly. She licked her own suddenly dry lips and cleared her throat. "Care to explain what you mean?"

He shook his head and tilted it slightly toward Leigha. "I'll tell you about it later."

Her curiosity and everything else in her body piqued, Dix worked her way through the rest of that chocolate cone, anxious to get back to Stratford House to get to the bottom of that tongue—er, story.

Her cheeks heated. Even though she hadn't spoken her slipup aloud, she'd thought it. Was she insane? Daydreaming about a client's tongue couldn't possibly be one of the duties of a good bodyguard. She averted her gaze, staring out at all of the patrons of the café, wondering if one of them was the person who'd pushed Stratford off the cliff.

At that thought, she went from hot all over to a cold chill. She shivered.

"Cold?"

She gave him a weak smile. "Maybe a little. Must

be the ice cream." Or a creepy feeling the culprit was watching them as they enjoyed their dessert.

Leigha finished her cone and licked her fingertips. "I'm sleepy," she announced and leaned back in her chair. "Can we go home now?"

"You bet." Stratford finished the last bite of his cone and waited at the cash register while Dix took Leigha to the ladies' room to wash the chocolate off her fingers.

"Andrew Stratford?" a deep voice called out behind him.

Andrew tensed as he turned. "Yes."

A gray-haired man stood behind him, wearing nice trousers and a button-down, long-sleeved shirt. He held out his hand. "Nelson Clayton. I grew up with your mother."

Andrew held his hand up, displaying his stitches. "Nice to meet you, Mr. Nelson."

"Mr. Clayton," he corrected.

"My apologies." Andrew dropped his hand to his side. "How can I help you?"

"Heard you were back in town. Just wondered for how long. Seems you only ever came for the summers."

Andrew nodded. "You are correct. I came to spend summer vacations with my grandfather. When I was a child." He started to tell Nelson he was there for good, but Nora Taggert hurried over, wiping her hands on her apron.

"Mr. Stratford, I hope you enjoyed the meal."

He smiled at the woman. "We all did. And the meat loaf was excellent."

She beamed, took his credit card, ran it through the

machine and handed him the slip to sign. "I hope you won't be such a stranger. We'd love for you to come back."

"You can count on it."

"Good." She handed him the receipt with a smile. "So, are you staying for the summer? Or are you here for good?"

"We're here for good, Mrs. Taggert. Thank you for dinner." He turned to Mr. Clayton. "Nice meeting you, Mr. Clayton."

The older man nodded. "Your mother is a special woman. We hated to see her leave Cape Churn."

Andrew didn't know how to respond to the man's remark and was saved from doing so by the sight of Leigha and Dix walking toward him. "Excuse me."

Clayton stepped aside, allowing him to pass.

He walked to the door and waited for Dix and Leigha to catch up. "Ready?"

"Yes, sir," Dix said.

He opened the door for her and Leigha. As Dix passed, he leaned close and said, "Please don't call me 'sir.' My name is Andrew."

"Yes, sir," she said automatically and then added, "Andrew."

He shook his head, his heart lighter than it had been in a very long time. What was it about Dix that made him feel things he hadn't felt for years? He touched his hand to her back, a shock of electricity running up his arm. He tried to ignore it, but he couldn't. "That's the military in you," he said, reminding himself she was a tough woman who was there to work.

"Hard to beat it out of a person," Dix said.

He stared at her, wondering what she meant by her remark. He started to ask, but he didn't get the opportunity.

Dix pushed her shoulders back and marched to the SUV like a good soldier.

"Dix, you're hurting my hand," Leigha said, pulling her out of her musings and back to the present.

Dix released the little girl's hand. "I'm sorry, sweetie." She bent to the child's level and rubbed her little fingers. "Better?"

Leigha nodded and raised her arms to Dix.

Scooping her up, she carried her the rest of the way to the SUV. After she'd buckled Leigha into the SUV, Dix straightened.

"Dix?" Leigha called from inside the vehicle.

Dix bent to look at the little girl.

Leigha patted the seat beside her. "Will you sit with me? Please?"

Andrew could imagine the look Leigha was giving her, with those big blue eyes that could melt the hardest heart. He gave Dix two seconds to think about it before she caved to Leigha's strong suit—mental manipulation. She could guilt anyone into doing exactly what she wanted.

Only one second had passed when Dix straightened again and captured Stratford's glance.

He nodded, pressing his lips together tightly to keep from grinning.

Score for Leigha.

Dix climbed into the backseat, next to Leigha, and took her hand.

Andrew slipped behind the wheel, started the engine and shifted into Reverse. He glanced in the rearview mirror to see two blond heads tipping toward each other. Again, he was reminded of how much they looked alike. He checked through the rear window and shifted his foot off the brake and onto the accelerator. No sooner had he started moving than a big white pickup darted behind him and stopped.

Andrew slammed on the brakes, bracing himself for the impact. When he didn't hear the sound of metal crunching into metal, he checked his side mirror and released the breath he'd caught and held. Then he pulled forward again, shifted into Park and got out of the SUV, anger burning through his veins.

The truck driver pulled into an empty parking space and got out.

Andrew walked up to him, fists clenched. "What the hell do you think you were doing?"

The man wasn't as tall as Andrew, but he made up for it in size. He had to be at least two hundred and fifty pounds or more. He puffed out his chest and snorted like a bull in a ring. "It's a free country. I have as much right to be in this parking lot as you rich folks."

"Not at the speed you were going."

The jerk made a show of looking around. "Don't see no speed limits posted."

"You don't need speed limits in a parking lot—you need common sense. People bring their children here. You could have run over one."

The man stepped around Andrew and shouted over his shoulder, "Then those people should keep their brats on a leash." He pushed the door to the Seaside Café open so hard Andrew was surprised the glass didn't break.

Sheriff McGregor and his wife stood just inside the door. The sheriff put out his hand and stopped the belligerent man as he entered. "Slow it down, Clayton, before someone gets hurt."

"You gonna give me a ticket for walking fast?" Clayton demanded.

"No, but keep it up and I will give you a ticket for destruction of property."

Clayton shook the sheriff's hand off his arm. "Either give me a ticket or leave me alone."

Andrew was halfway to the door, prepared to come to the sheriff's defense.

Taggert started to say something but Nora leaned close and whispered in his ear. The sheriff snapped shut his mouth, his eyes narrowing as Clayton stepped past him and walked into the café.

As Andrew reached the door, he asked, "Are you two okay?"

The sheriff nodded. "Yeah, but I got a real itchin' to take that fool down a notch."

"Tom," Nora warned. "I can handle him."

The sheriff turned to his wife and brought her hand to his lips. "If he gives you even a hint of a hard time, don't serve him, and call me."

She smiled. "I will. Now go on and let me do my job."

The sheriff glanced once more at the man he'd called

Clayton and stepped out onto the sidewalk in front of the café. "I don't know what's wrong with that boy."

"That boy" had to be at least thirty years old and he was bigger than a defensive football player. "Who is he?" Andrew wanted to make friends in Cape Churn, but not with that one. He needed to know whom to watch and avoid.

"That's Dwayne Clayton. His father is your neighbor, Nelson Clayton. They live on the other side of the ridge from you. Saw Nelson talking to you inside."

"My neighbors?" Andrew hadn't known that. With Stratford House surrounded by forty acres of forest and rocky shoreline, he hadn't run into anyone other than the man who'd pushed him over the cliff. He stopped to think about the size of his attacker. It had been so foggy, and happened so quickly, he couldn't be sure, but he didn't think the man had been as big as the younger Mr. Clayton. Though he wouldn't put it past Dwayne Clayton to push a stranger off a cliff. He'd have to make sure Leigha didn't stray onto Clayton property. The young Mr. Clayton had no love of children.

After her heartbeat settled to normal, Dix sat in the backseat of Andrew's SUV, holding one of Leigha's hands and resting her other hand on her full belly. Nora's meat loaf had been the best she'd ever had, and she'd loved her own mother's meat loaf. Up until that rude redneck nearly caused an accident, she hadn't felt that relaxed since before she'd gone to Ranger training.

Not long after they left town, Leigha nodded off, her head lolling to the side. She was a beautiful child with a sweet disposition. How anyone could hurt someone so precious was beyond Dix's comprehension. Every protective instinct inside her stood at the ready to defend this little bit of sunshine.

Dix leaned back and stared out at the sparkling night sky. She hadn't seen many stars in Vegas. The multitude of neon lights eclipsed nature's beauty. Here, along the Oregon coast, big, fluffy clouds chased the stars around the moonlit sky as a breeze blew in from the west, stirring up tiny white-capped waves in the cape.

"What a huge change from the city that never sleeps to a sleepy town on the West Coast," Dix said.

Andrew snorted softly. "Sometimes it can be too quiet. In New York City, all the noise drowns out the little things. Here, you can hear yourself breathe, and sometimes you think the house is alive with all the creaks and groans."

Dix smiled. "Vegas was like New York City. Noise and light all night long." She sighed. "You must love living here."

Andrew nodded. "I didn't realize how much I missed my summers with my grandfather until I came back. I wish I'd spent more time as an adult visiting him. He was an interesting man."

"What about your grandmother?"

"I never got to know her. She passed before I started coming to Oregon to visit my grandfather. I think she made him promise to get to know his grandson. My grandfather didn't talk much about her. I got the impression he missed her terribly. He never remarried. I went with him once to visit my grandmother's grave. He laid a single red rose on it and stood for a very long time."

Dix's heart squeezed hard in her chest. "He must have loved her so much. How did she die?"

"My grandfather told me she died of a broken heart. But my father said she died of a very aggressive breast cancer. By the time they found it, it had metastasized and spread throughout her body. She only lived two weeks after the diagnosis. My father flew out to be with her the last few days of her life. I remember him coming home looking much older and sad."

"I'm so sorry."

Andrew shrugged. "Now they're both gone."

"What about your parents?"

"Still alive. Still working for large corporations, living the fast-paced life in New York."

"What did they think about you having a daughter?"

His jaw hardened. "They asked for DNA results."

Dix drew in a long breath and let it out. After her conversation about the same thing, she understood Andrew's aversion to finding out if Leigha was really his.

Now that Dix had spent some time with the little girl, she understood. She'd hate to see her go into a state-run foster care system that was already overloaded with children. Andrew had sufficient money and a good home for her. Why tempt fate by checking her lineage? She had a father who loved her enough to provide a beautiful home and anything she could possibly want.

Before she knew it, they'd pulled through the gate of Stratford House and she'd gotten more out of Andrew Stratford that evening than she'd ever thought possible.

One thing was very clear: he would do anything for Leigha. Including risk his life for her. He had the scars to prove it.

Andrew parked the SUV and came around to the passenger side.

Dix had loosened the buckle around Leigha, but she stood back for Andrew to carry the child into the house.

Before he reached in for Leigha, he handed the key to the house to Dix.

Reminding herself she had the duty to protect, Dix glanced around the exterior of the mansion. Andrew had left the light burning on the front porch. Everything appeared too peaceful and untouched.

Dix unlocked the front door. As soon as she did, she could hear Brewer barking from somewhere in the house. They'd left him running loose. He would have been waiting at the door.

The hairs on the back of her neck rose. "Take Leigha back to the car," she ordered.

"What's wrong?" Andrew held Leigha close.

"Something isn't right," she said softly. "I need you to take Leigha back to the car and get inside. Let me check the house before you bring her in."

Andrew hesitated. "Maybe you should stay with Leigha and let me check the house. Or let me call the sheriff."

"Let's not waste time arguing about this. I have a gun. I'm trained on how to use it and I'm experienced in urban warfare." She slipped her hand beneath her skirt and pulled out the handgun. "Go."

She waited for him to leave the front porch and then

she pushed open the front door with the tip of her gun, standing to the side to avoid being the target of whoever might be on the other side.

Dix looked first then slipped through the doorway. Staying away from the moonlight shining through the windows, she moved from room to room, working her way to the back of the house to the kitchen. The back door stood ajar, as if someone had left in a hurry. From a quick inspection, Dix couldn't see any sign of a forced entry. She closed the door and locked it.

Brewer barked again, the sound coming from behind the basement door. Dix twisted the knob, pushed open the door and switched on the light over the stairs. Having been in the basement before, she wasn't sure she trusted the lights to stay on. Retreating to the kitchen, she pulled the rechargeable flashlight out of its charger on the wall by the back door. Armed with the flashlight and the gun, she inched her way down the stairs.

When she reached the bottom, she flipped the switch and illuminated the floor of the basement.

Brewer was tied to a beam in the middle of the basement, with a length of thin rope. He jumped and strained at the lead, his tail wagging.

For the moment Dix left him tied as he was while she made a complete search of the basement. When she was certain they were alone, she untied the dog.

He jumped up on her, planting sloppy kisses on her chin.

Her hands full of flashlight and a gun, Dix couldn't fend off the dog. When he'd greeted her to his own satisfaction, he raced up the steps to the kitchen.

Dix hurried up after him. One by one, she and Brewer searched the rooms until she was certain no one else was in the house.

Finally, she exited the front door and waved to Andrew. "All clear. Let's get Leigha in her bed. Then you can tell me what the hell's going on."

He got out of the car, gathered his daughter and carried her up the steps. Andrew brushed past her and hurried up the staircase.

Dix secured the front door and climbed the stairs.

He'd laid Leigha on her bed, pulled off her shoes and tucked the blankets around her. For a moment he stared down at his daughter, and then he bent and kissed her forehead.

When he straightened, his gaze met Dix's. "Let's talk," he said and led the way out of the bedroom.

Brewer started to follow.

Andrew pointed to the bedroom. "Stay."

The dog didn't cross the threshold of Leigha's room. After a moment he turned back and trotted toward Leigha's bed.

Her heartbeat fluttering, Dix followed Andrew to the first floor.

"Where do you want to talk?" Dix asked.

"On the back porch. I need some air."

"You sure that's a good idea?" Dix asked. "What if the intruder is out there? He could have a gun."

"I refuse to be confined to my house," he said. "If someone wanted me dead badly enough to shoot me, he'd have done it already." Andrew gripped her arm and guided her through what appeared to be a study toward a French door that led out onto a large patio with a view of the ocean.

"Here, let me have that." He took the flashlight from her and switched off the beam. Then he glanced at the gun in her hand. "Do you have to carry that?"

"If you want me to protect you and your daughter, I might need it." Her hand tightened on the grip.

He stared at her for a moment, his gaze slipping over her bare shoulders and down to the gun in her hand and lower. "Seems a little incongruous. You, looking beautiful in that white dress, carrying a gun that could kill a man."

Dix tilted her chin upward. "Don't judge a woman by her clothes."

He raised his hands in surrender. "Oh, I know that now. You can take down a full-grown man. I have the bruises to prove it." He waved toward the door. "Ladies with guns go first."

She stepped through the door, calling back over her shoulder, "I'm no lady."

His chuckle warmed her. "From where I'm standing, you're one-hundred-percent female."

Dix stood on the patio, peering into the shadows, wondering who had been in the house and had gone to the trouble of tying Brewer to a post.

A hand touched her shoulder. "Is everything all right?" Andrew asked. "What made you think something wasn't right?"

"My first clue was that Brewer didn't greet us at the door. I could hear him barking from the other side of the house."

"He could have gotten himself caught in a room and couldn't get out."

She shook her head, her lips pressing into a thin line as she stared up at Andrew. "I found him in the basement, tied to a post."

Chapter 10

Andrew's heartbeat stopped for a full three seconds and then rushed to catch up, thundering against his ribs. "I didn't leave him that way," he said.

"I didn't think you did. Does Mrs. Purdy ever tie Brewer in the basement?"

"Never."

"That's what I thought." She shook her head and descended two of the stone steps leading down to the garden and then sat on the top one. "The dog was in the basement tied up, and the back door was open, no sign of forced entry on any of the exterior doors. And, as far as I could tell, nothing appeared disturbed." She set the gun down beside her.

Andrew dropped to sit on the step, his thoughts roiling through his mind, searching for a reason. "Why?"

"Someone came into your house while you were gone and didn't take anything that I could tell." She shrugged. "If you have a safe or a stash of jewelry, you might want to check those."

"Hold that thought." He rose and reentered the study. He kept important papers and valuables locked in a wall safe behind a portrait of Leigha. He stepped behind his desk and slid the portrait to the side, exposing the safe.

"That portrait of Leigha is completely captivating," Dix said from behind him.

"I commissioned Kayla Davies, Gabe McGregor's wife, to paint it."

"It's nothing less than breathtaking," Dix whispered as she lifted her skirt up her thigh to slide her pistol into the holster.

Andrew swallowed hard and fought to remember what she'd just said, when all he could think about was that smooth, sexy thigh. She'd mentioned something about the painting. "I love the artist's work," he said, twisting the tumbler on the lock. "Only I think Leigha appears too sad."

"The painting captures her. When I first met Leigha, I got that sense from her. She seemed sad."

Andrew's fingers twisted too hard and missed the number he was aiming for. Dix had hit the problem on the head. Leigha seemed too sad for a girl of six. "I've given her everything she needs. I just don't know how to make her happier." He started the pattern all over, his heart pinching inside his chest. He'd brought Leigha to Stratford House to give her the home she deserved, but he didn't know how to make the house a home to the little girl.

"I'm not a parent, so I don't know everything. But I would think most kids just want to be loved and to feel safe."

Andrew turned to the last number, grabbed the handle and pushed it down. The door swung open. "Yeah, well, I love the girl, and I have *you* now to help her with the safe part."

"Safe isn't all about having a bodyguard. It's about knowing the ones you love aren't going to disappear on you. Or, in her case, aren't going to leave her or try to kill her."

Andrew grabbed a stack of documents and turned toward Dix. Even though her skirt was down around her knees, he couldn't get the image of her thigh out of his mind. "You mean she might think I'll leave her or try to kill her?"

"I doubt she'd think you'd try to kill her after saving her from the fire. But she might be afraid to love you for fear of losing you."

"So she calls me Mr. Stratford, even though she knows I'm her father," he said.

"Maybe." Dix touched his arm. "Or maybe she's waiting for you to give her permission to call you Daddy. Or maybe I'm reading too much into it." She took the stack of papers and laid them on the desk. "Forget it. I'm not a psychologist. I'm just a grunt who shoots guns and fights. I can't even analyze my way out of my own hangups." Her shoulders slumped and she straightened the pile on the desk, her hands shaking slightly.

This was the first sign of weakness Andrew had seen in Dix. Up until then, she'd been ready to charge into any situation, take on any challenge and kick butt. This chink in her armor made him look at her differently. What did he know about this woman other than what it said on her dossier?

She squared her shoulders and looked back at the safe. "Can you tell if anything is missing?"

Andrew tore his gaze from her and glanced into the safe. "I don't know. I never did an inventory on the contents. Most of my stocks and bond certificates I keep in a safe-deposit box in a Portland bank. I don't have any jewelry, other than a pair of diamond cuff links my parents gave me at my college graduation."

"So what is all of this?" She waved to the items on the desk.

"Things that meant something to my grandfather." Andrew sifted through the collection. There was a ledger his grandfather had kept to note expenses pertaining to the house, a bundle of letters tied with a string and a few large envelopes.

Dix lifted the bundle of letters that had yellowed with age. "The postmarks on these go all the way back to the 1930s."

"They do?" Andrew slipped the string off the bundle and took one of the letters.

Taking a couple of them off the top, Dix pulled them from their envelopes. "These letters all begin with *My Dearest Thom* and end with *All my love, Rowena.*"

"Thomas Stratford was my grandfather's name. Rowena was my grandmother."

Dix smiled. "These are love letters between them. How sweet."

Andrew dug into the pile again and found a small leather-bound book. He ran his fingers over the smooth surface and opened it. Each page had a date written on one corner and an account of what had happened on that date.

Third night at sea and thus far we've not run into the coast guard or any other privateers in the waters. The sea has been fairly calm with the wind out of the Northwest. Luckily, we've had no storms or fog with which to contend. At our current rate, it won't take long to get to San Francisco with our cargo.

Dix leaned over his shoulder. "What have you got?"

Her nearness made him warm all over. "I believe it's a captain's log for a boat or ship." Andrew turned the book over and opened it to the inside cover, searching for the name of the author. None existed. He opened to another page and read.

My love and I had to abandon our vessel at the dock when revenuers descended on our decks. Thankfully, we were in town at the time. Fortunately, our first mate was able to escape and find us, giving us sufficient warning. We were able to get away, but had to leave behind all of our belongings. Our cargo was declared contraband and was confiscated. We had invested every penny we owned in those barrels and now we are destitute. True, we are without means, but not without our wits and love.

Andrew shook his head. He knew this story. His grandfather had told him the adventures of a certain pair of rumrunners who'd dodged the law so often they'd made quite the reputation for themselves. The book must have been where he'd gotten the stories.

He turned the page and read on.

After hiding in the roughest neighborhoods of the city and being constantly on the lookout for revenuers and lawmen, we got word our buyer had been the one to inform the police of our illicit activities. Not only had he turned us in, he was secretly given our cargo as payment for the tip. We will have our revenge!

"Turn the page. I want to know what happened next." Dix leaned over his arm, her body warm next to his.

Andrew's pulse quickened and his groin tightened. The woman had no idea what she was doing to him. In that dress, her bare arm touching his, she was stirring up so much lust inside him, he could hardly breathe, much less focus.

"Finished reading that page?" she asked.

He nodded.

She turned the page for him, her fingers brushing against his. His nerve endings lit like Fourth of July fireworks, sparking desire throughout his body. His vision blurred. Thankfully, Dix read the next passage aloud.

"Today, revenge is ours. We have recovered, in worth, all that has been taken from us. Now the race is on to escape SF before we are discovered, and make our way north. I have never met a more ingenious woman, or one who is as willing to embark on a dangerous mission as my love. She amazes me at her resilience and cunning. I have met my match and am blessed to call her my wife."

Andrew flipped to the next page but he was happy to let Dix continue to read the words in her throaty voice.

"It has been many months since my last entry. I thought I had lost this journal in our struggle toward a new life and a new home. Alas, I found it buried among the few items retained from our past. We have made many sacrifices and started over—new names and a new home, in a beautiful town that has welcomed us with open arms. We live by the sea, which will always be a part of us, even if we don't traverse its waters anymore.

My love is expecting a child and I cannot begin to describe how full is my heart. I know there is much to do to ensure a stable life for the baby and for my love, but I have work at the local mill and I'm climbing the ranks quickly. I hope to own a business of my own someday. Our secrets, with our treasure, are safely stowed until such a day as they might be needed. For now, we are happy and have all we could wish for…each other."

Again, turning the page, Andrew was disappointed to find the rest of the book empty. He could have gone all night listening to Dix.

"That's it?" Dix exclaimed. "I want to know what happened to them."

Andrew closed the book and laid it on top of the other documents, not ready to move away but sure it was the right thing to do. "I know what became of them."

Dix touched his arm again, sending a pulse of electric shocks through his system. "You know?"

He drew in a steadying breath and let it out before answering. "Yes."

"You mean you know who they are?"

"I'm pretty sure." Though the journal had no name written on it or inside, he knew who'd written it. "My grandfather used to tell me stories of a daring pair of rumrunners who risked it all to make their fortune."

"Who were they?"

He smiled. "My great-grandparents. To the people of Cape Churn they were known as Margaret and Percival Mason. I suspect the journal was a family secret passed from their daughter, Rowena, to my grandfather, her husband, Thomas."

"A more modern-day Wild West?"

"Exactly. It was during the Prohibition era. You see, before Margaret and Percival came to Cape Churn, it would appear they had built a reputation as notorious rumrunners Peg and Percy Malone. On their last run from British Columbia to San Francisco, the man to whom they were to sell their whiskey double-crossed them. He turned them into the law. Their ship was confiscated and the rum disappeared."

"Into the cellar of their stool pigeon?" Dix offered.

Andrew nodded. "Peg and Percy were never caught. Two days after their ship was confiscated, the San Franciscan who'd turned them in reported a robbery at his jewelry store and claimed it had to be Peg and Percy Malone. Every town along the coast was alerted, and a reward was offered, but the authorities never caught the infamous pair."

"Because they no longer existed." Dix grinned. "Good for them. What happened to the jewels from the heist?"

Andrew shrugged. "You read it. They hid it until such a time as they needed it."

"You think they ever needed it?" Dix's eyes narrowed.

"If they had tried to sell the jewelry, they risked being caught. With a baby to think about, they couldn't take that risk."

"Are you sure that's all that was in the safe?" Dix walked over to peer inside. "No fancy jewelry? No treasure?"

Andrew paced across the room and back. "You think it's possible someone broke into the house looking for the jewels?"

"It's a valid motive."

"You have to remember, this house wasn't here when

Peg and Percy hid their treasure. My grandfather built this house for his bride, Rowena."

"Could Rowena's parents have given her the treasure to hide in the house?"

"Maybe, but I doubt it. They died when she was twelve."

"Taking their secret to their graves." Dix sighed. "So somewhere in or around Cape Churn is a treasure."

"Theoretically." Andrew placed all the documents and the journal into the safe and closed the door. "The treasure could be in the bay. If they arrived to Cape Churn in a boat, they could have scuttled the boat at the bottom of the bay."

Dix's eyes widened. "Is that what those two guys in the café were doing with the maps?"

Andrew nodded. "Seems they found what was supposed to be a fictional account of Peg and Percival's escapades and they're convinced the boat is at the bottom of the bay."

"Do you think that's where they hid the treasure?"

"I really hadn't thought about it. As a kid, I thought the stories my grandfather told were really just stories to entertain me."

"And now?"

He frowned. "Now I think he might have been telling them to me for a reason."

"He wanted you to know there was a treasure out there. If not for you to find, then for your heirs." Dix tilted her head. "And you don't want to get to it first?"

"I have to admit, the twins sparked my curiosity. But what do I need with the money? I have all I can use."

"I contend that it's not about the money. It's about the legacy."

"If my great-grandparents had wanted that legacy to carry on, they would have told someone where the treasure was. They couldn't unearth the treasure without risking exposing themselves. But their heirs could."

"But you said they died when Rowena was twelve. Then their secret would have died with them."

"True."

"Here, let me play devil's advocate." Dix leaned her bottom against the desk and crossed her arms over her chest. "If you let someone else find it, that's a legacy you let pass you by that could have gone to Leigha or Leigha's children."

Sweet heaven. When Dix crossed her arms, it plumped her breasts and drew Andrew's attention to those two lovely mounds. He dragged his gaze up to her full, lush lips. "Did anyone ever tell you that you're beautiful when you're so intense?" Andrew couldn't resist tucking a strand of Dix's hair behind her ear.

She captured his finger in her hand.

For a moment Andrew thought she might break his finger in two.

"No one has ever told me I was beautiful." Her brows descended and her gaze met his. But she didn't let go of his hand.

"Someone should have."

She shook her head slowly. "What were we talking about?"

"Legacies." He raised his other hand and brushed his thumb along her cheek, careful not to bump his stitches.

"Legacies?" Her voice came out in little more than a whisper and her hand tightened on his.

"What I don't understand is why Fontaine sent me a beautiful bodyguard." He tipped Dix's face upward and slid his thumb across her lips.

"I'm not beautiful," she said, her voice so soft she could barely hear it herself.

Andrew ignored her protest. "Did he not realize how distracting it could be?"

Her lips puckered ever so slightly against his thumb, but she said, "We should concentrate on the issue at hand."

"If I weren't such a messed-up bastard, I'd kiss you right now."

Dix shook her head and raised her hand to cup his scarred cheek. "We all have our scars."

He circled her waist with his injured hand and the back of her neck with the other, bringing her closer until her belly pressed against the hard ridge beneath his trousers. "Some more so than others."

She tipped her head and stared into his eyes. "Some have deeper scars on the inside. Scars that can't be seen but still hurt."

Andrew bent to claim her lips in a long, slow kiss.

She wrapped her hands around the back of his neck and deepened the kiss, opening her mouth to him.

He slid his tongue along the length of hers, caressing it with long, slow thrusts. She tasted of chocolate ice cream, sweet and too tempting to pass up.

When he finally remembered to breathe, Andrew leaned his forehead against hers and whispered, "What happened to you, Dixie? What scars are hiding beneath that beautiful, tough exterior?"

As the words left his mouth Andrew felt Dix's body go from soft and receptive to stiff and resistant.

She pushed away from him and scrubbed a hand over her face. "Mr. Stratford, that should not have happened."

"But it did."

"And it won't happen again."

"No?" He reached for her.

She moved away. "Look, we're better off keeping our relationship on a professional level." Then in her coldest, most distant voice, she said, "It's been a long day. If you'll excuse me, I'd like to check on Leigha before I call it a night."

With those parting words, she left the study and walked up the stairs, her back straight, her head held high.

Andrew watched her until she disappeared. Then he sat at his desk and called himself every kind of fool in the book.

No matter how tempting her lips or how perfect the curves of her body felt against his.

You don't kiss the help.

Chapter 11

Dix held herself together all the way up the sweeping staircase, counting each step as she went to take her thoughts off the man in the study below. But each riser represented one step farther away from what she really wanted. And that was to run back down and throw herself into Andrew's arms and kiss him again like they might not see another tomorrow.

But she wasn't there to kiss the client. And she had too many hang-ups with her past to let herself dare to fall for a guy. Every time she thought she could settle down, she got that itchy feeling to move. The longer she stayed in one place, the more she wanted to leave. Ever since she'd been held captive, she couldn't stand to be confined. She'd barely spent any time in her apartment in Vegas. If she wasn't out on the street running, she was hiking in the hills or working out at the gym.

No. Just no.

She couldn't wish herself on anyone.

Stick to the job. Leave the emotions out of it.

Dix checked on Leigha. The little girl lay curled into the blankets, still wearing her sundress.

In keeping with her need for continuous motion, she strode to the child's dresser, rummaged around quietly and found a soft jersey nightgown. As carefully as possible, she undressed Leigha and slipped the nightgown over her head. Dix went to the bathroom, wet a cloth with warm water and returned to wash Leigha's face and hands. When she was done, she pulled the blanket up to the little girl's chin and bent to press a kiss to her forehead.

A smile curled the corners of Leigha's mouth and she tucked a hand beneath her cheek and slept on.

If only it were that simple to fall asleep. Dix turned to find Andrew standing in the doorway, his gaze on her.

"She should be okay for the night. I'll leave my door open and listen for sounds," Dix said.

"Thank you for taking care of her."

"It's not difficult. She's a wonderful person. Anyone would do the same."

Andrew's mouth tightened. "Not everyone."

Dix's gut burned.

He was right.

Jeannette had tried to kill her own daughter. And Dix thought *she* was messed up. Jeannette had been one deranged woman. Too bad she'd let her crazy loose on her daughter. How much had that damaged the child?

Dix shook her head. The three of them were so much alike in many ways. Each damaged by the actions of others. Each of them suffering some form of PTSD. Yeah, Dix didn't need to add to the Stratford family's problems with ones of her own.

She strode toward the door.

Andrew didn't move until the last minute, turning sideways to let her through.

Just when she thought she might make good her escape, he touched her arm and stopped her.

"Dix?"

She froze, unable to move. If she were honest with herself, she was *unwilling* to move, afraid that she would do something she would regret like throw herself into his arms. Flames ignited where his hand touched her bare skin and spread through her body like wildfire. She stared at that hand, willing it to release her.

"I'm sorry if I took advantage of you," he said. "But I'm not sorry I kissed you."

Her belly clenched and heat pooled at her core. "Damn you," she said between her teeth. "Why couldn't you leave it?" That unnamed "it" hung between them like something physical and alive.

"Tell me you didn't feel it and I'll leave you alone."

She dropped her chin to her chest to keep from looking at him. Her gaze fell to his scarred hand and she remembered the way the grafted skin felt against the back of her neck. Smooth, cool and so tender. "I didn't feel anything." She lied to him. To herself.

He raised his hand, cupped her chin and lifted her face, forcing her to see him. "Look me in the eye and tell me you didn't feel anything," he whispered, his breath warm on her cheek, tingling against her lips and smelling of chocolate ice cream.

She fell into his ice-blue gaze, her resolve crumbling with every breath. Dix, the MMA fighter, Army Ranger and all-around tough gal, melted into goo as she stared into Andrew's eyes.

That urge to move hit her like a freight train. She popped up on her toes, grabbed his cheeks between her hands and kissed him hard, and then she ran. Down the stairs, through the study and out into the garden, her eyes burning from holding back the tears. Since her capture, she'd refused to cry. *Ever.* Nothing could be as bad as being tortured by the enemy, never knowing if you'd live to see another day. *Nothing.*

Not even this heart-pounding, gut-wrenching certainty that she could never love again. As a person, as a partner, she was too broken to allow someone else into her world for any length of time.

A few minutes stretched into fifteen as Dix stood in the chilled night air, her skin bathed blue in the moonlight, her face turned to the sky. She counted over three hundred stars before her pulse returned to normal and she could face going back into the house and its constrictive walls.

Up the stairs and into her room, she moved quietly, grabbing clean underwear and her soft sleep T-shirt. Then ducked into the bathroom.

During her years in the military she'd honed her

bathing skills to make her movements swift and efficient in the shower. She made mental images of her problems, imagining them washing down the drain with the shampoo and soapsuds. When she rinsed clean she almost felt normal. Except for the hollowness in her chest.

She'd get over it. Having survived a lot worse, Dix knew she could get over anything, given enough time.

When she stepped into the hall, soft sobs caught her attention. They emanated from Leigha's room.

Wishing she'd brought a pair of shorts, Dix tiptoed down the corridor to Leigha's room.

The little girl lay on her side, curled in the fetal position, her hand on her face, tears slipping down her cheeks.

Dix could hear the shower going in the master suite through the open connecting door. Quickly, she slipped between the sheets and gathered the girl in her arms. "Shh, baby. Everything is going to be all right."

Leigha's sobs subsided as she snuggled against Dix. Soon she lay quiet and still, her breathing deep and restful.

For a long time Dix stared at the ceiling, her lips tingling and places farther south burning inside. All the while, the man who'd stirred the embers settled in the king-size bed in the connecting room, a short distance away.

What would he think if she walked into his room and slipped between the sheets of his bed?

She closed her eyes and tried not to let her thoughts stray in that direction. The last thing she needed was to sleepwalk into Andrew Stratford's room and climb into bed with him. She would be completely powerless to resist her body's desire.

Andrew lay for hours, staring out the window at the star-filled sky. He knew the minute Dix had returned to the house because he couldn't rest until she was safe inside the walls. He'd gone down to the kitchen on the pretext of getting a glass of water, when, in fact, he'd known he could see the garden from the kitchen window. He watched like a voyeur as Dix stood staring at the sky, her skin and the white dress turned a mystical blue in the moonlight.

He'd wanted to join her there, pull her into his arms and kiss away her doubts. But who was he to woo the woman? He was scarred, damaged and ugly.

Dix deserved a man who didn't frighten children with his face. A man who had a lot more to show for his life than a bank account and a huge mansion that was too big for a family. Like she said, it might as well be a hotel. And he also came with strings attached. Whoever loved him had to love his daughter, too. She'd also have to understand that no matter what, Leigha was his number one priority.

What would a former Army Ranger and MMA fighter want with a broken-down stockbroker, a mansion on the edge of nowhere and a little girl?

Yeah, that was Andrew's life and he wouldn't have it any other way. He'd earned his scars saving his daughter, and he'd do it all over again. Leigha was worth every bit of the pain he'd suffered through skin grafting. Physically, she'd come out of the incident with a mild case of smoke inhalation, which was better than he could have expected. Inside, she'd take a little longer to heal.

They had all their lives to heal together.

Eventually, Andrew fell into a fitful sleep where fires burned. This time, not only was Leigha's life at stake, Dix was trapped behind a wall of flame. Her pretty white dress caught fire and she writhed in pain. Only she didn't scream or cry. She looked at him and told him to save Leigha. Just save Leigha.

No.

He couldn't let Dix die in the fire. Burning to death would be the most painful way to die. Having burned his hand, he knew the amount of pain flames could inflict on a body. He couldn't leave her to die like that.

But first he had to find Leigha and get her to safety. He searched the room, even looking beneath the bed. Instead of Leigha, he found Jeannette, laughing at his desperation. She flung a flaming blanket at him. It covered his head and he couldn't see his way out of the flames.

"Andrew," someone called.

He struggled to open his eyes. If only he could see, he'd follow whoever was calling to him out of the fire. But no matter how hard he tried, they wouldn't open.

"Andrew. You're dreaming. Wake up." A hand touched his shoulder and stroked down his arm. "Wake up. You're dreaming."

He grabbed the hand in his and held on, pulling himself out of the flames and into his bedroom. With what felt like a mighty effort, he forced his eyes open and stared up into the moss green eyes of the woman who'd sacrificed herself in the dream fire so that he could save his daughter.

"No," he said, his voice hoarse. He sat up, swung his legs over the side of the bed and pulled her against him, holding her tight. She was safe. Thank God, she was safe.

"It's okay," she said, stroking his hair, talking in a soothing tone. "You were dreaming."

As he surfaced from the lingering effect of the dream, he realized she wore only a T-shirt.

She stood between his legs, her skin pressed against his.

His pulse, still racing from the terror of the dream, continued to pound through his veins now for an entirely different reason.

He ran his uninjured hand up her back and down to the swell of her bottom. Her curves were soft, but the muscles firm beneath her skin.

"Are you awake now?" she whispered.

"Sweetheart, I'm so awake, my body is on fire." He gripped her hips, careful not to disturb his stitches, and set her away from him. "You'd better go now. If you stay any longer, I don't know if I'll be able to keep my hands to myself."

Dix stood still, staring into his eyes, her hands resting on his shoulders, her bottom lip caught between her teeth.

Andrew wanted to suck that lip into his mouth so badly he groaned.

"Are you okay?" she asked, her hands rubbing circles on his shoulders.

"No, I'm not okay. You're standing in front of me in only a T-shirt, and I'm fighting an uncontrollable urge to rip it from your body, toss you in the bed and make love to you."

She continued to worry that bottom lip, until finally she let go of it and removed her hands from his shoulders.

Andrew resigned himself to the need for a very cold shower and watched as she backed out of the V of his legs.

Dix shot a glance toward the connecting door to Leigha's bedroom. Nothing stirred in that direction. Then she grabbed the hem of her T-shirt and yanked it up over her head.

She stood in front of him wearing nothing but a pair of lace panties that left very little to the imagination.

Andrew's heart stood still, his lungs seized. Blood rushed through his veins and he sucked in a ragged breath. "I never would have thought a former Ranger and MMA fighter would wear lace panties."

Dix chuckled. "I might be tough on the outside, but I'm all female on the inside." She held out her hand. "I'm not asking you to fight your urges. I'm finding I have a few of my own."

"I won't do anything you don't want me to," he said, pulling her to stand between his legs again.

"Just take it easy on me. I haven't done this in a long time."

He smoothed his hands over her hips and upward to cup her breasts. "You're even more beautiful with your skin kissed by moonlight."

She wove her fingers through his hair and bent to press her lips to his. "You taste like chocolate ice cream."

He clamped his arms around her and lay back on the bed, pulling her with him. Then he rolled to his side, easing her onto the mattress. "Say the word and it all stops here."

She reached for his cheek, laying her hand across the ragged scar.

He fought his natural instinct to flinch, but held steady and let her trace the line from his temple to the corner of his mouth.

"This hurt, didn't it?" she asked.

"Not as much as it would have hurt if my daughter had died in that fire."

Her eyes narrowed. "This isn't a burn scar."

"No."

Dix's brows lowered. "*She* did that? Jeannette?"

He nodded. "She fought to keep me from saving Leigha."

Her finger slipped over his lips. "If she were still alive, I'd kill her."

"Even I didn't have that satisfaction."

"What happened to her?"

"She dove, headfirst, out of the eight-story building."

Dix shook her head and leaned up to press her lips to the corner of his mouth where the scar began. "Was that what you were dreaming about?"

"Some." Her mouth moving across his jaw scrambled his wits. "I was back in that apartment. I couldn't find Leigha. Jeannette was there…and you."

Her eyes widening, Dix stared up into his eyes. "Was I helping or hurting?"

"You told me to save Leigha."

"You should have let me fight off Jeannette."

"Enough about my dreams. Why were you awake?" He smoothed a strand of blond hair away from her eyes and kissed the tip of her nose.

"I have dreams of my own."

"About?"

She shrugged. "Doesn't matter. They were just dreams."

"Bad enough to wake you." He nodded. "When you're ready, I want to know what you dream about. I don't know enough about you." He brushed his thumb across her bottom lip where the thin line of a scar marred an otherwise beautiful face. "Like where did you get this little scar? In the fighting ring?"

She shook her head and pulled him closer to kiss his lips. "No. In a much darker place," she whispered against his mouth. Then she kissed him harder, thrusting her tongue through his teeth to connect with his.

Andrew tasted, twisted and stroked until he was forced to come up to breathe. He stared into her eyes, wondering what had caused the shadows in their green depths. There were so many unanswered questions about this fighting woman.

But for now, she wasn't willing to share her story. However, she *was* willing to share her body and she'd asked for him to be gentle.

Taking it slowly, he kissed a path from her lips along her jawline to the sensitive area beneath her earlobe.

Dix laced her fingers in his hair and guided him lower.

Andrew skimmed his mouth along the long line of her neck and pressed a kiss to the pulse beating at the base of her throat. Unable to stop there, he moved lower, at first kissing and then tonguing the swell of her breast until he reached the rosy nipple puckering beneath his touch.

Dix arched her back and pressed her hands against the back of his head, urging him to take more.

Flicking, licking and nipping at the beaded tip, he teased her until she writhed beneath him.

Then she took his head between her hands and dragged him to the other breast.

He treated that one to the same, until the tip beaded and Dix moaned.

With increasingly difficult restraint, he plied kisses and nips to each rib, working his way slowly down her torso to the thatch of curls covering her sex.

His body on fire, he fought to keep it slow, steady and controlled, when all he wanted to do was part her legs and thrust inside her.

As if she heard his thoughts, she spread her knees farther apart.

Andrew moved over her, positioning himself between her legs, slipping farther down her body until he hovered over the juncture of her thighs.

Dix pushed her panties over her hips.

Taking over from there, Andrew dragged them down to her ankles and off. Then he stroked the inside of her calves and thighs with the tip of his finger, drawing a line toward her glistening center.

Her chest rose as she dragged in a ragged breath. "I feel like I'm coming apart at the seams."

"Maybe you need to. Maybe we both need to." Andrew thumbed her entrance swirling around the inside, collecting the musky juices. From there, he dragged his wet digit up to that special place. Parting the curls and the folds, he stroked that little nubbin of flesh.

Dix moaned, lifted her knees, dug her heels into the mattress and pushed upward. "Oh, dear heaven, there!" she whispered.

He bent and tongued that very spot, flicking, licking and teasing.

Dix's back arched and her hips rose. "Yes!" she cried, her voice hushed but no less strident. Her body tensed beneath his and her fingers curled into his scalp. She stayed that way for a prolonged moment.

Andrew continued to caress her with his tongue until she fell back to the bed on a sigh, gripped his hair in her fingers and dragged him up her body.

"I need you inside me." She kissed his jaw and slid her hands over his shoulders and downward to slip beneath his boxers. Hooking her fingers into the elastic, she tugged the shorts downward.

He rolled off the bed, dropped his boxers and reached into the nightstand, praying he had at least one condom there. Since moving from New York City, he hadn't even thought about making love to a woman. After the horror of Jeannette, he wouldn't consider a one-night stand.

But the drawer had been packed and moved full. Thankfully, he found a string of packets and tore off one.

"Glad one of us is thinking." Dix took the packet from him, opened it and swung her legs over the side of the bed to face him. With deliberately slow movements she rolled the protection over him, her hands gliding down the length of him to the base. With a sassy half smile, she looked up. "Ready?"

Sweet heaven.

He growled deep in his throat, scooted her back on the bed and climbed up between her legs. Nudging her with the tip of his erection, he said, "You tell me if I'm ready."

"Mmm." She clutched his buttocks, widened her knees and guided him to her. "I'd say yes."

Gently he eased into her, careful not to hurt her. Her slick entrance made it easy and soon he was all the way inside. Her channel contracted around him, sending electric currents throughout his body. Going slowly would kill him. But she'd asked him to go easy. And he would.

"Can you go faster?" she asked, her voice tight, breathy.

"Are you sure?"

"Oh, yeah." She tightened her hold on his buttocks and pushed him, slamming him right back in. Again and again, setting the pace.

When Andrew took over, he plunged in and out, increasing the rhythm and intensity.

Dix let go of him and clutched the comforter in her fingers. She buried her heels in the mattress and raised her hips to meet his every thrust.

The tension built inside Andrew. The ripples of fulfillment started from where he touched her inside, spreading through his body and outward to the very tips of his fingers. He thrust one last time and buried himself deep.

Dix wrapped her legs around him, holding him as close as two people could get.

Waves of sensations washed over him and he shook from the force. When he finally came back to earth, he lowered himself on top of her and rolled to the side, taking her with him. "Wow. You are amazing."

Dix let go of a long breath and lay back against the pillow, a smile teasing the corners of her lips. "You're not so bad yourself."

He leaned up on his elbow and twirled a strand of her hair around his finger. "So where do we go from here?"

Dix stared up at him, her green eyes darkening. "I don't know that we go anywhere. I can't…" She rolled out of the bed and gathered her clothes.

Andrew's chest tightened. "Can't what?"

"I can't do this."

He shook his head. "Do what?"

"I don't know. Trust me. You don't want to start something with me. I'm damaged goods."

He frowned and sat up. "*You're* damaged goods?"

"Yes." She pulled her T-shirt over her head and down past her hips. "Can we just leave it at 'wow'?"

Andrew shook his head. "I don't think I can."

She walked around the room, staring at the floor. "Where are they?"

Andrew rose from the bed and plucked her panties from the floor. "Looking for these?"

She snatched at them.

He raised them out of her reach. "Talk to me, Dix."

"There's nothing to talk about. I'm not the girl for you." She tried again to reach the panties. When she couldn't get to them, she shook her head. "Keep them." And she spun, running out of the room and down the hall to her own.

Andrew stood with a pair of sexy panties in his hand, wondering what the heck he'd done wrong.

Chapter 12

Dix put on a pair of underwear and jogging shorts, and waited a few minutes before opening her door again. She wanted to listen for any sounds in Leigha's room. Then she lay on the bed, staring up at the ceiling, cursing the wickedly delicious ache between her legs. She wanted more than anything to go back into Andrew's room and tell him she wanted to be with him. But she was afraid.

Afraid she'd feel confined and need to bust free. Afraid her nightmares would make her lash out.

Andrew and Leigha had enough healing to do without having her add her own problems to the mix.

Stick to the job. Don't get involved. Don't fall in love.

Dix clapped a hand over her mouth to keep from crying out. No. She couldn't be falling for Andrew Stratford. He deserved someone who wasn't broken. He'd have no problem finding a wife who could love him and Leigha. The father and daughter were perfect, everything a woman could want in a husband and child.

Eventually she slept, waking with a start when she heard the sound of little footsteps padding down the hallway.

Leigha stood in the doorway to Dix's bedroom, wearing her nightgown.

"Hey, sweetie."

"Are you awake?" she asked.

Dix pushed back the covers and got out of bed. "I am. Are you hungry?"

Leigha nodded.

"Let's get dressed and brush our hair before we go downstairs." Dix went to her suitcase and unearthed a T-shirt and a pair of jeans.

Leigha entered the room and wandered around, touching the few toiletries Dix had brought with her. "Do you like it here?" she asked.

Dix put on her bra beneath her nightshirt. When it was in place, she shucked the shirt and dragged the T-shirt on before responding. "Yes, I do."

The little girl tilted her head to the side and stared at Dix with her big blue eyes. "Why?"

"For one, I like *you*." Dix kissed the top of the child's head.

Leigha smiled. "I like you, too."

Dix walked to the window and stared out at the incredible view. "I also like that you can see the ocean from here."

"Me, too." Leigha lifted Dix's brush and ran it through her hair. "Do you like Mr. Stratford?"

The girl's question caught Dix by surprise and she dropped the jeans she'd been holding. Where was Leigha going with her questions? "Of course I do. Your father is a good man."

"I know. I just wondered." She laid the brush back on the dresser and skipped to the door. "I hope Mrs. Purdy is making pancakes this morning. I love pancakes." She left the room and ran back to her own.

Dix finished dressing and followed Leigha.

The child had dressed herself in jeans, a T-shirt and sneakers. She was brushing her hair, though she struggled with the tangles.

"May I?" Dix held out her hand.

Leigha laid the brush in it. "Did your mommy brush your hair?"

"Yes, she did."

She stared at her reflection in the mirror. "Mine didn't."

Stumped again, Dix didn't know if she should comment or let Leigha's announcement pass. "Would you like me to braid your hair?"

She smiled. "Yes, please."

Though never a girlie-girl, Dix could dress up and do her hair when she had to. As a female MMA fighter, the sponsors and television networks had certain expectations of the lady fighters. Though they were punching, kicking and knocking each other out, they had to look good in the process. Hair, makeup, athletic clothes and toned bodies.

Dix had just wanted to hit something, but she'd been forced to look good while she did it. She'd gotten good at French braiding her hair.

Leigha's long blond hair was easy to braid, and so very soft. When Dix finished twisting the strands, she secured the end with an elastic band. "Ready?"

The child nodded. "I'm hungry."

"Me, too."

As she stepped out into the corridor, Dix's breath caught and held until she realized the hallway was empty. What had she expected?

Even though Andrew lived there, she wasn't destined to run into him every time she came out of her room. She released the breath she'd held and willed her pulse to return to normal.

What was it about the man that made her heart beat faster? He was just a man. Her client. Hell, he was more than that. Tall, dark, incredibly attractive even with the scars. He made her stomach flip whenever they were in the same room. And after last night... Boy, was she in trouble. He was an excellent lover.

Dix's belly tightened and her sex ached from the night before. Though she knew it was wrong to have slept with her client, she couldn't help reliving it over and over in her mind.

Mrs. Purdy was in the kitchen stirring batter in a big bowl. She beamed at Dix and Leigha. "Anyone up for pancakes this morning?"

Leigha raised her hand and shouted, "I am! I am!"

"Well, then, if you two will set the table, I'll make

them fresh and hot for you." Mrs. Purdy nodded toward an upper cabinet. "Plates are in there."

Leigha went for the flatware.

"How many do I plan for?" Dix asked, her belly knotting.

"Just you and Leigha. I ate breakfast at home with my husband, and Mr. Stratford ate an hour ago and left for Portland. He said he had some business to take care of."

Dix's heart slipped into her gut like a ten-pound weight.

Andrew had gone to Portland without telling her. Not that he was obligated to inform her of his movements, but after last night, she'd thought he would at least say something to her this morning.

Like what? *Great sex.* Or worse, being there and being caught in a painful silence where neither could look the other in the eye.

Dix sighed. Andrew had chosen the right option. Leave and avoid an awkward moment altogether.

Mrs. Purdy served them blueberry pancakes and blueberry syrup.

Leigha dug in, smearing blueberry juice across her smiling lips.

Her appetite a bit curbed by Andrew's departure, Dix ate at a more sedate pace. The pancakes were light, fluffy and heavenly. Even her mood couldn't dampen her enthusiasm for her breakfast. The next thing she knew, her plate was empty and she was licking the sticky syrup off her lips.

Dix and Leigha cleared the table, taking their empty plates to the sink for Mrs. Purdy to wash.

"Let's brush our teeth and then we can decide what we want to do today," Dix suggested.

Leigha ran up the stairs ahead of Dix.

Dix followed close behind, finding the little girl's eagerness contagious. She could explore the house and the grounds more thoroughly without Andrew around. She wouldn't be tense about running into him at every turn.

A few minutes later Dix entered Leigha's bathroom, where the little girl was wiping toothpaste from her mouth.

"What do you want to do today?" Leigha asked.

"I'd like to explore the house and yard," Dix said. "I want to see all of the places you like to play."

Leigha's eyes brightened. "Bennet will be so excited. He doesn't get many visitors where he is."

Dix frowned. "Just where is Bennet?"

"I'll show you." Leigha led the way down the stairs and through the beautiful entryway to what Dix would describe as an old-fashioned parlor or sitting room.

Brewer followed, his toenails tapping on the marble tiles.

Leigha aimed for the far side of the sitting room and a massive fireplace. Fresh logs were laid out on the hearth, but no signs of ash could be found. Dix doubted the fireplace had been used lately.

When Leigha didn't slow, Dix frowned. Where did she think she was going? It wasn't as though they would climb up the chimney.

Leigha walked right next to the stack of logs and

turned to the side where she pressed on one of the bricks. A door big enough for Leigha opened inward.

Dix had been in that parlor before and hadn't noticed the secret door.

Leigha entered, pulled a string above her head and a light blinked on, illuminating a room or passageway beyond. She turned and waved for Dix to follow. "It gets bigger once you go through the door."

Before Dix could take a step forward, Brewer shot through the opening and past Leigha, disappearing into darkness beyond.

Feeling like Alice in Wonderland falling down the rabbit hole, Dix followed Leigha through.

She waited for Dix to clear the little door and straighten before she turned and led the way through a narrow tunnellike corridor.

"Does your father know about this place?" Dix asked.

Leigha shook her head. "No. Bennet didn't want anyone to know."

A shiver of apprehension slipped across Dix's skin. "Why?"

"He said it was our secret."

Alarm bells went off in Dix's head. Anyone asking a child to keep such a big secret had to have nefarious plans. "Then why are you showing it to me?"

"Bennet trusts you. He said I could bring you and it would be okay."

"But not your father?"

She stopped for a moment, her chin dropping to her chest. "Sometimes Mr. Stratford doesn't like me very much."

Dix dropped to her haunches in front of Leigha. "Oh, sweetie, he does like you a lot. He loves you so much, he brought you here to live. He wanted you to have a great place to run and play."

Leigha scuffed her foot on the wooden flooring. "I like it when he reads to me," she conceded.

"Then ask him to do it more."

"He always seems too busy."

Dix made a mental note to tell Stratford to spend more time getting to know his daughter and making her feel more comfortable around him.

"You really should tell your father about this. What if you fell and got hurt? He wouldn't know where to look for you."

Leigha's brows dipped. "Do you want to come or not?"

Dix nodded, knowing she'd pushed far enough. If Leigha didn't show her father the secret corridors, Dix could show him later. She hated to think of Leigha wandering around and possibly getting hurt and no one knowing how to find her.

As she followed Leigha through the narrow corridor, Dix caught occasional glimpses through peepholes in the walls. At one point, she could see into a study through a narrow slat in the wall. She memorized the angle of the view. Next time she was in the study, she'd look for the hole in the wall that allowed her to see into the room.

Dix would have loved to take her time and explore more thoroughly, but Leigha appeared to be a child on a mission. After a while, the wooden flooring ended at a door. Leigha opened the door and the path gave way to hard-packed earth beneath their feet. The tunnel no longer was the wooden slats of antique walls but carved-out rocks and dirt.

Leigha stopped long enough to retrieve a flashlight from a cubbyhole in the dirt wall. She flicked the switch and aimed it into the darkness of the tunnel.

"How did you find this place?"

"Bennet showed it to me."

Walking behind the child who held a flashlight, Dix stumbled several times over the rugged ground. Eventually the small tunnel emerged into a cavern the size of a school auditorium.

In the middle of the cavern was a clear stream, meandering its way through.

Leigha hopped across the narrow strip of water and kept walking.

"Sweetheart, I'm not so sure this is a good place for you to play."

"Why?"

"Rocks could fall on you. There could be an earthquake that shakes this hillside and blocks the entrance."

"There's another way out."

"Still, it's not the best place a little girl could play alone."

Leigha frowned. "But I'm not alone. I have Brewer and Bennet."

The child's declaration didn't make Dix feel any better. "Where is Bennet?"

"He's here." Leigha smiled and waved her hand toward the cave wall.

Dix stared in that direction, wondering what the girl was seeing that she couldn't. "I don't see him." Yes, the girl had an imaginary friend. But just for grins, Dix asked, "Could you take me to him?"

Leigha giggled and turned to Dix. "He's right next to you."

A chill rippled down Dix's spine. "May I have your flashlight?"

Leigha handed her the device.

Dix spun in a circle. Still, she couldn't see anyone beside her, behind her or anywhere else. Willing the gooseflesh rising on her arms to subside, she pulled herself together. "I take it only you can see Bennet?"

Leigha giggled. "He's right beside you."

Standing in a dark cave, with only the beam of the flashlight cutting through the darkness, Dix was ready to grab the child and run back to the lit corridor. The creep factor was really high.

Brewer trotted up to Dix and stopped a couple of steps away, tail wagging and tongue lolling. He didn't seem to be looking at Leigha or Dix. Instead he appeared to be staring at the empty space beside Dix.

Another chill rippled across Dix's skin. "He's here now?"

Leigha nodded. "He says you're a gorgeous dame." Leigha tilted her head and shifted her gaze to Dix. "What's a dame?"

"A woman." Dix bunched her fists. If she had to hit someone, who would it be? She had to be able to see the person to hit him. But then, if he were a ghost, what good would it do to take a swing at him? Hell, what was she thinking? Ghosts weren't real. Or were they? "Wow, this is getting a little too weird, even for me." She took Leigha's hand. "We should probably go back to the house."

"But I haven't shown you the place I like to play."

Dix's brows rose. "This isn't it?"

Leigha shook her head. "Of course not. It's too dark."

Dix handed the child the flashlight with a resigned feeling of dread. "Show me. Then we're going right back to the house."

Leigha took the light and headed for another tunnel on the opposite side of the cave from the one leading toward the house.

Dix prayed she'd remember which one would get them back. All she needed was to get lost in a maze of tunnels and caves with the little girl she was supposed to be protecting. Call her crazy, but she followed Leigha. She couldn't wait in the cave for the little girl. Not in pitch black. Not with a ghost called Bennet calling her a gorgeous dame.

Brewer walked beside Leigha as she led the way through the tunnel. Soon a faint light appeared at the end of the tunnel and grew larger as they neared.

Dix closed the distance between her and Leigha. Having no idea where the tunnel came out, she didn't want Leigha to fall over a ledge or be captured by the unknown threat Dix was hired to protect her from.

Leigha held up her hand. "You have to go slow here," she said. With her back to the side of the tunnel, she slipped around the corner.

Dix stepped into the bright light streaming into the

tunnel entrance and let her eyes adjust. Then her heart screeched to a halt and her breath hung in her lungs. "Holy sh—shenanigans!" she said and stepped back, her hand going to the cave wall. Before her was the ocean and a one-hundred-foot drop to the rocky shoreline below. One more step and she would have gone over the edge and crashed to her death on the rocks.

"Leigha!" she shouted, her voice rising. "Leigha!"

Leigha appeared around the corner, her pretty brow furrowed. "What's wrong?"

Dix clutched the little girl's hand. "That's a deadly fall."

"I know. That's why I go around the side." She smiled at Dix. "It's okay. There's a path you can follow all the way down to the beach. That's where I like to play."

Dix wasn't so sure about sliding around the edge of the cave. One misstep and she'd be free-falling to the ground.

Leigha laughed.

"It's not funny," Dix grumbled.

"Bennet thinks so. He's making me laugh." Leigha slipped around the corner with Dix's hand in hers.

Dix either had to follow or let go of Leigha.

She followed, hugging the cliff side with her body as she inched her way around the corner.

Once out of the cave and onto a path, the trail widened and led a few feet away from the sheer drop-off. Leigha clicked off the flashlight and skipped ahead with Brewer.

Dix glanced up and couldn't see the top of the cliff above. From what she could surmise, they had exited the cave halfway down the side of the cliff. Stratford House was another one hundred feet above them.

The trail wound along the face of the cliff with its own pockets of trees and grass. Before long, Leigha came to a set of steps leading downward. Carved out of stone, the steps were partly natural with a few obviously chipped out by man.

As they neared the bottom, the trail narrowed again but the drop-off was less frightening.

At last, Leigha hopped off the last stone step onto a thin strand of beach.

"The tide is out. If the tide was in, the beach would disappear beneath the water."

"And your father doesn't know about this place?" Dix glanced at the sixty feet of beach.

"No," Leigha called out and darted away, running along the sand, chasing Brewer.

Dix shook her head and stepped onto the sand. First thing when she got back and Andrew returned home, she would show him what Leigha had shown her today.

If he wasn't concerned, he had no business being a father to a curious little girl. The child shouldn't be coming to this little beach alone. Wandering through a cave and a couple of tunnels alone was bad. A beach that disappeared at high tide was equally bad.

Dix's mind went through all of the horrible situations that could have happened. But there was Leigha, alive and happy, running across her favorite place to play. She'd be mad at Dix for telling her father about her secret place, but someone needed to let Andrew know what his daughter was up to. He probably had no clue.

Since Leigha never left the house through any of the known doors, and Andrew hadn't found the hidden door himself, no one could have known what Leigha was up to without dogging her every step.

She would burst that bubble later. For now, Leigha was safe. Dix would make sure they got back to the house without mishap.

The sun shone down on the little beach. Leigha threw a stick for Brewer and he retrieved it twelve times before he got tired of the game and wandered along the sand, sniffing.

Dix found a boulder to sit on and watched the waves roll up on the beach. The continuous ebb and flow mesmerized her. She could stare at the waves and the ocean for a very long time and never get bored.

A shout drew her attention. Only the shout wasn't the high-pitched call of a little girl. Instead it was a man's voice.

Dix dragged her attention away from the waves, Leigha and Brewer to locate the sound. Out in the bay, she spotted a dive boat. A man on the deck waved toward her. From the distance, she wasn't exactly sure who it was. Not wanting to appear unfriendly, she gave a little wave back.

The dive boat swung around. For a moment Dix thought it was pulling away from the shore, but it made a complete circle and slowly moved toward the spot where Leigha and Dix were.

Fifty yards from the shoreline the boat captain stopped the boat, dropped an anchor and stared down at the water. He wore a dark wet suit, unzipped and peeled down around his waist, exposing a thick, muscular chest. He glanced up and yelled, "Can you hear me?"

Dix nodded. She could just hear the captain's voice.

"There are two divers down there. They should have been up by now. I'm going to down to find them. If I don't come back up in thirty minutes, could you send for help?"

Dix climbed down from the boulder. "Yes, of course."

The man quickly shoved his arms into his wet suit and zipped. In under a minute he had on his buoyancy control device, tanks, regulator, masks and fins. Shoving his regulator into his mouth and pulling his mask over his face, he gave Dix the okay sign and stepped off the back of the boat.

Leigha came to stand beside Dix. Brewer stood at the edge of the water, staring toward the boat.

Dix counted the minutes. Searching the surface of the bay for bubbles. Unfortunately, the bay had just enough wave action to keep her from spotting any.

"Where did that man go?" Leigha slipped her hand in Dix's.

Dix shifted her empty hand to feel for the small handgun she'd tucked beneath her lightweight jacket before she'd left her room that morning. If the man who'd gone under planned to stage an attack via the bay, he'd have a surprise waiting for him. A lone woman and a little girl might look like easy prey, but Dix could take care of herself and the child.

Fifteen minutes passed and still the man in the wet suit hadn't surfaced.

Dix moved closer to the shore, Leigha at her side.

"Is that man going to drown?" Leigha whispered.

Dix slipped her arm around the child's shoulders. "No, sweetie. He knows what he's doing." At least, she hoped he knew what he was doing.

A second later a head popped up out of the water. Then another and another only ten feet from shore.

One of the three men gave an okay sign and pulled his regulator out of his mouth. "I'm sending these guys up with you. They're too tired to swim back to the boat and the boat can't get any closer to the shore. Too many submerged rocks in the area. Can you get them to a telephone?"

"Sure," Dix said, not too happy about the unexpected company on the beach. Especially considering there would be two of them against her and one little girl.

The two men swam toward the shore, the third man shoving them from behind. When they could stand, the third man trod water a little away from the shore. "Are you from the Stratford House?"

Dix nodded.

"I'm Dave Logsdon. I'll call to check on them later. Thanks for helping out. I'd stay and make sure they got back to Cape Churn, but I need to take my boat back to the marina before the fog rolls in."

Dix nodded and waved to Dave.

He slid his mask in place and turned toward the boat.

Dix rested her hand on the gun beneath her jacket and waited for the two men to emerge from the surf.

They sat in the shallow water, pulled off their fins and tossed them to the shore. Then they stood and walked toward her and Leigha.

"Thanks for letting us come ashore. I don't think I could have made it back to the boat." The diver's voice sounded familiar. When he pulled off his mask and wet-suit hat, he grinned. "Hey, you're the lady who was with Stratford last night at the café."

Dix recognized the guy as one of the twins who'd been at the table next to them.

Leigha slipped behind Dix's legs.

Reminded of her duty to protect, Dix smiled, but kept her hand on her H&K .40-caliber pistol. "What happened?"

"We got hung up in kelp," the young man closest to Dix said. "By the time the dive master found us, we were almost out of air."

His twin added, "Thank goodness he did find us. I was beginning to think we weren't going to make it."

Both men dropped to the thick sliver of sand and pulled off the gear they'd been wearing, leaving on the wet suits.

Leigha tugged her hand. "That man made it to his boat." She smiled up at Dix, the relief evident in her eyes.

"Yes, sweetie, he did." Dix turned to the two men. "The tide is starting to come in. I know you're tired, but we need to move you and the gear to higher ground before the beach disappears beneath the water."

The two men lurched to their feet, gathered their tanks and other gear.

Dix nodded toward the path. "Follow the trail up the hill. You can drop your gear when you get to where the path widens. It should be well above the watermark and safe."

"We can retrieve it later, after we rest," one of the twins said. "Right now, I just want to lie down for a couple of hours."

"Me, too," the other twin said. "But I don't want to lose the gear. We don't have it in our budget to replace it."

"No, we don't."

They reached the widened area of the trail and set the gear up against the rising bluff, as far away from the drop-off as they could get it.

When his hands were free, the first twin stuck one of them out. "By the way, I'm Jared Kessler." He elbowed his brother. "He's my brother, Joe."

Dix released Leigha's hand and took Jared's cautiously, prepared to take him down if he tried anything. He shook her hand and let go.

Joe offered his and did the same.

Not letting her guard down for a moment, Dix said, "You two can lead the way up the trail. We'll follow. When you get to the top, you'll have to squeeze around the side of a cave entrance. Be careful. A fall could prove deadly."

The twins nodded in unison.

"Got it," Jared said. He took a deep breath and let it out, and then started up the hill.

Joe followed.

Dix fell into step behind them, holding Leigha's hand and balancing her other hand on her gun. Brewer brought up the rear.

The trip up the trail took longer and was more strenuous than the descent. Still in good shape from all of her training as an MMA fighter, Dix didn't even get winded.

The twins were slow, but steady, arriving at the cave entrance as the sun slipped behind a heavy bank of fog rolling into the cape.

After the two men eased around the corner of the cave entrance, Leigha pulled Dix to a stop and pointed to the fog creeping toward shore. "Bennet calls that the Devil's Shroud." She glanced up at Dix. "What's a shroud?"

"It's like a blanket or sheet they pull over dead people," Dix answered, her gaze on the fog closing in on them. She shivered and turned away. The sooner they returned to the house, the better. Her hand on the gun, she slipped into the tunnel.

Jared and Joe stood at the entrance staring out at what should have been a view of the bay.

"That's some wicked fog," Jared said.

"I've never seen anything like it move as fast or blanket everything so thickly," Joe added, his voice low, his eyes wide. "I hope Dave made it back to the marina before it got too bad."

"Yeah," Jared agreed.

Brewer ran ahead, disappearing into the dark tunnel. Dix put Leigha in the lead with the flashlight, positioning herself between the child and the two men. She didn't like being in front of them, but she wasn't going to hand them the flashlight.

She let Leigha get a few steps of a head start. Then

she turned toward Jared and Joe and said in a low tone, "Just so you know, I'm a trained fighter. I can kill people with my hands. Try anything against me or that little girl and I won't hesitate to kill." She stared into their eyes in the limited light from the cave entrance. "Understand?"

The twins nodded.

Jared grinned. "What kind of fighting? Tae Kwon Do? Jujitsu? Boxing?"

"Army Ranger and MMA."

Joe smiled. "Bro, you don't want to mess with her. She means business."

Jared nodded. "We're not going to hurt you or the girl. We're just happy you were here to get us out of the water. I've never been more scared of drowning in my life." He nodded toward Leigha. "But we better get moving before we lose sight of the only one here who has a flashlight."

Dix gave them a hard stare.

Jared and Joe both raised their hands.

"Seriously," Joe said. "We're not here to hurt you."

Only slightly convinced they were telling the truth, Dix turned and hurried after Leigha, who'd reached a corner in the tunnel. As soon as she turned, the light became so dim Dix could barely see the walls and floor. She put her hand out and lightly skimmed the cool stone surface, moving as fast as she could to catch up to the girl.

Footsteps and muttered oaths behind her indicated the twins were doing their best to keep up.

When she turned the corner, she could see the light ahead.

"Leigha, wait up," she called, tired of tripping over rocks.

The little girl stopped and shone the light back into her eyes.

Dix held her hand up in front of her face. "Other way, sweetie. Turn the light the other way. You're blinding me."

"Sorry." Leigha pointed the light at the floor.

The two men behind Dix caught up and they continued, entering the cavern with the stream.

"Are you sure you know where you're going?" one of the men said from behind.

"No, but the girl does," Dix reassured him.

"Seriously?" the guy said.

Dix chuckled and stepped over the stream.

Leigha entered the tunnel Dix recognized as the one she'd come through earlier. Before long they came to the door to the hidden corridor inside the house. Leigha flipped a light switch and left the flashlight in a small hole from the dirt wall.

"Now we're talking," Jared said.

A few minutes later they ducked through the door in the fireplace and emerged into the formal sitting room.

Jared and Joe grinned and laughed out loud.

"I would never have guessed we'd come out in a place like this," Joe said.

"I thought we'd end up in an ancient torture chamber." Jared stared around the room. "Where are we?"

"Stratford House," a deep voice said from across the room.

Dix spun toward the sound and her body heated at

the sight of Andrew standing with his arms crossed over his chest, glaring at her. "Please explain yourself, Miss Reeves."

Chapter 13

Andrew had left that morning for Portland to meet with his attorney and accountant. But the farther away he got from Stratford House, Leigha and Dix, the more his chest tightened and his hands gripped the steering wheel. He'd had the overwhelming urge to turn around and go back.

Someone had attacked him on the cliff. Dix might be a trained soldier and a former MMA fighter, but she was smaller than most men. She could be overpowered. Then she *and* Leigha would be in danger. And he'd be too far away to help.

An hour and a half out of Cape Churn, he'd made a U-turn in the middle of the highway and exceeded every speed limit to return to Stratford House.

"I've been all over this house from top to bottom

looking for the two of you. I even called Sheriff Taggert. He's on his way out here now." He drew in a deep breath and demanded, "Where have you been? And what are these two men doing in my house?"

Leigha came out from behind Dix and faced her father. "It was my fault. I wanted to show Dix where I like to play. It took longer than I thought it would."

Dix placed her hands on the girl's shoulders. "It's okay, Leigha. You don't have to defend me." She lifted her chin and stared at him. "We were playing outside when these two men got into a bit of trouble." She turned toward them. "You remember them from last night?"

Jared held out his hand. "Mr. Stratford, we're sorry to drop in on you like this."

Andrew recognized Jared and Joe from the café the previous evening, but he wasn't in the mood to be nice. He ignored the outstretched hand. "I thought I told you I didn't like people to just show up at my house."

"Sir," Joe said, "we were diving in the bay off the nearby shoreline when we got caught up in kelp."

"It was all we could do to get to shore," Jared finished. "Our dive boat captain helped us ashore and then went back to his boat. He had to get to the marina before the fog set in."

Joe ran a hand through his hair, standing it on end. "Miss Reeves brought us up to the house to use the phone. As soon as we can call for a taxi, we'll be out of your hair."

"No one's going anywhere," Andrew said. "A taxi

won't be able to get here and back to town before the fog gets too thick. You'll have to wait until it clears."

"That's fine. We can wait out on the road," Jared offered, inching toward the door.

Dix frowned at the twins. "Don't be ridiculous. You're exhausted and probably on the verge of hypothermia. We can get some dry clothes for you and you'll stay here until the fog clears." She faced Andrew, her mouth set in a thin line, her chin high, as if daring him to kick her out with the guys.

Andrew loved the fire in her green eyes and the way she stood with her feet slightly spread, her fists bunched tightly. Ready for a fight.

Now that he knew Dix and Leigha were all right, his heartbeat was well on its way to returning to normal, but he wasn't letting Dix off easy. He narrowed his eyes and glared at her. She needed to fear his ire so that she didn't run off to God knew where with his daughter. She'd scared several years off his life. "Don't run off again without telling anyone where you're going," he said, his tone low, as intense as he could get it. He didn't want to be that scared ever again. "Understood?"

She glared back at him, giving him as much guff as he gave her. Then her mouth loosened into those full lush lips he'd kissed the night before and she nodded. "Understood. I'm sorry we upset you. It won't happen again." She ran her hand over the top of Leigha's hair. "Right, Leigha? You won't disappear without telling someone where you're going, will you?"

Leigha glanced up at Dix and then turned her gaze to her father. "No, I won't." She raised a hand, curled her fingers and extended the last finger and took a step toward him. "Pinkie swear."

Andrew stared at her hand, not sure what she was talking about.

"You heard her," Dix said. "Pinkie swear." Her lips twitched at the corners.

"I don't know what you mean."

Dix dipped her head sharply toward Leigha. "Go on."

Leigha and Dix obviously knew what a pinkie swear was, but Andrew didn't have a clue. Not to be shamed by the bodyguard, Andrew dropped to his haunches. "Show me."

Leigha took his uninjured hand, curled his fingers into a fist and then pulled out the last one. Then she hooked her pinkie with his and smiled. "I pinkie swear that I will always tell someone where I'm going before I leave."

"That's it?" He glanced up at Dix.

Her lips had spread into a full-blown grin. "You've officially been graced with a pinkie swear. Leigha knows she can't break that promise."

Leigha nodded. "I won't."

"Okay, then." Andrew straightened and ruffled Leigha's hair. "Now, go tell Mrs. Purdy you're okay and you would like to have two beds made up in the west wing for our guests."

As his daughter started to pass him, Andrew scooped her up and hugged her tightly. "Don't scare me like that again." He held her away from him and stared into her face. "I was very worried."

Leigha caught his face between her palms and kissed

him on the forehead, like he'd done putting her to bed. "I'm okay."

"Good." He set her on her feet and brushed the hair out of her face.

Leigha skipped out of the sitting room with Brewer keeping pace, leaving Dix, Jared and Joe for him to contend with.

Andrew waved a hand. "Dix, you can go."

Her brows dipped. She opened her mouth but snapped it shut instead and left the room.

A chuckle rose up his throat but he swallowed it back. He'd hear about that later. Frankly, he looked forward to it. But now he had a couple of men in his house for what appeared to be overnight. Once the Devil's Shroud moved in, it wouldn't recede until the following morning.

His eyes narrowed and he glared at Jared and Joe. "What are you really doing in my house?"

Both young men started talking at once.

Andrew held up his hand. "Jared."

Jared nodded. "We were searching for the ship Peg and Percy Malone scuttled when they arrived in Cape Churn. We thought we saw it when we got caught up in the kelp."

"And you thought it would be okay to waltz into my house and make yourself at home?"

"No, sir," Joe said. "We would have gone back out to the dive boat, but we'd used up all of our scuba air and just didn't have the strength to swim back out. Dave told us to stay on shore. We were lucky enough to find Miss Reeves and your daughter on the beach."

"On the beach?" Andrew stared at the men as if they'd grown horns. "What beach?" In all the years he'd visited Stratford House, he'd never known there to be a beach on the property. The cliffs were too rugged to climb down.

The twins exchanged glances.

Joe faced Andrew. "There was a little bit of a beach at the base of the cliffs and a trail leading up to a cave. Tunnels in the cave led to the house and this room." He shrugged. "You should ask your daughter. She led the way."

He couldn't believe what he was hearing. A dull ache started in his temples and radiated through his head and down into his shoulders. The drive toward Portland and his subsequent confrontation with Dix and these men had taken their toll. "You two can stay, but don't touch anything or go anywhere you're not invited. And if you so much as harm a single hair on my daughter's head, I'll kill you with my bare hands."

Jared and Joe backed up a step, raising their hands. "We really don't mind standing out by the road until the fog clears, Mr. Stratford."

Joe elbowed his brother. "Speak for yourself." He faced Andrew. "You don't have to worry, Mr. Stratford. We won't hurt your daughter. She's a smart little girl. I can't believe she led us through those tunnels and cave. What makes it more amazing is that she can't be more than seven years old."

"Six," Andrew said, his anger spiking at what the men were telling him. It meant Dix had allowed his daughter to wander around dangerous caves, cliffs and beaches while he'd been away. He would have a few choice words for Miss Reeves.

Dix followed Leigha to the kitchen, where Mrs. Purdy was pulling a roast out of the oven. "Thank goodness you two showed up when you did. I'll just call Sheriff Taggert and tell him it was a false alarm."

The older woman lifted a phone out of a receiver on the wall and dialed the sheriff's office. "Gabe? Good. I'm glad it's you. Could you put a call out to Sheriff Taggert that Miss Reeves and Mr. Stratford's daughter are home and safe? No, they weren't lost, just out exploring. Thank you, Gabe. How are Kayla and the baby? That's nice. Glad to hear it."

Mrs. Purdy hung up and turned to Dix. "I'm just finishing dinner preparations and need to get to town before the fog's too thick to see the road. Leigha can show you to the west wing. I have a couple of bedrooms I keep aired out in case we have guests. We just need to put sheets on the beds. Do you two mind helping?"

"Not at all," Dix said. The woman had her hands full with pots on the stove and bread baking in the oven. "Where can I find sheets?"

"In the linen closet at the end of the hallway. Leigha will show you, won't you, darlin'?" Mrs. Purdy smiled at Leigha. "She knows where everything is in the house. I'll finish up here and be on my way."

Dix had to agree with the housekeeper on that statement. Leigha had shown her places Dix hadn't dreamed existed. She wondered if there were other secret passages that led in and out of the house. If so, there might be more entries and exits that could be used by bad guys hoping to pay a surprise visit to the Stratfords. While she had Leigha alone upstairs, she'd ask the child if she knew about other secrets.

Leigha, with Brewer, once again in the lead, took Dix up to the second floor of the huge house and turned right instead of left to their wing of bedchambers.

"Bennet said he used to sneak into the house when the owners were sleeping and smoke cigars in the study downstairs." Leigha glanced back at Dix. "What's a cigar?"

"It's like a big, fat brown cigarette, only it smells a lot worse." The child had no limit to her curiosity. "Leigha, are there other secret tunnels or corridors in the house?"

Leigha shrugged and opened a cabinet door. "I don't know." The little girl's face reddened. "Here are the sheets."

Dix took out two sets of sheets and followed Leigha to the bedrooms Mrs. Purdy had designated. Inside, the rooms were spacious with rich, mahogany furnishings and light, airy curtains and comforters.

Dix suspected Leigha knew more than she wanted to admit about other secrets in the huge old mansion. "Will you show me the others tomorrow?"

Leigha took one end of the sheet and dragged it across the mattress. "Okay."

Dix played down her enthusiasm. "Thank you, Leigha."

To protect the family, Dix needed to know everything about Stratford House and its surroundings. She might even take a trip to the local library to see if they had any history on the place that could warrant someone wanting to get rid of the Stratfords. Secret passages leading to caves and the sea had to have had some basis in smuggling.

Between the two of them, Dix and Leigha made the beds in the rooms and put fresh towels in the bathroom across the hallway.

Andrew joined them in the hallway, carrying a stack of clothing.

Dix leaned to look behind him and raised her brows.

"Mrs. Purdy is filling them full of hot cocoa to warm them up."

"The beds are made. I'll sleep with Leigha tonight."

Leigha smiled and clapped her hands. "Yay! We can have a slumber party. I've never had a slumber party."

Dix's heart squeezed in her chest. The little girl should have friends to play with instead of the imaginary one. She shivered. Or ghost.

Never having believed in anything she couldn't see for herself, Dix refused to start now. Leigha had a wonderful imagination and a sense of adventure. Why not an imaginary friend? Maybe if she had real friends, she wouldn't need to make up a friend named Bennet.

When the house settled in for the night, Dix would have a heart-to-heart with Andrew. He needed to know about the hidden passageway in order to close it off to keep others from entering the house.

Dix held out her hands for the stack of clothing.

As he handed the items to her, Andrew caught her gaze. "We need to talk."

A thrill of excitement slipped through her veins.

"Yes. We do." Had nothing else happened that day, she might have thought they would talk about what they'd shared in his bed the night before. With the twins in the house and she and Leigha having been missing for a couple of hours, Dix was almost certain he had a more serious conversation in mind.

Andrew's eyes narrowed briefly and then he turned and walked to the staircase. His expression had been unreadable.

She handed half of the clothing to Leigha and pointed to a bedroom. "You can put these on the bed in that room." Dix entered the other room and set her stack on the bed.

She met Leigha in the hallway. "Do you think Mrs. Purdy would make cookies and popcorn for our slumber party?"

Leigha's blue eyes lit up. "I'll ask."

"Don't just ask, Leigha. Offer to help. Grown-ups love to have company and help when they're cooking."

"I love baking cookies with Mrs. Purdy. She makes the best!" Leigha and Brewer ran ahead and descended to the first floor.

Dix held her breath until the child made it to the bottom without tumbling all the way down in her rush to the kitchen.

"How do parents do it? I'll be a nervous wreck by the time this gig is up," Dix muttered.

"You do the best you can to protect them, but you have to let them have some freedom or you'll make them afraid to live."

Dix spun to face Andrew. He stood so close behind

her, she took a step back. Her foot met air and she would have fallen down the stairs if Andrew hadn't reached out and grabbed her, slamming her body against his.

Her breath caught in her throat. Dix couldn't breathe and didn't want to. She was in Andrew's arms. If she inhaled, she'd take in the heady scent of his aftershave.

She closed her eyes, recalling the feel of his skin on hers, as they lay naked in his bed. Sweet heaven, Dix wanted to drag him back to that bedroom and do it all again.

Wrong, wrong, wrong! her logical thoughts warned her even as her fingers curled into the fabric of his shirt.

Andrew dipped his head, his mouth skimming her temple. "Are you all right?"

No, she wasn't. She was in her client's arms, lusting after him when she should be downstairs looking after his daughter.

"I'm fine," she forced out through constricted vocal cords, with barely enough air to make a sound.

His hands splayed across her lower back, pressing her closer.

She could feel the hardness of the ridge beneath his fly nudging her belly. *Holy hotness.* How could she extricate herself when all she wanted was to be even closer?

"Mr. Stratford?" a male voice called from below.

Dix pushed against Andrew's chest and stepped away, careful not to fall down the stairs. She shoved her hair back from her face and resisted the urge to fan herself as heat radiated throughout her body.

"Up here," Andrew responded.

Jared started up the stairs with his brother, Joe, right behind him. "Mrs. Purdy said you would be able to show us to the rooms we'll occupy tonight."

"I can do that."

"I'll go check on Leigha." Dix turned away but was caught up short by a hand on her arm.

"I'm serious," Andrew said, his voice soft enough only Dix would hear. "We need to talk."

She nodded, her pulse hammering, electric currents racing from where his hand held her arm through her body, dropping low into her belly.

When Andrew released her, Dix ran down the steps as if the devil himself was chasing her. Not that Andrew was the devil. Her own lusty thoughts were sending her into a tailspin she wasn't sure she could recover from.

She had begun to wonder if she was really needed there. In the couple of days she'd been at Stratford House, nothing had happened to make her think Leigha and Andrew were in danger. In their talk, she'd ask him if he'd made any progress on finding a permanent bodyguard to replace her.

The thought made her chest tighten and her eyes sting. Already, she'd formed an attachment to Leigha. But the connection she had with Andrew wasn't good. Even though it felt really good when they'd been together in his bed.

Chapter 14

Dinner had been festive with their two guests. Jared and Joe were entertaining, talking of some of the adventures they'd been on during summer break from their studies at Washington State University.

Andrew wasn't ready to think they were harmless. Not with his daughter's welfare at stake, but he did get caught up in their tales of archaeological digs in Africa, where they'd unearthed remnants of ancient civilizations. And then there were the dinosaur bones they'd found in North Dakota.

By the time they'd finished the roast beef and mashed potatoes Mrs. Purdy had left for them, the two young men were ready to call it a night. They headed for their respective bedrooms.

Leigha yawned and rubbed her eyes. "Are we going to have a slumber party?"

"If you stay awake long enough," Dix said. She gathered the plates and cups from the table and laid them in the sink.

"We'll see how you feel after a bath." Andrew lifted her in his arms and started for the stairs.

She laid her head on his shoulder and snuggled into his strong arms. "Are you coming to my slumber party, Mr. Stratford?"

"If you want me to," he answered, his voice catching in his throat. This was the first time his daughter had wanted him to participate with her in any activity. He'd sleep on a bed of nails if she asked him. Anything for her smile, for her acceptance.

He carried her to her bedroom and set her on her feet. "I'll get your bath started. You grab the pajamas you want to sleep in."

"Okay."

Dix had followed them into the bedroom, but she stood by the door. "Want me to take it from here?"

"No need. I can manage a faucet." He entered the adjoining bathroom, started the water and checked the temperature, and when it was right, he filled the tub.

Leigha entered behind him, carrying her night-clothes.

Andrew turned off the water and straightened. "I'll be back to kiss you good-night."

"And to stay for my slumber party?" she asked, looking at him with expectant eyes.

He smiled and ruffled her hair. "And to stay for the

slumber party." Andrew didn't think she'd make it fifteen minutes after her bath before her eyelids closed and sleep claimed her.

He left the room and walked down the hall to the master suite, where he stripped out of the trousers and white shirt he'd worn for his aborted trip to Portland. In minutes, he'd showered and changed into a pair of sweats and a T-shirt. He padded barefoot through the connecting door into Leigha's room.

His daughter had dressed in her favorite pajamas and was sitting in the bed. Brewer lay curled up next to her.

Dix sat behind her wearing that darned T-shirt and a pair of athletic shorts, braiding Leigha's hair. She glanced up, her gaze raking over him. Then she returned to the braid she was working, pink spots of color glowing in her cheeks.

Leigha patted the bed. "Sit here. You can read a story while Dix braids my hair."

"Shall we pick up where we left off with *Island of the Blue Dolphins*?"

Leigha smiled. "Yes, please."

Andrew plucked the book from the shelf and settled on the edge of the bed. He read and Dix braided. Between the two of them, they had Leigha yawning by the time Dix secured the braid and Andrew finished the chapter.

Leigha slipped between the sheets and tucked her hand under one cheek. "Don't stop reading," she whispered. "I'm awake, just resting my eyes."

Andrew hid his smile.

Before he'd read another paragraph, he could see his daughter had fallen asleep.

Dix scooted to the edge of the bed, dropped her feet to the floor and exited the bedroom.

Andrew waited a moment or two more before he rose and set the book back on the shelf. He pressed a kiss to his daughter's forehead and pointed at Brewer. "Stay." As if he needed to tell the dog to stay with Leigha. She was his human and he'd protect her at all costs. Andrew tiptoed out of the room, closing the door behind him.

Dix had disappeared.

Andrew frowned. He'd specifically told her they needed to talk. Well, they were going to have that conversation, even if he had to drag her out of bed to do it. The thought of Dix lying in bed in that unflattering T-shirt made his groin tighten and blood burn hot through his veins.

He raised his hand to knock on her door but it opened before he could.

Dix's eyes widened when she spotted him standing there with his fist raised to knock. She'd been pulling a sweater on over her T-shirt and she'd put on a pair of sneakers. "Oh, there you are. We should go downstairs to the study or out on the porch. Do you think Leigha will be okay with the Kessler twins on the same floor?"

Andrew nodded. "If they try anything, Brewer will raise a ruckus and we'll hear them."

Dix glanced down at his bare feet. "You might want to put on some shoes."

"Why?" Andrew asked.

"Just trust me on this."

Andrew returned to his room, slid into some boat shoes and returned to the hallway.

Dix studied his shoes, hesitated for another second, seemed semi-satisfied with his footwear choice and led the way down the stairs.

He hadn't noticed just how taut her calves were or how narrow her ankles. He could imagine how those legs would feel wrapped around his waist again. And there he went, diving into his imaginary fantasy with his lusty thoughts of Dix naked.

When she reached the bottom of the stairs, Dix turned and walked past the study. She led him to the sitting room he'd found all of them standing in earlier that day. It wasn't his choice of places to conduct a conversation, but it would suffice.

Dix stopped in the middle of the room and faced him. "Now that Leigha isn't here, you need to know what she showed me today. But, first, do you have a padlock?"

He frowned. "Padlock?"

Dix nodded.

He held up a finger. "Don't go anywhere. I'll be right back."

Andrew left the sitting room and returned a minute later with a combination padlock.

Dix was standing next to the fireplace when he returned. She held out her hand and he placed the lock in it. "Do you know the combination?"

He nodded.

"Good. We'll need it." Then she did something peculiar. She ducked low and stepped into the fireplace.

Granted, the logs weren't burning, but her actions were perplexing.

Dix pushed a brick and frowned. She pushed another and another until the last brick she pushed slid inward and the rest of the wall of brick slid open.

Andrew swore softly. "I've been all over this house and never knew that was there. How did you find it?"

She raised her brows. "I asked Leigha to take me to her favorite place to play."

"And this was it?"

Dix shook her head. "You haven't seen anything yet. Hold on to your hat—I'm about to tell you what your daughter has been up to when you weren't watching her."

Andrew tensed, ready to tell Dix he didn't need an outsider telling him how to raise his daughter. But then she disappeared through the small door.

His pulse quickened and he leaned across the hearth, peering into what looked like a very narrow corridor. Andrew ducked through the door and stood up straight. The ceiling of the corridor was as high as the ceiling of the sitting room. "Well, I'll be damned."

Dix snorted. "Babe, you need to see the rest."

His heart sped at her use of the word *babe*. He tamped down the urge to reach out and crush her against him. But she moved away.

"I don't feel comfortable leaving Leigha for any length of time, but we need to go to the end of this corridor and lock the door to keep Leigha from going out and strangers from coming in. The Kessler brothers know about the tunnel now, but we don't know who else could have found it or will find it."

"Thus the need for the lock," Andrew stated. "I don't like leaving Leigha, either. Go," he urged her.

Dix hurried along the wooden floor to the end where it dropped out of the house and into the hillside tunnel.

Andrew went a few steps farther, studying the solid walls of the tunnel. "I can't believe this has been here all along and I didn't know. Makes me wonder if my grandfather knew. If so, why didn't he tell me?" He stared back at Dix.

She shrugged. "You said you were a lot like Leigha. Maybe your grandfather knew it was dangerous for a small child to wander around the caves and tunnels. He probably didn't tell you to keep you from getting lost or falling off the cliff."

Andrew's heart skipped several beats. "I thought Leigha was safe as long as she played in the house." He shook his head. "I didn't know she'd found a way out. But how?"

Dix frowned. "When I asked her how she found the tunnels, she said her imaginary friend showed her."

Andrew pounded his hand into his fist. "Her and that damned imaginary friend."

"She might have dreamed him up because she's lonely. Kids need other kids to play with."

"I know. I'm going to fix that. But it takes time." Andrew scrubbed a hand over his face and turned back to the narrow corridor. "For now, we need to block this passageway."

"Tomorrow, you need to follow it to the beach."

"What beach?" Andrew's head spun with the discoveries he'd never expected. He thought he knew his own home.

"You'll see when you follow the tunnels all the way out to the ocean." Dix's lips twitched into a smile. "You might have to have Leigha show you the way to keep from getting lost." She moved backward as Andrew re-entered the corridor.

He turned and pulled shut a door, slipped the padlock through the hasp and closed the lock. Then he leaned on the door and swore. "My six-year-old daughter has been wandering around in caves and out on cliffs and I sat in my office as if she were in a padded playroom."

Dix laid a hand on his shoulder. "She needs attention, and she's a little afraid of you."

Andrew jerked his head up. "Afraid? Of what?"

"You are pretty intimidating when you raise your voice."

"Damn it! I'm not intimidating!" His voice echoed in the long passageway.

Dix raised her brows and stood with her arms crossed. "I'm an adult, but I can see where she's coming from." Her lips quirked upward. "You can be downright scary to a six-year-old."

Andrew wanted to wipe that smile off her face.

With a kiss.

He started to step past her in the tight confines. His body brushed against hers and he couldn't resist. He turned and grabbed her, smashing her against him, his lips crashing down on hers.

She gasped, her mouth opening enough to let him

thrust his tongue past her teeth and sweep along the length of hers.

At first her hands pressed against his chest, pushing him away. But the longer he kissed her the less she resisted.

Soon Dix's hands slipped up his chest and wrapped around his neck. Her body melted into his and her leg curved around the back of his.

Andrew moaned and leaned her against the wall, his hands slipping down her back, over her buttocks and lower still to cup her thighs. He lifted. And, oh, those legs wrapped around his waist and squeezed tight.

He broke the kiss and drew in a deep breath. "You drive me crazy."

She laughed. "I think you have that backward." She brushed her thumb along the scarred side of his face and leaned in to kiss him again.

All that stood between them was the stretchy clothing they wore. It wouldn't take much to remove them…

Dix sighed. "We can't leave Leigha for long. I don't feel comfortable with her all the way up the stairs and us in this corridor where we wouldn't hear her if she screamed."

"You're right." He lowered her legs and helped her straighten her shirt. Then he took her hand and led her to the door in the fireplace.

Once they were in the sitting room, Andrew tilted his head to the side and listened for any sounds of distress.

The house remained silent. But that didn't mean anything. Even silence was threatening when it came to his daughter.

He didn't wait for Dix. He strode out of the sitting room and climbed the stairs two at a time, his heart beating faster as he neared the top.

He couldn't relax until he pushed the door to Leigha's room open and saw the girl lying in her bed, her hand tucked beneath her chin and Brewer looking up at him as if to reassure him that he was on the job.

Dix touched his shoulder. "I'll stay with her tonight."

"No." He turned and rested his hands on her hips. "You'll stay with me. We'll leave the door open between the two rooms."

She cocked her brows. "Is that an order?"

"That's a strongly worded invitation I hope you will accept."

She stared at him for a long moment, her head moving slowly in a negative.

His heartbeat slowed to a stop and he held his breath, wondering if he'd pushed her too far. He'd never been good at asking people to do his bidding. As a businessman, he'd told people what he wanted and they did it. Not Dix.

"Say 'please,'" she whispered, her hand rising to cup his face. "Say 'please' and I'll think about it."

He swallowed, his groin tightening so hard he was glad he'd worn the sweatpants. "Please," he said through gritted teeth. He wasn't sure how much longer he could hold back from unleashing his passion on her.

Dix touched her lips to his and said, "Okay."

Andrew swept her up in his arms and carried her toward his bedroom, pulse pounding and every nerve in his body on fire, ready to make love to this incredible woman.

As he reached for the doorknob, a small voice called out.

"Mr. Stratford? Dix?"

With a groan, Andrew held tightly to Dix for a moment and waited to see if Leigha would go back to sleep.

"Dix?" she called out. "Mr. Stratford?"

"I'll check on her." Dix wiggled free of his grasp and dropped to her feet. She leaned close, kissed him and pressed her finger to the spot she'd warmed with her lips. "Hold that thought."

She disappeared into Leigha's room.

Andrew stood still, willing his body to calm before he entered his daughter's room.

Dix lay on the bed beside Leigha, holding the child. "She's thirsty. Do you want to stay with her while I go down for a glass of water?"

"I want you to stay." Leigha clung to Dix, snuggling into the curve of her arm. "Please, Dix. Stay with me."

Andrew raised a hand. "Stay here. I'll go."

Dix frowned. "Are you sure?"

"Yes." He performed an about-face and walked along the dimly lit landing to the stairs. Perhaps Leigha's request was just what he needed to keep him from losing his head over Dix.

At the bottom of the steps, he turned toward the kitchen. Strategically located night-lights provided just enough light to see where he was going. When he arrived in the kitchen, he pulled a glass from the cabinet and filled it with cool water. He filled another for Dix and started back toward the stairs.

A sound in the sitting room caught his attention. His pulse quickened. What if someone had come through the secret corridor? He shook his head. Not possible. Not with a lock on the door.

Another sound made him stop and set the glasses of water on a side table. Had the twins come down to snoop around the house?

Anger burned in Andrew's gut. He'd invited the two young men into his home. If they'd wanted to look around, all they'd had to do was ask. With words poised on the tip of his tongue, Andrew marched into the sitting room and reached for the light switch.

Before his fingers touched it, something hit him in the back of the head. He yelled, pain blinded him, and he dropped to the floor, complete darkness blocking out the soft glow of night-lights.

Chapter 15

As soon as Andrew left the room, his daughter had fallen back to sleep.

Dix rose from the bed and paced the length of the little girl's room. The walls seemed too close, so Dix stepped out into the hallway. What was keeping Andrew?

What should she do about his request for her to stay in his room through the night? It was a recipe for disaster. The more time she spent with him, the harder it would be to leave. And she would leave. That itchy feeling she got when she stayed in one place too long would drive her away.

Dix leaned over the railing, searching the shadows below for signs of Andrew. As big as the house was, she doubted she'd hear the sound of him rustling around in the kitchen. Leaving Leigha again didn't seem like a good idea, but Dix was getting nervous.

A muffled shout sounded from somewhere below followed by a heavy thud. "Andrew?" Dix called out. He didn't answer. "Andrew!"

She ran back to her room for her gun and then raced for the stairs.

Two doors opened down the hall and the Kessler twins' heads popped out.

"What's wrong?" one of them asked.

"I don't know. I thought I heard someone yell." Dix dashed down the stairs, her heart pounding against her ribs. "Andrew?"

Footsteps sounded behind her as the two young men followed.

She hurried toward the kitchen, flipping light switches wherever she could find them.

The kitchen was empty with no sign of Andrew.

"I found him!" one of the twins yelled. "Call 9-1-1!"

Dix's heart sank to the bottom of her belly as she followed the sound of the young man's voice into the sitting room they'd all been in earlier.

Andrew lay on the floor, completely still.

Dix dropped down beside him, laid her gun on a table and carefully shook his arm. "Andrew."

Jared pressed a hand to the base of his throat. "He's got a pulse."

Joe pointed to the knot forming on the back of Andrew's head. "Looks like he was hit with something. Hit hard. That's a big goose egg."

Andrew groaned.

"Andrew?" Dix leaned close. "Can you hear me?"

"Shh," he said. "You don't have to shout. I've got a splitting headache." He pushed against the floor but only managed to roll onto his back and wince. "Sweet heaven. That hurt."

"You have a lump on the back of your head," Jared said. "What happened?"

Andrew pressed his fingers to the bridge of his nose. "I don't know. I got a couple glasses of water to take upstairs. Heard a noise in the sitting room. Then nothing." He sat up and swayed.

Jared and Dix slipped arms around his back and steadied him.

"We're calling an ambulance," Joe said.

"No." Andrew shook his head once and cringed. "I'm okay…just need to wait until the room quits spinning."

"We're calling 9-1-1," Dix seconded. "You could have a concussion or swelling on the brain."

A scream silenced all of their arguments.

"Leigha." Dix grabbed her gun, leaped to her feet and ran out of the room, calling back over her shoulder, "Don't let him get up."

"Like hell," Andrew said.

She glanced back to see him lurching to his feet.

Jared and Joe slipped Andrew's arms over their shoulders and ran with him.

Satisfied Andrew wouldn't run up the stairs on his own, Dix raced to the second floor and burst into Leigha's room. She sat up in bed, her eyes wide, tears streaming down her face.

"What's wrong?" Dix asked, hurrying to her bedside.

"Fire was all around me. I couldn't breathe because of the smoke. I was so afraid." Leigha bent over, sobbing.

Dix slid the gun onto a dresser and then sat beside the child, pulling her into her arms. "Oh, sweetheart, it was just a bad dream."

"No." She shook her head, her eyes squeezing shut. "It was real. I was there. I couldn't get out."

"You're okay now. Open your eyes. See? No smoke. No fire. Just your pretty bedroom."

"Where's my daddy?"

"I'm here." Andrew broke free of Jared and Joe's hold and walked slowly into the room. "I'm here, Leigha. I'll always be here for you."

She reached her arms up.

Andrew lifted her into his embrace.

Dix stood, ready to assist if Andrew passed out.

He didn't. He held Leigha close, talking soft, soothing words.

"You saved me. I know it was you. I remember," she said. "You saved me…" Leigha's voice faded and she laid her cheek against his chest.

"Is everything okay?" Jared asked from the door.

"Is the little girl all right?" Joe whispered.

Dix nodded, her eyes stinging. "She had a bad dream."

Jared stepped back. "We'll check the house and make sure whoever did this is gone."

Dix shot a glance at Andrew and Leigha and then walked over to the Kessler twins. "I'd rather you stayed to make sure Mr. Stratford doesn't fall down holding his daughter." She eased past them, snagging her gun from the top of the dresser. "I'll check the house."

Jared followed her out into the hallway and grabbed her arm. "You can't do that. You could be hurt, too."

Dix held up her gun. "I'll be okay. I know how to use this."

Jared raised his hands. "I believe you, but at least take one of us with you. Two sets of eyes are better than one."

She didn't need Joe or Jared getting in the way if she had to fire her weapon. But Jared was right. "Then *you* come with me. Joe can stay with Andrew and Leigha."

Jared nodded, whispered instructions to his twin and followed Dix down the stairs.

They moved from room to room, checking everywhere. They didn't find anyone or anything out of place.

Dix stood in the foyer, shaking her head. "After Leigha showed me the secret passage in the sitting room, I'm willing to bet there's one, maybe two, more. Mr. Stratford and I checked all the windows and door locks. Whoever hit him had another way into the building."

Jared stood with his back to Dix. "I don't like it. He could still be here, listening to us talking."

Dix didn't like it, either. She'd have to stand guard through the night to make sure no one else was hurt. In the meantime, Andrew needed someone to look at him. He could be suffering from concussion. He might feel all right now, but if he had any swelling on his brain, he could be dead in minutes.

She sent Jared up to check on his brother, Andrew and Leigha while she called Tazer.

The SOS operative answered immediately. "I hear

you have houseguests. Dave told me what happened earlier in the bay."

"Dave?"

"My fiancé," Tazer clarified. "He's the dive boat captain who took the Kessler twins out today."

"Oh, was that him?" Having just met Tazer, she hadn't had the chance to meet her fiancé.

"Yeah," Tazer said. "He said he got really worried about them when they didn't come up on time. I can't believe they were caught in kelp."

"They're lucky Dave went in after them. I take it Dave got back all right?"

"The Devil's Shroud almost had him, but he made it back in time to see the marina."

"I'm glad." Dix drew in a deep breath and let it out before continuing. "I called because we had another attack here at Stratford House."

"Want me to send the team over?"

"No. I think we have it under control. But Mr. Stratford refused to go to the hospital. I'm afraid he might have a concussion from being hit in the back of the head."

"I'll send Creed's girl over. She's a nurse at the Cape Churn hospital. Maybe she can convince one of the doctors to make a house call. Either way, she can at least check him out. He might listen to her if she thinks he needs to go to the hospital."

"Thanks." Dix started to hang up.

"Are you sure you don't need reinforcements?" Tazer asked.

"No. I'll stand watch tonight."

"You need sleep, too," Tazer reminded her.

"I've pulled all-nighters before in worse places than this. Try standing knee-deep in a foxhole filled with freezing water, while a thunderstorm rages overhead. This will be a cakewalk."

Tazer snorted. "Must be all that Ranger training." She paused. "Okay, but I'll be over in the morning to give you a break. Even Rangers need to sleep. Be on the lookout for Emma Jenkins. If I can get her on the phone, she'll be out there within the next thirty minutes."

Dix ended the call and hurried back to Leigha's room.

Jared and Joe stood out in the hall, talking softly. When she approached, they straightened.

Jared stepped forward. "Mr. Stratford lay down with his daughter. We're not sure that's a good idea. Aren't you supposed to keep concussion victims awake for a couple hours?"

"I'll take care of it," Dix said. She smiled at them. "You two can go back to bed. Lock your doors. I'll stand guard in the hallway until morning. No one else is getting hurt on my watch."

Jared nodded. "I'd offer to take the next shift, but I don't think you want me handling a gun. I'd probably shoot myself."

She shook her head. "Thanks, but I can handle it. I have a nurse coming to check Mr. Stratford. If she thinks he needs to go to the hospital, we might be packing up and heading into Cape Churn."

"Do you want us to stay and babysit Leigha?" Joe offered.

"No," Dix said. "She'd come with us."

"Let us know." Jared shot a glance at his brother. "We might go with you."

Dix's lips twisted. "I wouldn't blame you. Who wants to stay in a big house where the owner is attacked?"

"Exactly." The two men spoke in unison and laughed.

Dix returned to the bedroom.

Leigha lay curled against her father's side, her breathing slow and steady.

Andrew lay on his back.

Dix checked to see if his chest was moving up and down. When she couldn't tell, she leaned over him and listened for his heartbeat.

A hand smoothed over her hair. "Don't worry—I'm alive," he said, his voice rumbling against her ear.

She straightened. "How do you feel?"

"Got a headache. I don't suppose you'd get me a couple of pain relievers?" he asked, closing his eyes.

"I'd rather wait until the nurse gets here," she said, brushing a strand of his pitch-black hair back from his forehead.

"Should we move to a hotel?" he asked.

"Not tonight." She stood by the bed, smoothing Andrew's hair back from his forehead. When the clock on the nightstand indicated it had been twenty-five minutes, she bent to whisper in Andrew's ear, "I'm going to check on that nurse."

He caught her hand. "I don't need one. I need you."

She smiled. "I'm not a nurse."

"There's a phone in my room. Call from there."

Dix left his side and crossed through the connecting doors into Andrew's room. She called Tazer.

"I was just about to call you. I hate to tell you, but Emma couldn't make it out to you. The roads are socked in with the Devil's Shroud. She tried, but she almost ran off the road a couple times before she left town. If she could have made it, she would have. It's just not safe for anyone, including an ambulance, to drive out to you."

"Anything I should do to monitor him?"

"She said he should get plenty of rest. If he is nauseous, has trouble with balance, is dizzy or incoherent, you might have to get an ambulance out there."

Dix resolved to wake Andrew every two or three hours just to check to see if his condition was worsening. "Can I give him some pain relievers?"

"You can give him acetaminophen. Nothing else. You need to know if the pain is getting worse."

"Okay."

"I'd offer to come out and help, but I looked outside. Emma was right. It's really bad out there. The worst I've seen it since I've been here."

"I think we'll be okay. I'm going to keep an eye on Stratford through the night. If anything changes, I'll call."

"Thanks for keeping me informed," Tazer said. "I'll see you in the morning as soon as the fog clears."

Dix ended the call and returned to Leigha's bedroom. Andrew raised his hand.

Dix captured it in hers. "How are you feeling?"

"Like I was hit by a train."

"I'll bet you don't feel better lying on your back. Do you need help turning onto your side?"

"No, but I could use a hand getting into my own bed."

"You're not going anywhere."

He stared up at her, his lips twisting. "I guess this means we're not making love tonight."

"Absolutely not. No contact sports for you until we know for sure you don't have any bleeding on the brain."

His grip tightened on her hand. "At the very least, why don't you join us?" He started to scoot over.

Dix bent to kiss his knuckles. "I'm not sleeping in here."

His brow creased. "Then where are you sleeping?"

"I'm not." She laid his hand on the bed. "I'm pulling guard duty until morning."

"That's ridiculous. You can't stay awake all night."

"I can if I'm on my feet, checking all the rooms."

Andrew pushed the blanket back and started to get out of the bed.

"Where do you think you're going?" she asked.

"To a hotel. This place is too big for one person to guard all night. I won't have the same guy who attacked me attacking you."

"Andrew Stratford, get back in that bed before I put you there." She spoke in a soft yet urgent tone, afraid she'd wake Leigha if she raised her voice.

He sat on the side of the bed, staring at her. "You can't do it alone."

"I'm a trained soldier and an MMA fighter. I can protect myself and you two. That's why I'm here. Relax before you make your injury worse. I can't make my rounds if I'm worrying about you."

His frown deepened. "I'm getting rid of this place."

"The hell you are. It's part of your family heritage. You just need to find all the secret passages and seal them. We can work on that tomorrow."

Leigha turned over and sighed.

"I need to leave you two so you can sleep."

"Can't you stay here with us? You can keep your gun on the nightstand."

"What if someone goes after the Kessler twins?" she asked.

"Maybe one of them was the one who hit me."

"No. They were in their rooms when I heard you yell. They couldn't have hit you and run up the stairs without me seeing them."

"So it's not them. Then who was it?"

"That's what we need to find out. We need to discover who would want to hurt you and why."

"Do you think they're after the same thing the Kessler boys are?"

"You'd think your grandfather would have found that treasure before he died. *If* it really exists and isn't some big, whopping lie told to make Peg and Percy Malone more glamorous. I'm going to check the library tomorrow. And maybe Jared and Joe will show me what they're basing their exploration on."

"We'll figure this out."

"Yes. We will. In the meantime, you need to rest and let your head recover from that blow."

He shoved his hand through his hair and felt the back

of his neck. Andrew winced. "That's some bump. But I'll live."

"Go to sleep. I'll check on you in a couple of hours."

"Wake me up. I want to know you're okay, too."

"I will." Once more, she tried to leave but he caught her hand and dragged her back to his side.

"Be careful out there." He pulled her to stand between his legs. "Leigha is getting used to having you around." Andrew wrapped his hands around her waist.

"She's a sweet kid." Dix leaned forward and kissed him on the lips. "Sleep. We can talk more in the morning." Once more she bent to kiss him.

He circled the back of her neck with his hand and drew her closer, deepening the kiss, his tongue teasing hers.

Using all of her resolve, she pulled free of his grip and backed out of his reach. If she continued kissing him like that, she would never leave the room. "Rest. I'll be back later." Dix spun and walked out without looking back. She couldn't do her job if she couldn't focus. She couldn't focus when she was around Andrew Stratford. Clearly, making love to her client was a conflict of interest and left her and him vulnerable to attack.

She'd call Fontaine in the morning and ask him to relieve her. Falling in love with a client was not conducive to keeping him and his daughter safe.

Chapter 16

Andrew lay beside Leigha on the little girl's bed, counting the minutes until Dix returned. He didn't like being confined to a bed, but when he sat up, his head hurt and his vision blurred. Granted, it wasn't quite as bad as when he'd first woken in the sitting room. But he wouldn't be of any use to Dix if he fell down the stairs running after her.

Leigha needed someone to fight her dream dragons. Or, to be more precise, rescue her from the fire that had nearly ended her life.

Even as worried as he was about Dix wandering the house searching for bad guys, Andrew couldn't stop his heart from swelling at what Leigha had called him when she'd been so frightened from her nightmare.

Daddy.

He'd told himself it didn't matter that she referred to him as Mr. Stratford. But hearing her call him Daddy had melted every bone in his body and swelled his heart to twice its size. He'd move heaven and earth for that little girl. She was *his* little girl. She had his eyes and his name was on her birth certificate.

He turned onto his side to relieve the pressure on the lump at the back of his neck. It gave him a chance to study his daughter in the soft glow of the night-light plugged into a wall socket.

Part of him wanted to know for certain whether or not she was his child biologically. But another part of him knew she was his whether they shared the same DNA or not. Leigha needed him as much as he needed her.

Brewer stood, turned around three times and lay across Andrew's ankles.

The dog had proved to be a great companion to Leigha, but she really needed some human friends, too. Andrew would consult with Mrs. Purdy about the best way for Leigha to get the interaction she needed. His housekeeper knew everyone in town. Surely she had a contact who could steer him in the right direction.

Tomorrow he'd also go to the local school and enroll his daughter for the coming fall. She'd be old enough to attend first grade. She would make friends with other little girls and, eventually, she might give up her imaginary friend.

The biggest task for the following day would be to find the bastard who was threatening them. Once he was arrested and sent to jail, Andrew, Leigha and Dix could stop jumping at shadows. They wouldn't need bodyguards to protect them. Dix wouldn't have to work for him and he could kiss her all he wanted.

Andrew must have fallen asleep.

A hand on his arm gently shook him awake.

"Hey," a gravelly voice whispered in his ear.

He opened his eyes to stare into Dix's green gaze. "Hey, yourself."

"How do you feel?"

He blinked and thought about it. "My head doesn't hurt as badly and my vision isn't blurry."

"That's a good sign." She took his hand and held it in hers. "You can go back to sleep."

"What time is it?"

"Four o'clock. The sun won't be up for another two or three hours, assuming the fog clears soon."

"Any problems?"

"Not so far."

"Good." He yawned and patted the bed beside him. "I don't suppose I could talk you into staying?"

"Not tonight." She pulled out of his reach, rounded the bed to Leigha's side and pressed her hand to her forehead. "Has she had any more nightmares?"

"She hasn't called out in her sleep, so I assume no."

"I'll check with you again in a couple hours."

"I don't like you wandering around this big old house by yourself."

"It's my job. Let me do it."

His gaze followed her every move. She tiptoed around the room on silent feet, the sway of her hips making him crazy with need. "And if I fire you?"

"I'd still do it. I don't want anything else to happen to you or Leigha."

Andrew sighed. "I'll be up tomorrow and we're going to find out how that guy got in and back out without being seen."

"I think Leigha might be able to help us with that effort. Somehow she knows about this house's secrets."

"She's amazing," Andrew said, staring at his daughter as she slept. "And I haven't paid nearly enough attention to her."

Dix left Leigha's side and walked toward the door. When she reached it, she looked back at them. "Sleep."

Andrew wasn't going to fight her on this. She was the trained professional. He wasn't. In the morning, he would turn the house inside out if he had to.

He closed his eyes, knowing she would take care of them. What bothered him was who would take care of Dix?

He closed his eyes and slept, hoping that by morning, the power of rest would have restored him to full functionality. He'd need it to tear the big old mansion apart to find what he was looking for.

"Daddy?"

A hand on his shoulder woke him from a dream about running through dark, narrow corridors, searching for Dix and Leigha.

When he opened his eyes to see Leigha smiling down at him, he drew in a deep breath, his pulse returning to normal.

Brewer crawled up the comforter, his tail wagging, eager to be a part of a morning wake-up.

Andrew smiled at his daughter. "Hey, sweetheart."

She grinned. "You stayed the whole night of my slumber party."

He nodded, the pull of swelling at the back of his head reminding him of the attack. "I did."

Leigha glanced around the room. "Where's Dix?"

Andrew had been wondering the same. "She probably got up early to help Mrs. Purdy in the kitchen. I can smell bacon."

Brewer woofed at the mention of bacon.

Despite his determination not to feed the dog anything but the special-blend dog food he'd purchased from the vet, Andrew knew he was given treats by the women in the house. He'd caught Leigha sneaking bits of bacon to him beneath the table. She thought he didn't know. He did, but he hadn't said anything. Mrs. Purdy was just as bad. When she filled the dog's bowl with his dry dog food, she poured bacon grease on the top.

The dog barked again.

"I think Brewer wants to go down for breakfast," Leigha said. She flung her arms around Andrew, kissed his cheek and rolled out of the bed onto her bare feet.

Andrew pressed a hand to his cheek. He couldn't recall a time when his heart was as full as it was at that moment.

He pushed to his feet, happy that he wasn't dizzy. Other than a dull ache at the base of his skull and a knot the size of a guinea egg, he felt as close to normal as a man could after being attacked in his own house.

Andrew opened the curtains to a cloudy day. But the fog had cleared and he could see the bay. "How would you like to spend the day exploring?"

Leigha looked up from rummaging in her dresser. "With you?"

"Yes, with me." He had yet another reminder that he hadn't spent nearly enough time being a father to this child.

"And Dix?" she persisted.

"And Dix." After she had the opportunity to rest. Andrew left Leigha to dress by herself and hurried into his room to shave and put on some clothes. By the time he was ready, Leigha had already left her room with Brewer.

Andrew stepped out into the hallway. He could hear voices below. As he descended the stairs, he looked at his home with a keener eye. Hidden passages had never occurred to him. Now that he knew one existed, he had to know if there were more.

He followed the voices to the kitchen, where it looked like a party going on. The Kessler twins were playing with Brewer, scratching his belly and throwing one of his favorite plush toys for him to retrieve.

Dix stood to one side, talking to the woman Andrew had met the night he'd brought Dix to his home.

The tall, svelte blonde stepped away from Dix and held out her hand. "I don't know if you remember me from the other night. I'm—"

"Nicole Steele." He touched her hand with his injured and scarred one. When she didn't flinch, he added, "Tazer."

She smiled. "I must have made an impression. I hope it was a good one."

He nodded, his gaze going to Dix. "Everything all right?"

She had shadows beneath her eyes, but other than that, she appeared alert and ready to go. "The night was quiet after everyone went to bed."

"I told Dix I'd hang out until she caught a couple hours' sleep." Tazer turned to Dix, her lips twisting. "She says she doesn't need it."

"How are you this morning?" Jared stepped up to Andrew. "That was some nasty bump on the head."

Andrew rubbed the back of his neck. "It's already going down. I'll be fine." His attention remained on Dix. Her gaze hadn't left him since he'd entered the room. "I agree with Tazer. You need rest. Leigha and I can hang out in the study until you've had a chance to sleep."

Dix was shaking her head before he could finish his sentence. "I'm fine. I want to spend some time exploring the house and, if we have time, I'd like to visit the library in town. There has to be more information about your family inheritance."

"Anyone hungry?" Mrs. Purdy plowed through the middle of the adults, carrying a platter full of fluffy scrambled eggs and setting it in the middle of the table. "You might save this conversation until later. Little bits have big ears."

Andrew glanced down at his daughter, who'd been

quietly following the conversation like a spectator at a tennis match. Mrs. Purdy was right. They didn't need to give the curious little girl any more fodder to fuel her imagination.

The others shot glances at Leigha and nodded.

"You've gone to all the trouble of cooking for all of us. Let us help by setting the table." Jared grabbed a plate of bacon and one of toast and added them to the offering on the big kitchen table.

Everyone joined in, helping to set the table with orange juice, glasses, butter, jelly, plates, knives and forks. For the next twenty minutes the conversation centered on food and local festivities.

When the plates and platters had been emptied, they all helped carry the dishes to the sink.

"Let us do the dishes," Joe said.

"No, you all need to talk. Leigha can help me." Mrs. Purdy handed Leigha a towel. "I'll wash. You can dry. If we do a really good job, we can have one of those cookies we baked yesterday when we're done."

"Cookies for breakfast?"

"Shh." Mrs. Purdy pressed a finger to her lips and winked. "Don't say it too loud or everyone else will want one and there won't be any left for us."

Leigha grinned and set to work drying.

"We'll be out on the porch," Andrew said.

Once they were all outside, Andrew turned to the twins. "I get the feeling whoever has been attacking me knows something about this house and what might be hidden inside. Do you think the Malones stashed their treasure somewhere around here?"

"That would be my bet." Dix had had all night to think of a motive for someone to attack Andrew Stratford. "You say you moved here with Leigha less than a year ago. Was there a gap between when your grandfather died and when you arrived?"

"My grandfather died two years ago. I came out for the funeral and to secure the house. I had no intention of moving here at that time."

"Then you found out about Leigha and moved here," Dix stated. "There were several months that the house sat empty. Someone could have been in here, looking for the treasure. They could have found some of the secret passageways."

Andrew nodded. "That's possible. When I got here, one of the door locks wasn't working. I had to replace it."

"Who, besides you, knows about the Malone legacy?" Dix asked.

Jared chuckled.

"Practically everyone in town. We went through every newspaper article in Cape Churn related to Peg and Percy Malone. We also looked at everything we could find on Margaret and Percival Mason," Joe offered. "We know for certain that the theft took place. Where they stashed the ill-gotten gains is a mystery."

"We spent time in the Oregon State Library in Portland before coming here and dug up everything we could find," Jared added. "You're welcome to our file of data."

Jared's eyes narrowed. "I don't suppose your family has a blueprint of the Stratford House?"

Andrew shook his head. "If they did, I have yet to find it."

"We'd like to look through the caves a little more thoroughly. There were other tunnels besides the one leading to the beach."

"I have no problem with you looking through the caves. Just be careful."

"You'll be the first to know if we find anything."

Mrs. Purdy stuck her head out the door. "Dave Logsdon is here to pick up the Kessler boys."

Jared grinned. "That's our cue to leave. We'll head back to our hotel and grab what we need for spelunking and come back in our own car."

"I don't know if there are other ways into and out of the cave," Andrew said. "You might have to come through the house. In which case, I'd rather be here when you are."

The Kesslers nodded.

"We understand," Jared said.

Dix probably wouldn't have been as generous as Andrew, but then, the young men hadn't been the ones to hit him and they had helped get him up the stairs after the attack. Her gut told her to trust them.

The twins left a few minutes later.

Leigha slipped between Dix and Andrew and grabbed a hand from each. "Are we going exploring today?"

Andrew smiled down at his daughter. The love shining from his eyes was apparent.

It made Dix's heart squeeze hard in her chest.

"Where are we going?" Leigha asked, looking up at Andrew and then Dix.

Dix knelt beside Leigha. "Remember how you showed me the secret hallway in the sitting room?"

Leigha nodded.

"You said there were others like it." Dix stared into her eyes, forcing a smile when she felt tension building inside. "Could you show us another?"

Leigha's brows knit. "I don't know."

"Why?" Andrew asked. "Have you forgotten where they are?"

She shook her head. "No. But I promised Bennet I wouldn't tell anyone where they are."

Andrew frowned. "Who's Bennet?"

Dix shot Andrew a stern glance and gave a slight shake of her head before she faced Leigha with a smile. "But you showed me the one yesterday."

Leigha twisted the hem of her T-shirt in her fingers. "Bennet said it would be okay."

"Could you ask Bennet about the others?" Dix persisted.

"Yes." Leigha let go of their hands and ran from the room, calling out over her shoulder, "I'll be right back. Stay there."

Andrew and Dix started to follow Leigha. When they reached the door, Dix noticed Leigha was going up the stairs. Brewer followed. "Let her go. She's heading for her bedroom."

Andrew's frown deepened. "Who's Bennet?"

Dix grinned. "Bennet is her imaginary friend."

"Are you sure he's imaginary?"

Remembering that creepy feeling she'd had in the cave, Dix chewed on her bottom lip. "I'm not ready to believe in ghosts, so I'm calling him an imaginary friend."

"Explain," Andrew demanded.

She told him about the trip through the cave and how Leigha had insisted Bennet was in the cave with them, standing beside her.

Andrew shook his head. "I'm enrolling her in school today. And I'm going to find some activity center she can go to during the day so that she can make friends with kids her own age."

Dix nodded.

A door slammed and tiny footsteps sounded on the floor above.

Leigha came running down the stairs, Brewer keeping pace. She skidded to a halt in front of Dix and Andrew.

Andrew dropped to his haunches and caught Leigha in his arms. He hugged her and chuckled, the sound warming Dix's heart. "Well? What did Bennet say?"

Dix was glad Andrew hadn't tried to tell Leigha that Bennet didn't exist. He seemed to know she needed Bennet, even if he wasn't real.

Leigha's face split in a big grin. "He said it was okay. I could show you and Dix, but no one else."

"Great." Andrew lifted her in his arms and turned around in the foyer. "Which way should we go? And do we need anything like a flashlight or a loaf of bread?"

Her little brows wrinkled. "Bread?"

"You know. To leave a trail of bread crumbs so that we can find our way back."

Leigha giggled. "I have a flashlight where we're going. But we don't need bread. I know the way back. And if we lose our way, Bennet will help us get home."

Andrew shot a glance toward Dix over Leigha's head. "Oh, good. I feel so much better, knowing Bennet will be there."

"He's very nice and he takes care of me and Brewer."

Andrew's lips thinned.

Dix could tell he was kicking himself for leaving Leigha to fend for herself while he worked.

Leigha wiggled in Andrew's arms. "Put me down. I'll show you where we start."

Andrew set the child on her feet.

She darted toward the back of the house and turned toward the west wing. "Follow me!" she called, her hair flying out behind her.

"You heard her—follow Leigha." Dix took off at a slow jog, afraid that if she let the child get too far ahead, she might disappear.

Since she'd spent a good portion of the early morning hours searching rooms, touching walls and feeling for hidden doorways or panels, she still hadn't a clue as to where the other secret passageways were located. They were at the mercy of a six-year-old and a ghost to find them.

Leigha ran halfway down the first-floor hallway of the west wing and stopped in front of a small alcove with an arched entrance. A life-size statue of a Roman woman holding a baby took up the majority of the space.

Dix remembered running across her as she'd patrolled the halls in the middle of the night. She'd walked all the way around her, searching for a doorway, a lever or a switch. The only switch she'd found was a button. When pressed, the light over the statue came on.

Leigha pushed the button and waited.

The light came on. Leigha turned to the statue and grabbed the baby's toe.

Dix leaned closer and noticed the toe moved into the statue.

Still nothing major happened.

Then Leigha pushed the button on the wall again and the alcove, statue and all, rotated into the wall, exposing a doorway.

Leigha started to enter when Andrew grabbed her arm and held her back.

"Wait." Andrew tipped his head toward the wood floor of the hallway.

Dix stared hard at the dark wood. Then she saw them. Footprints. "Sweetheart, let me go first." Her hand went to the gun beneath the blazer she wore.

Leigha looked up at her. "But you don't know the way."

"Brewer does, doesn't he?"

"Yes."

"Then I'll follow Brewer. You can hold your father's hand and help him find the way."

She considered Dix's words and nodded. "Okay. But you'll need this." She reached around Dix and plucked a flashlight from a cubbyhole in the secret passage, switched it on and handed it to Dix. "This hall doesn't have a light switch."

"Nice to know." Dix balanced the light in her left hand, keeping her right hand free to pull her gun, if needed. She focused the beam down the narrow corridor and stepped into the passageway. "Did you put the flashlights in the corridors?"

"No," Leigha said from behind. "They were here. Bennet showed me how to find them."

"Bennet seems to be a handy friend to have," Andrew muttered.

"He's very smart and knows his way around the house and caves."

"I'd like to meet him someday." Andrew's voice carried to Dix.

She almost laughed, wondering how he'd react if Leigha introduced him to Bennet the same way she'd introduced him to Dix.

The corridor made a ninety-degree turn to the left and another to the right. At one point it ended in a T-junction.

"Which way?" Dix asked.

"If you go to the right, it leads to the garden," Leigha said. "Left leads you to a staircase that takes you up to the tower. You can see all the way to Cape Churn up there."

"I'll take your word for it. Are there any other corridors off either of these choices?" Dix asked.

"No."

"Then let's go to the garden." Dix turned right and walked approximately fifty feet to a door. She held her hand up, hoping Andrew would hold back Leigha while she checked to see what was on the other side of the door.

A glance over her shoulder proved he'd understood. He held on to Leigha's hand, pulling her back behind him.

Dix turned the doorknob and swung the door open. Brewer ran out.

Light filtered through a veil of vines.

Dix passed through the door and parted the vines. She stood still, scanning the garden, the bushes and shadows for movement.

Brewer trotted along a stone path, his nose to the ground, sniffing. When he came to a low stone wall, he reared on his back legs, planted his front paws on the wall. The dog looked over the top, his tail still for several seconds, and then he wagged it. Apparently satisfied no one was lurking on the other side, he dropped to the ground and turned back toward Dix as if to say *The coast is clear.*

Dix felt a little bit of relief, but she wouldn't be much of a bodyguard if she based her actions on what she thought the dog was thinking. Dix moved into the open, crossed to the wall and glanced over the top.

She noted the small patch of dirt on the other side. Everywhere else was covered in grass or moss. Peering closer, she could swear the patch of dirt had a shoe print in the middle.

Dix vaulted over the wall, deliberately landing on the grass. Hugging the bushes, she made a one-hundred-eighty-degree sweep of the area around the wall, moving farther into the woods just to be certain no one was out there who could harm her or her clients.

When she was as sure as she could be, she returned to the wall and squatted beside the dirt patch. Definitely a footprint. The pattern indicated some kind of work boot. She straightened and swung her legs over the stone wall.

Andrew stood with Leigha near the vines. "Anything?" he asked.

"It's a lovely garden." Dix bent to pick up a stick. "Leigha, does Brewer know how to play fetch?"

Leigha nodded and held out her hand. "Want me to show you?"

"Please."

She took the stick, walked a few feet away and threw the stick.

Brewer raced after it, snatched it up with his teeth and dropped it at Leigha's feet. She giggled and did it again, moving a little farther away from where Andrew and Dix stood.

"What did you find?" Andrew asked.

"I didn't find the perpetrator, but I did find a boot print in the dirt on the other side of the wall. Whoever hit you last night probably left through the secret passage."

"I suppose I need to stock up on locks."

"You might consider installing a security monitoring system."

"It's on my list of upgrades, as soon as the contractor can get to me."

"You might want to move it to the top of your priority list."

He nodded. "Leigha, are there any more secret hallways in the house that lead to the outside?"

She threw the stick for Brewer once more and came to stand beside Andrew. "None that lead outside. Only this one and the one that goes through the cave."

"Let's go back inside. I want you to show me the one you showed Dix yesterday."

"Okay." She ducked through the vines, disappearing into the house.

If Dix hadn't known where the door was, she wouldn't have known it was there. The vines and shadows completely hid the door. She was surprised Andrew hadn't discovered it as a boy exploring his grandfather's house.

Brewer followed Leigha, Andrew went next and Dix brought up the rear, closing the door behind her. When she turned, she nearly ran into Andrew.

He hadn't moved far into the narrow corridor. "I'll come back with a lock after she shows me the cave."

Her heart hammered against her ribs. Standing as close as she was to Andrew, she could smell the sexy scent of his aftershave.

He reached out to brush a strand of her hair away from her forehead. "I'm sorry things didn't work out the way we'd planned last night."

She fought the urge to lean her cheek into his palm. Instead she stared up at him, forcing herself to be professional. "It's probably just as well our plans didn't happen. Not that I wanted you to be hurt. It's just that I'm here for the short term. What good is it to start something we both know we can't finish?"

"How do you know?"

"I'm not the right person for you and Leigha. I have too many issues."

"And we don't?"

"Three wrongs don't make a family."

"So that's it?" He tipped her chin up and stared into her eyes in the dim glow of the flashlight he carried in his other hand. "You're not even willing to see what might come of us?"

"I told you—"

"I know. You're damaged goods. I hope someday you'll explain to me how different you are from me and Leigha." He bent his head until his lips hovered over hers. "The way I see it, we have a lot more in common than you're willing to admit." He brushed his lips lightly over hers. "Resist all you want. I like what I know so far, and I'm not ready to give up on you."

Then he deepened the kiss, pushing his tongue past her teeth to tangle with hers. He lifted his head and smiled. "You might think you're all tough and hard as stone." He touched a finger to her chest. "But I'd bet my last dollar you're all soft and squishy on the inside."

"Are you coming?" Leigha asked. "We still have to go through the cave. And Brewer's hungry for one of Mrs. Purdy's cookies."

"Coming," Andrew answered. Then, to Dix, he said, "You heard that. Brewer needs a cookie. But don't forget— I'm not ready to give up on you." He turned and shone the flashlight ahead of him.

Dix stayed rooted to the floor, her lips tingling from his kiss, her heart squeezing so tightly in her chest she was afraid it would implode.

You might not be ready to give up on me, Andrew Stratford. But it's not you I'm worried about. I don't know if I have what it takes to stay.

Chapter 17

Leigha wasted no time leading them to the sitting room and through the hidden doorway in the fireplace. When they reached the door that would lead into the cave, they paused while Andrew worked the combination lock.

Dix led the way through the tunnel, carrying the flashlight.

Andrew was shocked when the tunnel emptied out into the cavern and even more disturbed by the next tunnel's exit over a cliff and down the trail to the beach. The tide was out, so he could see the little strip of sand, just enough for someone to beach a skiff.

"How did I not know about this?" Andrew said as he watched his daughter and Brewer play on the sand.

"The bigger question is how Leigha found it." Dix shook her head. "I can't imagine she found those two passages on her own. Someone had to have shown her the triggers to open the hidden doors."

"But who?" Andrew didn't like it. "All the while I was working in my office, she was wandering through secret tunnels and caves. She could just as easily have slipped off a cliff or gotten lost in the woods."

"At least you know now and can keep her safe."

He rubbed his scarred hand through his hair and winced when his stitches snagged. "I wish parenting came with a how-to book."

Dix chuckled. "She's amazing. I can't imagine a book would be adequate."

Leigha ran back to the two of them, her hair in disarray, her jeans wet from kneeling in the sand. "Brewer is ready for his cookie."

"What about Bennet?" Dix asked.

"That's silly. Bennet doesn't eat cookies."

"Why not?" Andrew asked.

"He can't." Leigha started up the stone steps. "He's a ghost," she called out over her shoulder. "Everyone knows ghosts don't need to eat."

And so Andrew was schooled on what ghosts could and couldn't do. Never in a million years would he have guessed he'd be living at his grandfather's estate in Oregon, talking to a six-year-old who believed in ghosts. *His* six-year-old daughter.

Leigha hurried them back through the tunnels and cave to the house. Once she emerged from the fireplace, she made a beeline for the kitchen, skipping across the marble-tiled floor, Brewer racing ahead.

By the time Andrew and Dix entered, Leigha was at the table with a cookie and a glass of milk.

"You two look like you need a cookie. Would you prefer coffee or milk?"

Dix and Andrew replied as one. "Milk."

Dix turned to Andrew. "Really? I would have pegged you for a coffee drinker."

"And I am. But nothing goes better with one of Mrs. Purdy's cookies than milk." He leaned close to her as he stepped around her. "Yet another thing we have in common." Before she could protest, he reached for the cup and cookie and took the seat beside Leigha. "Mrs. Purdy, are any of my grandfather's cronies still alive?"

She brought a cookie and a glass of milk and set it on the table across from Andrew and motioned for Dix to take the seat. "Why do you ask?"

"I'd like to talk to them about my grandfather and this house."

She tilted her head and stared at the far corner for a moment, and then her face brightened. "As a matter of fact, Mr. Giddings, the owner of the hardware store in Cape Churn, is still alive and kicking. I think the man is going to outlive us all." She shook her head. "He and your grandfather met for coffee once a week at the café. I believe they used to play cards here at the house when they were younger."

"And he still works at the hardware store?"

"He does. He's got to be pushing ninety. But he likes feeling useful and he knows everything there is to know about lumber, hardware and fixing things. He works a shorter day than his son. If you want to see him, you should go in the next hour or two."

"Leigha, how would you like to go to town with me and Dix?" Andrew asked. "We could run by the school and get you registered for first grade."

"I can go to school?" Her face lit and she practically bounced in her chair. "With kids like me and a teacher?"

Andrew laughed. "Yes. With kids like you and a teacher."

"Yes, please." She leaped out of her chair and ran for the door.

"Leigha," Andrew said, his voice firm.

Leigha slid to a halt on the tiled floor. "Yes, sir?"

"We'll go after we finish our cookies and milk that Mrs. Purdy so nicely provided."

She walked back to the table, slid into her seat and proceeded to gobble up the rest of the cookie and drink her milk. When she set her glass down, she had a milk mustache and a smile. "Can we go now?"

Andrew finished the last bite of his cookie, upended his glass of milk and sighed. "Yes, we can go."

Leigha pointed at him and laughed.

Andrew looked around, pretending he didn't know he had a matching milk mustache. "What?"

"You have milk on your lip." Leigha giggled again.

"Oh, you mean like the milk on your lip?" He grabbed a napkin and wiped the milk from her mouth. "There."

Dix handed Leigha a napkin and she repeated the gesture, wiping the milk from Andrew's lip. "There," she echoed.

Andrew and Leigha turned to Dix.

"What?"

"Are you ready?" Andrew asked.

Dix shoved the last bit of her cookie into her mouth and drank her milk so fast she got milk on her upper lip.

Leigha dissolved into giggles, rolled out of her chair onto the floor.

Brewer saw his chance to lick her face, which made her giggle more.

Andrew loved the sound of his daughter's laughter. And he loved that Dix, the former Army Ranger and MMA fighter, had enough of a sense of humor that she could be silly along with a six-year-old and her father.

He applied a fresh napkin to her lip and wiped the milk away. Then he brushed a quick kiss where the white mustache had been. "Ready?"

She shook her head, but got up from her chair anyway.

Andrew knew it wasn't going to be easy to convince Dix to stay long enough to get to know each other. But he was up for the challenge. He'd been to hell and back. He could handle it.

Based on Mrs. Purdy's recommendation, Andrew gathered Leigha's birth certificate and immunization record. He, Leigha and Dix loaded into his SUV and drove into Cape Churn. They made their first stop at the school administration building, where Andrew registered Leigha for school. Leigha met the school superintendent and learned the name of the elementary school. She was so excited when they left, Andrew felt bad that he'd isolated her for so long.

After dealing with the school registration, they stopped at the hardware store.

In the front window of the store, someone had set up a display of a small chicken coop and populated it with live yellow chicks. When they went inside, Leigha planted herself in front of the chicken display while Andrew and Dix located Mr. Giddings, the elderly owner of the hardware store.

He was counting wood screws for a customer and dropping them into a thick paper bag. "That's fifty. Is there anything else I can get for you, Mrs. Laney?"

Andrew waited for the woman to pay for her purchase and leave before he spoke. "Mr. Giddings, do you remember my grandfather—"

The old man held up a hand and stared at Andrew through narrowed eyes. "You're the Stratford boy who inherited Thomas Stratford's place. Am I right?"

Andrew smiled. "Yes, sir." He held out his hand. "Andrew Stratford."

"Richard Giddings. But you can call me Mr. Giddings. You're too young to call me Richard."

"Yes, Mr. Giddings." He turned to Dix. "This is my… friend, Dixie Reeves. We'd like to talk to you, if you have time."

Giddings took Dix's hand in both of his and smiled. "Now, you can call me Richard if you like. Never could resist a pretty girl."

"Thank you, Richard." Dix shot a triumphant glance toward Andrew.

Andrew chuckled. "Mr. Giddings, I understand you

and my grandfather were good friends and spent some time together before he passed."

Mr. Giddings released Dix's hand and turned his attention to Andrew. "Thomas was a good man. Played a mean hand of poker, but he was a good man. What's been troubling you?"

"Sir, I've been attacked two times in the past week and I haven't a clue as to why. Once on the cliff behind Stratford House and once inside the house itself."

"Told Thomas his house was far too big when he first brought his plans to me."

"Plans?"

Giddings nodded. "He wanted a house big enough for a whole litter of children and his in-laws, if they wanted to stay."

"My grandfather had only one child that I know of," Andrew said. "My father."

Giddings nodded. "Rowena had several miscarriages before she gave birth to Benjamin. I don't think I'd ever seen her as happy as when she brought your father home." He stared into the distance, a sad smile curling his lips. "She was so proud of him."

"And the in-laws?"

"Friends from the church temporarily moved in with Thomas and Rowena to help with the baby, but Rowena never really got over Benjamin's birth. Oh, she lived to raise him, but her health was never the same."

"She died shortly after I was born," Andrew said.

"That's right. Young Ben came back to Cape Churn after he graduated from college. He met Laura, your mother, who was a few years younger, and they fell in love. Ben proposed and she said yes. It made your grandmother happy to know her son was happy and they'd be living close by so that she could watch her grandchildren grow up."

"Only my parents didn't stay in Cape Churn," Andrew said.

"No, they didn't. They would have, but your mother's old boyfriend made their lives hell. He stalked Laura, showing up everywhere she went. Your father came to blows with him after he'd cornered your mother in the grocery store."

"What was his name?"

"Nelson Clayton."

Clayton. The older gentleman who'd talked to him at the Seaside Café. "Isn't he my nearest neighbor?"

"Yes. He bought the property next to Stratford House. I remember he'd said he should have owned Stratford House. He claimed he was Thomas's bastard son, born before Benjamin. Therefore, he should have inherited Stratford House."

"What?" Andrew hadn't heard any of this. "From all the stories my grandfather told me about his wife, they were deeply in love. He didn't have eyes for any other woman."

"Which is true. But before your mother came along your grandfather was quite the ladies' man." Giddings leaned against the counter, warming to his story. "He was known to have a fling or two among the more promiscuous women. One in particular. Darla Landis. She set her sights on your grandfather and seduced him."

Andrew chuckled. "I'm having a hard time picturing my grandfather being seduced."

Mr. Giddings smiled and puffed out his chest. "You only saw him as an old man. When we were young, we were like you—good-looking, viral men about town."

"Oh, I believe you," Andrew said. "Please continue."

"Not long afterward—a couple days, maybe a week— Thomas met Rowena Mason and fell hopelessly in love. They hadn't dated more than two weeks before he asked her to marry him."

Dix snorted. "I take it Miss Landis wasn't too happy."

"Not at all. She tried to break up the wedding. Caused a big ruckus. But when the dust settled, Thomas and Rowena were happily married."

"What happened to Darla?" Dix asked.

"She married Oliver Clayton, an older man who owned a fishing boat. She never was very happy. She had a child right away. Old Man Clayton didn't live long after. He got caught out on the water in the Devil's Shroud and sank with his boat. Darla's baby was only a year old. She started spreading the rumor that her boy Nelson wasn't Clayton's baby after all."

Andrew shook his head and asked, "Could it have been Thomas's?"

Giddings shrugged. "She had the baby ten months after she and Thomas were together."

Dix's eyes narrowed. "I've heard of women carrying their babies for ten months instead of the usual nine."

"It's possible," Giddings said. "Meanwhile, Thomas's investments took off and he became a millionaire practically overnight. He built that massive house to show Rowena how much he loved her. Rowena didn't care about having a big house or fancy cars. She would have loved him if he'd been dirt-poor." Mr. Giddings straightened. "Look at me getting all nostalgic."

"Sounds like Thomas and Rowena had the perfect marriage," Dix said.

Giddings nodded.

"Why did Ben and Laura leave?" Dix asked.

"They didn't want to, but Nelson wouldn't leave them alone. The final straw was finding Nelson in the nursery with baby Andrew. It upset Laura so much, she insisted they move as far away from Nelson as possible." The old man sighed. "Losing her son and grandson threw Rowena into a tailspin. She was so sad. Nothing Thomas did could cheer her up. Then she was diagnosed with cancer and it was all downhill after that. Ben barely made it back before Rowena passed."

"No wonder my parents didn't want to come back to Cape Churn." Andrew had thought they were self-ish and hated his grandfather. He glanced up. "Did you know about the tunnels and secret passageways inside the house?"

Giddings frowned. "Tunnels, you say?" He shook his head. "I didn't see anything of the sort in the drawings. Wouldn't surprise me, though. Thomas brought in workers from Southern California to do the excavation and framing. They spent a couple years building that mausoleum. Most of the workers only spoke Spanish, so they kept to themselves. When they were done, Thomas sent them back to California." The old man chuckled. "That would be just like Thomas to do something like that."

Dix tilted her head. "Why?"

"Who knows? Some say he was just a little crazy. Others said he was into smuggling, though the Prohibition was long over. There were the lunatics who tried to convince everyone that Rowena's parents were the famous Peg and Percy Malone." Mr. Giddings's brow knit. "Which made an excellent motivation for Thomas to build tunnels out to the sea. If his in-laws were notorious thieves, they would have needed an escape route."

"And a place to stash the loot," Dix added. Her gaze captured Andrew's.

"Is there any reason someone would want me off my own property…permanently?" Andrew asked.

"No one thought you'd come back to live in Cape Churn." The hardware store owner scratched his head. "Other than Nelson Clayton, I can't think of anyone who'd want the Stratford House. It's got to cost a fortune to maintain. Your heating and electric bills alone would bankrupt most of us."

Andrew's lips twisted. "They aren't minimal." But he could afford it. So what would anyone have to gain by knocking him off? Unless… "Speaking of the Malones, what do you know about them?"

"They were a legend along the West Coast. Supposedly disappeared in broad daylight. They kind of became heroes among the working class. Not many around here were happy about Prohibition. When that big shot from San Francisco turned them in and then sold their whiskey, he got what he deserved."

"The theft of his jewelry store?" Dix added.

The old man nodded. "Since then, there have been treasure hunters who've scoured the coastline searching for the boat they stole." Giddings jabbed a finger in the air. "Just the other day, we had a couple of college students in buying supplies for their own treasure hunt. I heard they hired Logsdon to take them out in his dive boat." Giddings frowned. "I also heard they ended up staying last night at your place. You sure they weren't the ones who attacked you?"

Dix shook her head and answered for Andrew. "Mr. Stratford was attacked on the first floor. I was upstairs, as were the Kessler boys. It couldn't have been them."

Andrew understood how small towns worked. News traveled fast. Still, he was amazed at how fast it did travel. "Mr. Giddings, thank you for all the information."

The hardware store owner straightened slowly. "Wish I could help more. Thomas was a good friend. We played cards on occasion and had coffee once a week." He touched a finger to his chin. "Come to think of it, in the last few weeks of his life, Thomas talked about a journal he was keeping. Did you find it?"

Andrew frowned and shook his head. "I've been there for almost a year and haven't found anything like that. I've been through his file cabinets and desk drawers."

"If he was smart enough to build hidden passages and tunnels, he's probably got it hidden somewhere. But that's strange he didn't leave it where you could find it. I got the impression he was documenting things he wanted you to know should he die."

Andrew sucked in a deep breath to ease the tightness in his chest. His biggest regret was not coming back to Cape Churn before his grandfather died. "Again, Mr. Giddings, thank you for your help."

"I hope you find out who's been attacking you." Mr. Giddings straightened a stack of miniature flashlights on the counter. "Hate to think one of our own is causing you trouble."

Andrew and Dix collected Leigha on the way out.

"Could I have a baby chick someday?" she begged. "Please?"

Until he discovered who was trespassing and why, Andrew didn't feel good about bringing anyone, or anything, out to Stratford House.

On the drive home, Leigha fell asleep in the backseat.

Andrew glanced in the rearview mirror at his daughter and then shot a sideways glance toward Dix. "Should I move Leigha and you into a hotel in town?"

Dix shook her head. "Between me and Brewer, we'll take care of Leigha. *You're* the one I'm worried about. You're the one who's nearly been killed. Twice." She held up two fingers to emphasize her point. "Maybe we need to ask Fontaine for a bodyguard assigned to you. Three attacks might be a charm. And I don't mean that in a good way."

Andrew rubbed the knot on the back of his head and grinned. "If I'm not mistaken, you're worried about me. Does that mean you're coming around? Maybe you like me a little?"

Dix rolled her eyes. "That's never been what was holding me back."

"Ah! So you *do* like me." He smirked, his blue eyes bright in the interior of the SUV. "Good to know. Now, let's find my grandfather's journal. I get the feeling it holds the key to why someone would want me dead."

Dix pressed a finger to her lips. "Shh. You don't want to scare Leigha," she whispered.

Andrew wrinkled his brow. "Are you sure you weren't a mother in another incarnation?"

She held up her hand. "Not that I know of. Before I came to Stratford House, I didn't believe in the paranormal, but now…" She shook her head. "I don't know what to believe."

Andrew reached out a hand to her.

Instead of drawing away, she took his hand and held it all the way back to the house.

He called it progress. Now, if he could convince her his bed was the right place to be, he'd cinch the deal.

A glance at Dix's tight jaw and worried frown wasn't reassuring Andrew. But he didn't give up easily, not on something or someone worth fighting for.

Chapter 18

Leigha woke when they pulled into the yard. Though it was cloudy, night had yet to fall.

Dix helped Leigha out of the SUV and set her on the ground. She yawned and stretched. "We didn't get any ice cream."

"I bet Mrs. Purdy has some in the freezer," Andrew said. "Why don't we go inside and ask?"

Mrs. Purdy exited the front door, her purse and sweater draped over her arm. "I left a lasagna in the oven. There's a salad in the refrigerator and green beans in a pot on the stove. I'd stay, but Mr. Purdy is threatening to climb a ladder to clean a gutter on our house. If I'm not there to hold the ladder, he's likely to fall and hurt himself."

"By all means, Mrs. Purdy, you should hurry home," Andrew said.

Brewer squeezed past Mrs. Purdy's legs and ran straight for Leigha.

She flung out her arms and wrapped them around Brewer's neck.

Dix could remember the love she'd had for her dog when she was growing up. Seeing Leigha with Brewer surfaced some very good memories of her childhood. Her heart swelled and she wondered if she really could stay in one place and not feel as if she were going to come apart at the seams.

Mrs. Purdy paused before climbing into her sedan. "Oh, the internet has been out all day. I tried to bring up a recipe on my tablet and couldn't connect. I called the provider. They walked me through several quick fixes and determined the line has an interruption. They're sending someone out. He should be out anytime soon."

"We'll take care of it," Andrew said. "Thank you."

Mrs. Purdy drove away, leaving the three of them alone in front of the big old house.

Dix glanced at the sky. She could just see a bit of the bay beyond the house. Already the water was a steely gray and a wall of fog crept toward land.

"Will you and Leigha be okay if I go inside?" Andrew asked. "I want to check my grandfather's study for that journal."

Dix snorted. "Good luck. The man had a knack for hiding things." She glanced at Leigha. "Do you think Leigha could ask Bennet to find it for you?"

Andrew stared at his daughter for a minute before shrugging. "If you'd asked me that three days ago, I would have laughed you all the way back to Vegas."

Dix's lips pressed together. "Go on. I'll let Leigha and Brewer stretch their legs before we come inside."

Andrew glanced at the bay, his brows dipping. "Don't be too long. Looks like we're in for another foggy night."

"Trust me, I don't want to get caught in that any more than you do."

Andrew touched the side of her cheek and bent to kiss her lips. "Still working on you," he whispered and left her standing in the grass.

Dix touched her mouth where his lips had been. No matter how many times he kissed her, she felt that tingling sensation. Kissing Andrew never got old.

She closed her eyes for a second, wondering what it would be like to stay there. To become another member of the Stratford household. To be a mother to Leigha and a wife to Andrew.

Could they pull together and become a cohesive, balanced family unit?

Dix opened her eyes and glanced around just in time to see Brewer run around the side of the house, Leigha chasing him.

"Leigha!" she called out, already running after her. She didn't like letting the little girl out of her sights for a moment.

Dix raced around the corner. Her heart stopped for a second when she couldn't see Leigha or Brewer.

"Leigha?"

Brewer burst out of a grouping of rosebushes and raced toward Dix, carrying a long string of beads in his mouth. He ran past Dix and stopped, threw the string in the air, let it fall and pounced on it. He grabbed it in his teeth and shook it. The string broke and little white beads spewed across the grass.

"Brewer!" Leigha ran out of the same rose garden. "Give me that! That's mine!" She stopped short when she saw the mess Brewer had made of the beads. Her shoulders slumped. "Now you've broken it."

"We can string them back together. Help me find all of them." Dix dropped to her hands and knees to help Leigha gather the little white beads. As she collected them, she looked down. They looked like pearl beads, like those that made up the necklace her mother had worn with her best dresses. "Leigha, where did you find these?" She glanced up at the little girl and noticed the bright necklace around her neck. The stones were clear and multifaceted.

Dix's heart skipped several beats as she straightened, still on her knees, eye level with Leigha. "Where did you get that necklace?"

The child touched the jewels around her neck. "I found them."

"Yes, sweetie, but where?" Dix stared down at the pearls in her hand. "This isn't the kind of jewelry you play with. It's the kind grown-ups spend a lot of money on."

"They're mine. Bennet showed me where to find them."

"Oh, baby—"

Dix was cut off by the sound of Brewer barking. He was out of sight on the other side of the rosebushes. Suddenly he squealed and the garden grew silent.

"Brewer?" Leigha turned and ran toward the rose garden. "Brewer!"

Dread filled Dix's chest just as she heard the crunch of footsteps on the gravel path. "Leigha, wait!"

The little girl ran into the rose garden.

Dix leaped to her feet and ran after her. She got there too late.

A big man, wearing jeans and a uniform shirt for the internet provider, stood with his feet braced, holding Leigha around the middle with one arm, his other hand clamped over her mouth.

Brewer lay on the ground beside a marble bench.

Red flushed over Dix's eyes and she barreled toward the big man.

Before she reached him something caught her ankle and sent her flying forward. She hit the ground hard enough to knock the breath out of her. Then someone landed on her back, pinning her to the ground. A cloth covered her mouth and nose. When she tried to breathe in, she smelled something sweet with a hint of a chemical scent. Then the fog from the bay crept over her vision and the daylight blinked out.

Andrew hurried into the house and went straight to the study his grandfather had always used. The study he used now as his office since taking up residence at Cape Churn. He'd been through every drawer and cabinet, familiarizing himself with the paperwork his grandfather had felt important enough to keep.

He went through all of them again, moving swiftly,

not really expecting to find the journal Mr. Giddings had mentioned.

When he came up empty-handed, he sat in the big leather chair and stared at the room, wondering if there were any hidden doors, shelves or boxes in the room. He knew about the wall safe behind the portrait of Leigha, but there had to be more. And it had to be here. His grandfather had loved this room and spent hours working or reading there.

Andrew heard the sound of Brewer barking. He started to get up, but the dog stopped. He was probably playing catch with Leigha.

He tapped his fingers on the desktop.

Think.

Where would his grandfather have hidden a journal?

The more he tapped, the more he realized the sound was hollow in a place that shouldn't sound hollow. He'd always assumed his grandfather's desk was solid mahogany. But right in the middle where he was tapping his fingers, he heard a hollow sound.

He curled his fingers into a fist and knocked on the desktop in several places, always coming back to the center where it sounded different.

Andrew got down on his knees and looked beneath the desktop. It was a good three inches thick in the middle, much too thick. If it were solid, it would make a dull thump when he knocked. He felt around the underside of the desk but couldn't find a lever or switch. He opened the drawer on the right and emptied it of the papers and documents. Then he stuck his hand inside a drawer and felt the underside of the desk. Nothing. He repeated the same technique on the left-hand drawer. Just when he was about to give up, his finger touched what felt like a rounded wooden dowel. He pushed it. Something clicked and a shallow drawer slid out of the middle of the desk. In it was a small leather-bound journal.

Andrew's pulse picked up as his fingers curled around the leather and he lifted the book out of the velvet-lined drawer. He opened it to the first page and read.

To my dear Rowena,
You will always hold my heart in your hands. Just because you are gone doesn't mean we'll never see each other again. Our souls are destined to spend eternity together. Until then, you have all of my love. Thomas

Flipping through the pages, Andrew shook his head. This was it, the truth about his heritage, all neatly hand-written and documented for future generations of Strat-fords to read and know.

"Dix?" Andrew clutched the book in his hand and leaped to his feet. "Dix!" he shouted, running for the door. He couldn't wait to show her what he'd found. This could be what his attackers were after. It spelled out everything.

Andrew raced out the front door.

Dix, Leigha and Brewer weren't there. Then he remembered hearing the sound of Brewer's barking at the back of the house. Holding tightly to the book, Andrew ran around the side of the house and worked his way through the garden maze.

"Dix! Leigha! Brewer!" he yelled.

No response.

Had he missed them? When he went out the front door, had they come in through the back door?

He shook his head. Assuming Mrs. Purdy had locked up before she left, the only door unlocked was the front door, and they hadn't come through from that direction.

"Dix! Leigha!"

A soft woof sounded from the other side of a bank of rosebushes.

Andrew tiptoed into his grandmother's rose garden, crouching low, prepared to react should someone try to hit him again in the back of the head.

Nobody jumped out. Nothing moved but a black thumping tail sticking out from under a rosebush.

Checking the area carefully, Andrew didn't kneel down until he was certain nobody else was there. Then he reached beneath the rosebush, the backs of his hands scraped by thorns, and eased Brewer into the open.

The dog lay on his side, his tail twitching, but he didn't get up.

"Where's Leigha, Brewer?" he asked softly.

Brewer lifted his head and tried to get up, but he fell back. He tried again and this time rolled onto his side. He whined softly and shook his head. Then he lurched to his feet and staggered a few steps.

"That's right, boy. Find Leigha."

Brewer limped a little, fell, got up and limped some

more, heading through the garden to the west end of the house.

Andrew knew he couldn't risk going after Dix and Leigha without help. If someone had snatched them, he'd need backup.

He unlocked the door leading into the kitchen, grabbed the phone and entered Tazer's number.

"Yeah?"

"Tazer, this is Andrew Stratford. Dix and Leigha are missing. I think they're in trouble."

"Where are you?"

"At Stratford House. They were playing outside. Then they were gone."

"On our way. Wait for us to get there. We don't know what you might be up against."

"Can't wait. Just get here." He dropped the phone and raced after Brewer, who'd continued through the garden.

If Andrew had waited for the firemen to save Leigha, she would be dead. His instinct had been right to rush into the blaze. He might not be facing an inferno this time, but there were a number of other hazards inherent in living where he was with the cliffs, caves and sea nearby.

He prayed Brewer could track Leigha and find the two women before whoever took them harmed them. He shoved the journal into his back pocket. If he had to, he'd use it in trade for the lives of the two people he cared for.

Inside the journal, his grandfather had confirmed the identity of Rowena Mason's parents. Margaret and Percival Bennet Mason were, in fact, Peg and Percy

Malone, the infamous rumrunners who'd turned the tables on San Francisco big shot Willard Jameson, who'd been in cahoots with the law, stolen their contraband and sold it for pure profit.

The Malones had taken a significant haul when they'd robbed the jewelry store. Not only had they gotten away with thousands of dollars' worth of diamonds and precious gems, they'd taken Jameson's yacht since their boat had been confiscated.

The journal also contained detailed drawings of the locations of several stashes of the jewels from the heist.

Andrew didn't care what happened to the jewels. He'd trade all of them and everything he owned to get Leigha and Dix back alive.

He hurried after the dog, his only hope to find them, praying Leigha's imaginary friend would look out for them until Andrew could get there.

Chapter 19

A high-pitched shriek pulled Dix out of the gray fog swirling around her head. She lay against something hard and cool and, despite the clearing of the fog, she couldn't see much. Darkness surrounded her.

When Dix tried to sit up, she couldn't balance. Her hands were securely tied behind her back and rope bound her ankles.

"I told you—I'm not supposed to show anyone where I found those necklaces. Bennet made me promise. And give them back! They're mine."

Dix lay ten feet away from where the big man she recognized as Dwayne Clayton held Leigha trapped between his hands.

"If you don't want anything to happen to your friend over there, you'll tell us where you found this." The man standing in front of Leigha held out what Dix suspected was a diamond necklace.

As all gazes turned toward her, Dix closed her eyes and pretended to still be unconscious. She peered at the trio through her lashes, tamping down the rising panic of being held captive.

When the man across from Dwayne looked her way, she recognized him as the man who'd introduced himself to them at the Seaside Café. Nelson Clayton, Andrew's nearest neighbor.

Based on the darkness and cool, solid ground beneath her, Dix guessed they were in a cave. Around her were old wooden barrels with metal stays and what looked like the makings of an old still.

If she could get close enough to one of the metal stays, she might be able to rub against the jagged metal and cut the ropes tied around her wrists.

When the men redirected their gazes to Leigha, Dix inched her body toward the piles of metal and wood. Just a few inches was all she needed.

"You got these jewels from somewhere in this cave, didn't you? Who showed you where it was?"

Leigha tilted her chin and glared at Nelson. "Bennet told me. He's my friend."

"Where is this Bennet? Maybe we should ask him where you found the jewels."

She smiled. "Bennet's here in this cave. But he's not telling you anything."

Both men glanced around as if expecting someone to appear out of the darkness. When no one did, Dwayne frowned, twisted his fist in Leigha's hair and pulled.

Leigha stood on her toes, her face tensing. But she didn't cry.

Dix was so proud of her. She was probably scared and in pain, but she refused to cry. Dix's fists clenched. When she got loose, she'd take those two down for picking on a little girl.

She felt around behind her for the edge of a rusty stay. Once she found one, she sawed her arms back and forth, pressing down as hard as she could to cut through the rope chafing her wrists.

Every time Leigha or the men said something, Dix sawed hard at her bindings. When they were quiet, she grew still. But progress was slow and the men were getting impatient with the child.

Finally some of the strands snapped and the ropes loosened around her. More sawing took her the rest of the way through the rope and it broke free. Easing her legs up close to her hands, she untied the bindings around her ankles.

The men were so convinced Dix was out cold, they were fully focused on Leigha and the possibility of finding the jewels.

Dix waited to choose the best moment to surprise her captors.

Dwayne raised his hand, as if to strike Leigha.

That was when Dix came unglued. The mama bear came out in her. She rolled to her feet and charged Dwayne like she was on the defensive line of a football team zeroed in on the guy carrying the ball.

Dix hit Dwayne in the side, sending him staggering across the uneven cave floor. He dragged Leigha with him for a few steps before he let go, his arms flying out for balance. He teetered a moment and then crashed like a felled tree.

Leigha fell to the ground and lay for a moment, barely moving. Then she rolled to her hands and knees.

"Run, Leigha!" Dix shouted.

The little girl darted into the darkness, disappearing into a tunnel.

Dwayne roared and scrambled to his feet.

Dix was ready. The man had at least one hundred pounds on her. That didn't faze Dix. She went after him, landing a side kick in his gut.

The man barely doubled over before he came at her again.

Dix threw another side kick, hitting him in the gut again.

He snagged her angle and twisted, sending her flying to the floor. She jerked her foot free of his grasp and swept his legs out from under him.

Once again, Dwayne went down hard. He rolled to his side and started to get up.

Dix was on him before he could straighten, knocking him off his hands and knees. He splayed across the ground, his forehead bouncing off the stone cave floor. He lay dazed for a moment.

Seizing her opportunity, Dix grabbed his arm, shoved it up between his shoulder blades and straddled his back, pinning him to the ground.

"I think we've had just about enough of this," a voice said.

The cool, hard shaft of a gun barrel pressed to Dix's

temple. She froze but didn't ease the pressure on the man's arm.

"Get off him," the older Clayton demanded. "Now! Or I'll shoot."

Dix shook her head. "I guess you're gonna have to shoot me. You two have caused enough trouble. I'm not letting you hurt anyone anymore."

"You're not in a position to make that happen. The only position you're in at this time is your last position."

The explosion of gunfire echoed through the cavern.

Dix flinched and held her breath, waiting for the stabbing pain of the bullet to tear through her flesh.

Nelson Clayton staggered backward. The gun slipped from his fingers and dropped to the hard surface. Nelson crumpled beside it.

Distracted by Nelson, Dix loosened her hold.

The man beneath her bucked and rolled, throwing her off.

Dwayne grabbed for the gun Nelson had dropped, rolled to his back and aimed at the man diving toward him.

"Look out!" Dix yelled. She kicked out, catching Dwayne's hand a second after he pulled the trigger. The gun went off and then jerked from his hand, flying across the cave floor.

Still lying on the ground, Dix kicked again, catching Dwayne in the face. The crunch of bone and cartilage meant she'd hit her mark.

The big man slapped a hand to his eye as his nose spurted blood. He rolled to the side, screaming like a girl, and then passed out.

Dix leaped to her feet, secured the gun and ran to where Andrew lay on the ground, his hand pressed to his side. "You're hit!" she exclaimed.

"Either that or it's raining blood in here." He sat up and winced, pressing a hand on his wound. "Where's Leigha?"

"I don't know. When she got loose, she ran."

Andrew pushed to his feet. "We have to find her."

"You shouldn't be on your feet. Let me at least stop the flow of blood before you run any sprints."

"Leigha!" he shouted.

"How did you know we'd be here?" Dix pulled off her T-shirt, thankful she'd worn a sports bra that morning. With quick, efficient moves, she tore the shirt in two pieces and folded one.

"Brewer led me here." He glanced around. "Where'd he go?"

"Move your hand," Dix commanded.

"Bossy thing, aren't you?"

"When I have to be." She pressed the wad of cloth to the wound and placed his hand on top to hold it while she tore the rest of the shirt into a long strip. Wrapping her arms around his waist, she pulled the strip of cloth around him and tied it in a tight knot over the cloth pad. "That will have to do until we get you to the hospital."

"Leigha!" Andrew shouted again.

Dix turned in the direction the little girl had disappeared. "Leigha, where are you?"

"I'm here," she responded, edging out of a dark tunnel, struggling to carry a wooden box too big for one little girl to handle.

Brewer limped alongside her.

"Sweetheart, what have you got?" Dix started toward her.

Tears hovered on the child's eyelashes. "The treasure. I was going to give it to the men so that you and Daddy wouldn't get hurt." She stared at the blood on her father's shirt. "I didn't want my daddy to die." She sniffed. A tear slipped from the corner of her eye and slid down her cheek.

A flash of movement alerted Dix.

Dwayne rolled across the floor, grabbed Leigha's leg and jerked her hard.

Before she fell, Leigha threw the wooden box at the man's head. Once on the ground, she kicked him in his swollen eye and again in the face, hitting his broken nose.

Dwayne bunched his fist and pulled his hand back, ready to throw a punch.

Dix ran at him and kicked his arm so hard, the bone snapped. With so much forward momentum driving her forward, she tripped over the man and landed on her knees on the other side.

Dwayne roared and swung his good arm at Dix.

Andrew grabbed his wrist and twisted his thumb until he cried out. Then he pulled the handgun from his waistband and pointed it at the man. "Move a muscle and I won't hesitate to end it now."

Dwayne lay still.

Dix scrambled to her feet and away from Dwayne. She scooped Leigha up into her arms and hugged the child close. "You'll be okay."

"And Daddy?" she asked, her gaze going to her father. "He isn't going to die?"

Andrew shook his head, his focus on the man lying at his feet. "I'm going to be around long enough to embarrass you as a teenager. I love you, baby."

Leigha cupped Dix's face in both of her little palms, forcing her to look the child square in the eye. "Are you going to stay with us?"

Those blue eyes so much like her father's stared straight through her, pulling at her heartstrings so hard, Dix could barely breathe. "We'll see, sweetie. We'll see." She couldn't promise that she would stay. Too many variables were still up in the air. And now that they'd found the people responsible for the attacks, her services were no longer needed.

Dix's eyes stung and she fought to keep the tears from falling. Rangers and MMA fighters didn't cry.

But mommies of darling little girls did. At that moment she wanted to be Leigha's mother more than she had ever imagined possible. She didn't even want to think about how much she wanted to be with Leigha's father. A man who'd been through so much, saved his daughter not once but twice and now had saved her... Her heart swelled inside her chest, hurting so much she thought she might be dying.

"Dix! Andrew!" a female voice called out.

"Over here," Dix responded.

Tazer stepped out of the tunnel leading from the house and into the cave, a handgun in one hand and a flashlight in the other. "Did you save anything for us?"

Dix chuckled. "Just the cleanup." She nodded toward Andrew. "My client ended up saving me."

"After she saved Leigha and me." Andrew shrugged and grimaced, pressing his hand over his wound. "It only seemed fair."

Tazer crossed to where Andrew stood holding the gun on Dwayne. "I'll take it from here. You look a little worse for the wear."

"Thanks. I feel like I was hit by a train."

Tazer nodded. "A bullet in the gut has a way of making it real."

Gabe McGregor, Casanova Valdez and Creed Thomas emerged from the tunnel, all carrying weapons.

Dix grinned. "You brought the cavalry?"

Tazer nodded. "Damn right. I didn't know what we were up against when Andrew placed the call that you and Leigha were missing."

Nova shook his head, his gaze scanning the cavern as he crossed to where Nelson lay on the ground. He dropped to his haunches and checked the base of the man's throat for a pulse. "He's still alive." Jerking the man's jacket open, he tore Nelson's shirt and ripped off pieces of fabric to fashion a bandage to help stop the bleeding. "Great place to throw a party."

"If you like dark, cool places you can't find easily," Creed said.

"How did you find us?" Dix asked.

Gabe stepped aside. "I was questioning Jared and Joe Kessler when Tazer called. They thought they might be of some help if you were climbing around inside a cave." Gabe waved his hand. "I didn't know what they were talking about, but I'm glad they came along." His glance came to a halt on Andrew's shirt. "Are you okay?"

"I will be," Andrew said. "I don't suppose you brought a doctor with you."

"Will a nurse do until we can get you to the hospital?" Emma Jenkins stepped from the tunnel, carrying a red plastic box. "I grabbed the first-aid kit from Gabe's cruiser. Who needs it?"

"Andrew," Dix said. "He's been shot."

Emma pushed through the crowd and examined the pressure bandage Dix had applied. "This will hold until we get him out of here." She made her way to Nelson and applied a pressure bandage.

Gabe secured Dwayne by handcuffing his good arm behind his back, clipping the other cuff to the man's belt. His other arm hung at an awkward angle by his side, completely useless.

The odd group of SOS agents, sheriff's deputy and young archaeologists trudged out of the cave and back through the narrow passage.

Gabe and Creed stayed behind to wait for the first responders to arrive with the stretcher they'd need to carry Nelson out.

Tazer and Nova escorted Dwayne all the way out through the front of Stratford House, just as the ambulances pulled into the yard.

Andrew didn't want to ride in the back of the ambulance, but when the EMTs agreed to let Dix and Leigha ride with him, he acquiesced.

"But who's going to take care of Brewer?" Leigha asked.

Nova waved. "I've got Brewer. I'll take good care of him."

Dix buckled Leigha into the front seat with the driver while she sat in the back next to the EMT who worked over Andrew, checking his vital signs and establishing an IV with fluids.

The ride into town didn't take long, and before she had a chance to say anything to Andrew, she was asked to wait by the ER door until they unloaded him from the back. The driver brought Leigha to her. Together, they watched the EMTs take Andrew into the ER.

Leigha wrapped her arms around Dix's neck and hugged tightly. "I'm scared."

Dix was, too. Gunshot wounds were tricky. Everything depended on what damage the bullet had done inside Andrew. But she couldn't show Leigha how frightened she was.

"You are the bravest little girl I've ever known."

She sniffed and leaned back to stare into Dix's face. "Me?"

"Yes, you." Dix smiled and brushed a strand of spun-gold hair out of Leigha's face. "You went to get the treasure to save us. That was very brave of you, when you could have run all the way back to the house and stayed safe."

"But you and Daddy were still in the cave with those bad men."

"Yes, we were. And you saved us." Dix hugged her, her eyes stinging again. Whoever married Andrew Stratford would be one lucky woman. Not only would she be getting a wonderful, sexy, handsome man to spend her life with, she'd also get the huge bonus of being a mother to Leigha.

In that moment Dix envied a woman she didn't know and who might not even exist.

Shortly after Andrew was wheeled into surgery, Tazer arrived in the surgical waiting room. "I hear Stratford's in surgery."

Dix nodded, unable to say anything for the lump lodged in her throat.

She didn't have to. Tazer continued. "I checked on Nelson and Dwayne Clayton. Dwayne had his arm set, his nose splinted and he was escorted to the county jail. Nelson is next in line for surgery."

Dix didn't care about either of the men. As far as she was concerned, they could die and the world would be a better place.

Tazer arched her brows and stared at Dix. "Hmm. Real talkative, I see." She fished in her purse and pulled out a deck of cards. "You might want these to keep your mind off things."

Dix pulled the cards from the box and shuffled several times before dealing three hands of Go Fish.

"I reported what happened to Royce."

Dix glanced up. "He should fire me."

"How do you figure?"

Tipping her head toward the hallway, she said, "I'm not much good as a bodyguard. I mean, look where my client is."

"The way Royce sees it, you've proved yourself as an SOS agent. He's already looking for your next assignment."

Dix frowned. Anywhere else she'd been, she'd been ready to leave within weeks of getting there. The only reason she'd lived in Vegas so long was that her fighting had taken her all over the country and sometimes all over the world.

Staring down at Leigha's golden hair, her small hands holding on to the cards, Dix didn't want to leave.

"You do know that quite a few of us work out of Cape Churn. We leave to perform our assignments, but we always come back. It's home."

"Are you all from Cape Churn?"

Tazer snorted. "Hardly. But we've found our homes here." She smiled. "Strange how that old saying 'Home is where your heart is' holds true." She touched Dix's arm. "So, have you found your home?" She tilted her head toward the hallway.

The word *home* made Dix long for so much more than what she'd had since returning from the war. "I don't know. I've only been here a few days."

"Your heart knows. Trust it."

A man in green scrubs stepped into the waiting room, untying the mask from around his face. "Are you the family of Andrew Stratford?"

Leigha, Dix and Tazer stood.

"Yes," Leigha said.

"Mr. Stratford came through surgery just fine. The bullet managed to miss all of his organs. Other than losing a lot of blood, he should recover nicely."

"My daddy's going to be okay?" Leigha asked, tears filling her eyes and spilling onto her cheeks.

The doctor knelt in front of her. "He sure is." He lifted her little hand that still held cards. "Are you winning?"

She nodded and turned to Dix.

The doctor straightened. "The nurse will let you know when he's awake. You can visit, but not for long. He'll need rest." The doctor left them in the waiting room.

Dix lifted Leigha into her arms and hugged her. "You hear that? Your daddy is going to be okay."

Even if she didn't stay in Cape Churn, she'd leave knowing Andrew would be okay. The bad guys were neutralized and Leigha would have her father for a very long time.

When she thought of leaving, her chest felt hollow and her belly tightened.

Was Tazer right? Did her heart know what her head couldn't comprehend? Was she falling in love with her client?

Or had she already fallen?

Chapter 20

One night in the hospital was all Andrew could take. He barked at the nurses, growled at the doctor and nearly tore his stitches getting out of bed too soon after surgery. He was up and dressed by the time the doctor made his rounds the next morning to sign his discharge papers.

The doctor chuckled. "Anxious to get home?"

"I never liked hospitals," he grumbled. "No offense. You and the staff are doing a great job."

"You don't have to explain. I get it. I'm one of the worst patients when I'm sick." He scrawled his signature on the bottom of Andrew's chart. "You're free to go as soon as the nurse gives you discharge instructions. Remember when I told you not to fall off any more cliffs? Well, try not to catch any more bullets, as well."

The doctor left and the nurse came in to go over the discharge instructions, and still Dix hadn't shown up.

She'd been there the previous night up until the pain meds had kicked in and knocked him out. He'd woken once, and Dix had been by his side. She'd told him Molly had taken Leigha to the bed-and-breakfast. Brewer was at the vet's office overnight for observation. They said he had some broken ribs and a mild concussion, but he would be all right with rest.

A knock sounded on the door.

Andrew's heart sped up as he glanced up from the documents the nurse handed him. When he saw a fit man with white hair standing there, he couldn't help the disappointment welling in his chest.

"Mr. Stratford?" the man said.

"Yes," he said, carefully shrugging into his jacket.

The man entered with his hand held out. "I'm Royce Fontaine."

The feeling of disappointment turned to a solid ache. "Dix isn't here."

He smiled and nodded. "I know. I asked to be the one to take you home."

Andrew's eyes narrowed. "Why?"

"I wanted to get feedback on one of my newest agents, and to make sure you were okay." He held the door for Andrew and waited until he passed through.

The nurse stopped him before he could go three steps. "Sorry—hospital policy. You have to go down in a wheelchair."

Andrew growled. "I don't need one."

She smiled cheerfully and pushed a wheelchair in front of him. "Sorry—it's policy." She pointed. "Sit."

"I'll push it," Fontaine offered.

The nurse gave him a narrow-eyed glance. "All the way to the exit?"

Fontaine held up a hand. "I swear I'll keep him in the chair until we reach the vehicle."

She stared a moment longer and finally nodded. "Okay. Mr. Stratford, please follow the post-op instructions. I don't want to see you back here anytime soon."

Andrew eased into the wheelchair, muttering curses beneath his breath.

Fontaine stepped behind the chair and pushed it toward the elevator.

"So, what do you want to know?" Andrew started the conversation. "Did Dix do a good job? Was she professional? Would I do it all over again?"

Fontaine stopped the chair in front of the elevator. "For a start, yes."

Andrew punched the down button. "My answers are yes, yes, and I don't know." The door slid open.

Fontaine backed Andrew into the car and stood beside him, his brows knitting. "What do you mean *I don't know*?"

"Look, I have a little girl. I come as a package deal. What hurts my little girl hurts me. And I think it goes both ways."

Fontaine shook his head. "I still don't get it."

Andrew sighed. "I don't regret hiring Dix. She saved my girl and me. But I will regret losing her."

Fontaine chuckled and shook his head. "I don't think you have to worry about that."

It was Andrew's turn to frown. "No?"

"No." The elevator stopped and Fontaine pushed Andrew through the lobby to the exit where a rental car waited in the pickup area.

"We're out of the hospital. I can take it from here." Andrew stood and walked toward the car.

Fontaine pushed the wheelchair away from the curb and set the brake. Then he hurried to open the door for Andrew.

Andrew didn't like to have people fuss over him and he didn't even know Fontaine. But he needed his ride home and he didn't have another one waiting. He swallowed his pride and the curse words he wanted to let loose, and he got into the car, jolting his wound as he settled back against the seat. He winced and bit down hard on his tongue.

Fontaine slipped into the driver's seat and started the engine. "Ready?"

"I was ready an hour ago."

The older man smiled and drove out of the parking lot. "Though Leigha was worried about her father, she had a good time staying at Molly and Nova's place."

"If she's still there, could we stop by and pick her up?"

Fontaine shook his head. "Molly and Nova brought her home. Your housekeeper is watching her."

"What about Brewer?"

"Already home from the vet clinic. The vet observed him overnight, but by morning he was ready for release." Fontaine raised his hand. "Not to worry. Creed and Emma took him home. He'll be there with Leigha when you arrive."

Fontaine had mentioned Leigha and Brewer would be at home, but he still hadn't said anything about Dix. Had she been reassigned? Was she already gone from Oregon on her way to her next dangerous mission?

Andrew's chest hurt even worse. Not in the area of his wound, but in his heart. He hadn't known Dix long, but she was an amazing woman. With her gone, Stratford House would feel even bigger and emptier.

Dix had been right. He needed to turn the place into a hotel or bed-and-breakfast. It was too big for him and Leigha by themselves. It needed to be full of happy people.

He'd be happy to see Leigha and Brewer, but part of him didn't look forward to going home to the house with Dix gone. He sat in silence, dreading walking through the door and not seeing her smiling green eyes. Hell, he'd let her throw him again, if it meant she was staying a little longer.

Fontaine fell silent until they were well out of Cape Churn and almost to the gate to his estate. The quiet suited Andrew. He didn't feel much like talking.

And then Fontaine broke his silence. "You know, I was thinking, with as many of my agents out here on the West Coast, I could use an office with support staff here. I don't suppose you know of a suitable building that has sufficient room in a secure location?"

Andrew had to let Fontaine's question sink in before

he could respond. "I'm not that familiar with what Cape Churn has to offer."

"I've been thinking it would be even better to have an office away from town, in a secluded area. Maybe a gated location."

"Sorry." Andrew started to shake his head but then he frowned. "What are you asking for? Just spit it out."

"Mr. Stratford, would you consider leasing space in Stratford House for our West Coast operations?" Fontaine pulled up to the gate and turned to Andrew. "It would be a perfect location to set up computers and satellite communications."

Andrew's frown deepened. "My home is not for rent or lease."

Fontaine nodded. "Just think about it. No pressure. It just seems a shame to let all those rooms sit empty when you could put them to good use." The SOS leader leaned out the window and pushed the codes for the gate entrance.

"How did you know my code?"

"I have people who specialize in code cracking." Fontaine's mouth turned up on the corners. "And if all else fails, I asked the housekeeper, Mrs. Purdy. She's a wonderful woman and she cooks a mean meat loaf."

Andrew sat back in his seat, not sure he liked that Mrs. Purdy had given his gate code to a stranger.

When they rounded the last bend in the driveway, Andrew leaned forward. "What's going on here?"

Half a dozen vehicles lined the drive. He recognized two sheriff's SUVs and his pulse kicked up its pace. "Is everything okay?"

"As far as I know, everything is fine." Fontaine parked the car and rounded to the passenger side to open the door for Andrew. "A few people wanted to come by and wish you well."

The last thing Andrew needed was a houseful of guests. His chest hurt, his hand hurt, and all he wanted was to hug his daughter and spend time with her.

He sucked in a deep breath and climbed out of the vehicle. As much as he'd like to tell everyone to get lost, he had to remember they were part of the team that had helped him when he'd needed it. They were part of the community and he needed to get more involved with them. He couldn't let his scars hold him back. Nobody had seemed to be turned off by them. They'd helped him unconditionally. The least he could do was thank them.

When he walked through the front door, nobody was there to greet him.

He followed the scent of charbroiled steaks and hamburgers coming from the back of the house. He could hear voices in the kitchen and Brewer barking.

When he arrived in the kitchen, Mrs. Purdy was chopping onions, alone. "There you are. We were waiting to eat until you got home."

"We?" Andrew asked. "Where's Leigha?"

"In the garden with the others." She waved her hands at him. "Go on. I'm just finishing up the potato salad and then I'll be out there, too."

Andrew stepped out into the garden and followed the voices to the patio overlooking the cape.

More than a dozen people were seated in lounge chairs, at the tables or standing near the barbecue grill.

Gabe McGregor spotted him and shouted, "He's here!"

A cheer went up from all of the people there.

Andrew stood stunned for several seconds. Then Leigha grabbed his hand and pulled him into the crowd. "We're having a barbecue. Come sit with me and Dix."

His heartbeat ratcheted up, pounding against his ribs. Then he saw her and it was as if everyone else faded into the background.

Leigha led Andrew to where Dix sat at one of the tables.

As they approached, Dix stood, a smile spreading across her lips, her gaze sweeping over him. "You look great for having been shot," she said, her voice soft, controlled.

"I thought you'd left."

She shook her head. "I couldn't." Her eyes grew glassy and a single tear slipped from the corner. She brushed it away and reached for his hand. "I didn't think I could stay in one place without feeling as though I were a captive again in a Taliban village. But when I thought of leaving Leigha, Brewer, Stratford House…and you, I couldn't."

Andrew drew her into his arms and smoothed his hand over her hair. "I'm glad. You've only been here a few days, but this big place wouldn't be the same without you in it."

Leigha squeezed between the two of them and looked up. "Does that mean Dix is staying?"

Andrew held Dix's gaze.

Dix nodded. "Yes. If you two can stand to have me around."

Leigha hugged her around the middle for a long time and then turned and hugged Andrew.

"What about your job?" Andrew asked softly.

She smiled. "My boss tells me I can base out of the West Coast office of the SOS."

Andrew smiled. "That's perfect, because I'm going to lease the west wing of Stratford House to SOS for their new offices." He kissed Dix and stood back, grinning. "I told you I'd convince you to stay."

"Yes, you did. And just look at all the friends you've made in the past few days."

Andrew dragged his gaze away from Dix long enough to appreciate all the people he'd met.

Gabe McGregor, the sheriff's deputy, and his wife, Kayla Davies, were there with their teenage son and newborn daughter. Sheriff Taggert and his wife, Nora, were talking with Tazer and Dave Logsdon, the dive boat captain. The newlyweds, Molly and Nova, were laughing with Creed Thomas and Emma Jenkins. Even the Kessler twins had come by.

Royce Fontaine stepped up to him and laid his hand on his shoulder. "Glad you're on board with the whole SOS West Coast office being based out of Stratford House. Can't think of a better place."

Andrew nodded and smiled. "Me, either. It means I'll have Dix close by."

She leaned into his uninjured side and wrapped her arm around his waist.

Watching Leigha play with Nova and Brewer, Dix

pressed against his side, and new friends gathered around, Andrew finally felt like he'd come home to stay.

As the sun dropped below the horizon, the guests, full of steaks and hamburgers, left for their own homes, stopping to congratulate Andrew and Dix on a case closed.

When the last person left, Andrew walked Leigha up the stairs to her bedroom.

Dix followed, feeling more settled and happy than she had in a very long time.

"Daddy?" Leigha leaned up to kiss him good-night. "Do you think Bennet will ever disappear?"

"Since I haven't seen him, I couldn't say," Andrew said.

Dix smiled. "Even if he does disappear for you, Leigha, you will always have him in your heart." Dix dropped a kiss on her forehead. "Sleep tight, sweetheart."

"I will." Leigha yawned and rolled onto her side, her arm draping over Brewer's neck.

Dix walked with Andrew into the adjoining room. "After all that's happened here, have you changed your mind about ghosts?"

Andrew turned Dix to face him and touched his lips to the tip of her nose. "You mean, do I believe in them?"

Dix nodded, loving how tender he was.

"Jury's still out, but I'm leaning toward yes." Andrew brushed his lips across hers. "What about you?"

She captured his face between her hands and stared up into his eyes, loving the blue depths more and more.

"Yes. There's no other way to explain everything that has happened. And I kind of like the idea of having a benevolent ghost looking out for Leigha."

"And I like the idea of you being here with us. Anytime you feel the need for space, just let me know. I've got a yacht at the marina. We could sail away from everything."

"If it's all right with you, I'd just as soon stay here with you, Leigha and Brewer. I think I'm falling in love with all of you, and I'd like to see where it goes."

"I knew it the moment you threw me on my back—you were the woman for me." Andrew drew her into his arms and kissed her.

* * * * *

If you loved this novel, don't miss other
suspenseful titles by New York Times
bestselling author Elle James:

DEADLY OBSESSION
PROTECTING THE COLTON BRIDE
DEADLY ALLURE
DEADLY LIAISONS
DEADLY ENGAGEMENT
DEADLY RECKONING

Available now from Harlequin Romantic Suspense!

COMING NEXT MONTH FROM
Ⓗ HARLEQUIN®

ROMANTIC suspense

Available February 7, 2017

#1931 CAVANAUGH IN THE ROUGH
Cavanaugh Justice • by Marie Ferrarella

CSI Susannah Quinn has a secret that's made her build mile-high walls around her heart. Sexy homicide detective Christian Cavanaugh O'Bannon is determined to climb those walls and, at the same time, bring down the serial killer who is determined to make Suzy his next victim...

#1932 HER ALPHA MARINE
To Protect and Serve • by Karen Anders

When Neve Michaels is threatened by an international arms dealer out for revenge, she's set on handling it herself. But her brother's best friend, Russell Kaczewski, refuses to butt out, and now Neve is stuck with him. As they team up to bring down her enemies, their arguing takes a decidedly sexy turn. And yet they still need to get out with their lives intact.

#1933 THE KILLER YOU KNOW
by Kimberly Van Meter

FBI agent Silas Kelly has dedicated his life to finding his brother's killer, even when it means being forced to team up with ambitious reporter Quinn Jackson. As they close in on the truth, both of them begin to realize the killer might be someone *very* close, and more than their passionate attraction is at stake!

#1934 SHIELDED BY THE COWBOY SEAL
SOS Agency • by Bonnie Vanak

Cooper Johnson is on leave at his family's farm when he's asked to protect Meg Taylor from her abusive ex-husband. What he doesn't know is that the woman he's beginning to fall for is the CEO of the company responsible for his sister's death. Can they learn to trust each other long enough to bring down the man truly responsible?

YOU CAN FIND MORE INFORMATION ON UPCOMING HARLEQUIN® TITLES, FREE EXCERPTS AND MORE AT WWW.HARLEQUIN.COM.

HRSCNM0117

REQUEST YOUR FREE BOOKS!
2 FREE NOVELS PLUS 2 FREE GIFTS!

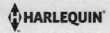

ROMANTIC suspense

Sparked by danger, fueled by passion

YES! Please send me 2 FREE Harlequin® Romantic Suspense novels and my 2 FREE gifts (gifts are worth about $10). After receiving them, if I don't wish to receive any more books, I can return the shipping statement marked "cancel." If I don't cancel, I will receive 4 brand-new novels every month and be billed just $4.74 per book in the U.S. or $5.49 per book in Canada. That's a savings of at least 12% off the cover price! It's quite a bargain! Shipping and handling is just 50¢ per book in the U.S. and 75¢ per book in Canada.* I understand that accepting the 2 free books and gifts places me under no obligation to buy anything. I can always return a shipment and cancel at any time. Even if I never buy another book, the two free books and gifts are mine to keep forever.

240/340 HDN GH3P

Name	(PLEASE PRINT)	
Address		Apt. #
City	State/Prov.	Zip/Postal Code

Signature (if under 18, a parent or guardian must sign)

Mail to the **Reader Service**:
IN U.S.A.: P.O. Box 1867, Buffalo, NY 14240-1867
IN CANADA: P.O. Box 609, Fort Erie, Ontario L2A 5X3

Want to try two free books from another line?
Call 1-800-873-8635 or visit www.ReaderService.com.

* Terms and prices subject to change without notice. Prices do not include applicable taxes. Sales tax applicable in N.Y. Canadian residents will be charged applicable taxes. Offer not valid in Quebec. This offer is limited to one order per household. Not valid for current subscribers to Harlequin Romantic Suspense books. All orders subject to credit approval. Credit or debit balances in a customer's account(s) may be offset by any other outstanding balance owed by or to the customer. Please allow 4 to 6 weeks for delivery. Offer available while quantities last.

Your Privacy—The Reader Service is committed to protecting your privacy. Our Privacy Policy is available online at www.ReaderService.com or upon request from the Reader Service.

We make a portion of our mailing list available to reputable third parties that offer products we believe may interest you. If you prefer that we not exchange your name with third parties, or if you wish to clarify or modify your communication preferences, please visit us at www.ReaderService.com/consumerschoice or write to us at Reader Service Preference Service, P.O. Box 9062, Buffalo, NY 14240-9062. Include your complete name and address.

HRS15

"Your time would be better spent coming up with answers regarding our dead woman," she said in a no-nonsense tone.

Our.

Her slip of the tongue was not lost on Chris. The grin on his lips told her so before he uttered a word. "Our first joint venture. We should savor this."

"What I'd savor," she informed him, "is some peace and quiet so I can work. Specifically, some time away from you."

The expression that came over Chris's face was one of doubt. "Now, if we spend time apart, how are we going to work on this case together?" he asked, conveying that what she'd just said lacked logic.

Suzie had only one word to give him in response to his question. "Productively."

With that, she went back to doing her work, but that lasted for only a few moments. A minute at best. Though she tried to block out his presence, he still managed to get to her.

He was standing exactly where he had been, watching her so intently that she could feel his eyes on her skin. It caused her powers of concentration to deteriorate until they finally became nonexistent.

Unable to stand it, she looked up and glared at him. "What do you want, O'Bannon?" she muttered. It took everything she had not to shout the question at him. The man was making her crazy.

Chris never hesitated as he answered her. "Dinner."

She clenched her jaw. "You can buy it in any supermarket," she informed him coldly.

He sidestepped the roadblocks she was throwing up as if they weren't there.

"With you."

This time Suzie was the one who didn't hesitate for a second. "Not at any price. Now please go before I take out my manual on workplace harassment and start underlining passages to get you banned from my lab."

"It's the crime scene lab, not yours," he reminded her pleasantly, taking a page out of her book. And then Chris inclined his head. "Until the next time."

"There is no next time," she countered, steaming even though she refused to look up again.

"Don't forget we're working this case together," he told her cheerfully.

He thought he heard Suzie say "Damn" under her breath as he left the lab.

Chris smiled to himself.

Don't miss
CAVANAUGH IN THE ROUGH by Marie Ferrarella,
available February 2017 wherever
Harlequin® Romantic Suspense books
and ebooks are sold.

www.Harlequin.com

Turn your love of reading into rewards you'll love with
Harlequin My Rewards

**Join for FREE today at
www.HarlequinMyRewards.com**

Earn **FREE BOOKS** of your choice.

Experience **EXCLUSIVE OFFERS** and contests.

Enjoy **BOOK RECOMMENDATIONS**
selected just for you.

PLUS! Sign up now
and get **500** points
right away!

Earn
FREE
REWARDS
Join
Today!
HarlequinMyRewards.com

MYR16R

JUST CAN'T GET ENOUGH?

Join our social communities
and talk to us online.

You will have access to the latest
news on upcoming titles and special
promotions, but most importantly,
you can talk to other fans about your
favorite Harlequin reads.

Harlequin.com/Community

 Facebook.com/HarlequinBooks

 Twitter.com/HarlequinBooks

 Pinterest.com/HarlequinBooks

THE WORLD IS BETTER
WITH
Romance

Harlequin has everything from contemporary, passionate and heartwarming to suspenseful and inspirational stories.

Whatever your mood,
we have a romance just for you!

Connect with us to find your next great read, special offers and more.

f /HarlequinBooks

🐦 @HarlequinBooks

www.HarlequinBlog.com

www.Harlequin.com/Newsletters

⬧ HARLEQUIN®

A *Romance* FOR EVERY MOOD™

www.Harlequin.com